DRIVEN BY FIRE

THE FIRE SERIES

ALSO BY ANNE STUART

ROMANTIC SUSPENSE

The Fire Series

Consumed by Fire

The Ice Series

On Thin Ice
Fire and Ice
Ice Storm
Ice Blue
Cold As Ice
Black Ice

Stand-Alone Titles

Into the Fire
Still Lake
The Widow
Shadows at Sunset
Shadow Lover
Ritual Sins
Moonrise
Nightfall
Seen and Not Heard
At the Edge of the Sun
Darkness Before Dawn
Escape Out of Darkness
The Demon Count's Daughter
The Demon Count

Demonwood
Cameron's Landing
Barrett's Hill
Silver Falls

Collaborations

Dogs & Goddesses
The Unfortunate Miss Fortunes

Anthologies

Burning Bright
Date with a Devil
What Lies Beneath
Night and Day
Valentine Babies
My Secret Admirer
Sisters and Secrets
Summer Love
New Year's Resolution: Baby
New Year's Resolution: Husband
One Night with a Rogue
Strangers in the Night
Highland Fling
To Love and To Honor
My Valentine
Silhouette Shadows

ROMANCE

Wild Thing
The Right Man
A Dark and Stormy Night
The Soldier and the Baby

Cinderman
Falling Angel
One More Valentine
Rafe's Revenge

DRIVEN BY FIRE

THE FIRE SERIES

ANNE STUART

Text copyright © 2016 Anne Kristine Stuart Ohlrogge
All rights reserved.

Published by Montlake Romance, Seattle

www.apub.com

Amazon, the Amazon logo, and Montlake Romance are trademarks of Amazon.com, Inc., or its affiliates.

ISBN-13: 9781503952010
ISBN-10: 1503952010

Cover design by Jason Blackburn

Printed in the United States of America

For Lynda Ward and Jenny Crusie—I couldn't have done it without you.

Chapter One

She never should have been there. Normally Jennifer Parker would have waited for the smoke to clear for a call for her services as a pro bono lawyer. She'd already acquired a small but stellar reputation for dealing with the poor and disenfranchised, and a cargo ship with seventy-three women and children bound for the sex trade would require her help sooner or later.

She had the perfect excuse to show up. She would have gotten a phone call from the DA's office, or the Red Cross, or any of a number of charitable organizations in need of her expertise, and if anyone questioned her presence, she could simply explain that she saw no reason to wait when she might be needed. The police and the FBI and their ilk were doing an excellent job clearing the ship, but these victims would be better off dealing with a sympathetic woman than a gun-toting police force.

But that wasn't her real reason for driving her ancient Toyota down to the docks and ferreting her way past the police barricades and news crews and gawkers.

"Do you want to be responsible for your brother's death?" Her father had thundered at her from the end of the phone line, the father she hadn't spoken to in three years. "I know you have no family feeling when it comes to most of us, but this is Billy, your baby brother! What would your mother have said if she knew you let him walk into a trap and did nothing to save him?"

"He got himself into it," she said, fighting back the guilt. "If he's been making money from sex trafficking, then he deserves whatever he gets."

"A bullet between the eyes? I may have spent a fortune paying off the New Orleans police but there are other agencies involved in this, including some mysterious foreign group called the Organization or the Committee. They won't hesitate to blow his brains out."

"There's nothing I can do that you can't," she said stubbornly.

"I can't do anything. He's not answering his cell phone, and if I or any of my men show up at the docks, they'll think we're a part of this mess."

"Aren't you?"

"Don't be disrespectful! I know better than to get involved in a half-assed scheme that crumbles so easily. Why else do you think I've prospered for so long?"

"Because you pay off the police?" she suggested brightly.

The silence at the other end told her she'd gone too far, but there was nothing left of her relationship with her father to salvage. Finally he spoke.

"Are you going to save your brother? You know someone had to have played him—he's the best of all of us," Fabrizio Gauthier said ruthlessly, ignoring his daughter's lifelong efforts to break free from her family's pernicious influence.

He was right, though. Billy was the baby, too young to be mired in the illegal activities of the rest of the infamous Gauthiers. The boy . . . no, man . . . she knew would never have involved himself in something as filthy as sex trafficking. Fabrizio was right—someone had to have set him up.

"I'll go," she said finally. "Not for your sake, but because he was Mama's baby. There's a chance he hasn't been totally corrupted yet."

She didn't expect a thank-you, and he didn't offer one, breaking the connection rather than spending one more moment with his recalcitrant daughter. That suited her fine—she would be just as happy never to exchange another word with the man she thought of as a sperm donor and nothing more. She'd always felt like a changeling in her family of criminals, and once her mother died, only Billy had felt like her real kin.

It hadn't taken her long to reach the crowded docks of the Port of New Orleans. Women and children were being herded onto a school bus, all of them looking dirty and pale and frightened. Instinctively she started toward them, then remembered she had come to find her brother. The people milling around were so busy that no one noticed when she slipped past the barriers and onto the container ship.

She came across the first body in the narrow stairway leading upward and she froze in horror, bile rising inside her. He'd been shot between the eyes, as her father had predicted, and his bowels had loosened with the suddenness of his death.

Holding her breath, she stepped over him, stumbling up the stairway. She found two more bodies on the next deck, and she almost turned around. In the distance she heard noise and shouting, and she wanted to run in the opposite direction, off this horrible boat with the stink of death all around her. How innocent could Billy be, with all the hideous things that were happening here?

She had just reached the next deck when she saw them—a group of men, some uniformed, some not. Three men were lying facedown on the deck, handcuffed, and another man lay bleeding up against a wall.

She darted into the shadows when one man turned, some preternatural sense telling him that he was being watched. She only had a brief glimpse of him—a tall man, in dark clothes, a gun in his hand.

She had no idea whether he'd seen her or not, but she wasn't taking any chances. She didn't hear his footsteps approach, but instinct told her he was the kind of man who wouldn't let anything go, and she managed to back into one of the cabins, closing the door silently behind her. She turned and came face-to-face with her baby brother.

He looked like hell. His face was smeared with smoke and blood, his mouth grim, and the look in his usually sweet brown eyes shocked her. For the first time he looked like their father, kingpin of the notorious Gauthier family of organized crime and political power, and in one hand he held what she recognized as a Glock 25, her father's gun of choice. He was texting furiously on the cell phone in his other hand, and she almost wanted to laugh at the absurdity of it. Even death and disaster couldn't pry Billy's cell phone from his sticky fingers.

He looked up and saw her, and suddenly he was her baby brother again, looking lost and troubled. "What are you doing here, Sissy?" he whispered. "You need to get out of here! I've screwed up, and they're going to kill me if they find me."

"Father sent me," she whispered, her voice just a breath of sound. "I'm trying to save your life! What the hell have you gotten yourself mixed up in?"

"I didn't know," he said helplessly. "By the time I realized what was going on I was in too deep to back out."

"Oh, baby, of course you didn't," she said, her heart breaking. "You can turn state's evidence—I can work something out . . ."

"I won't make it that far," he said with a trace of bitterness. "I'll be dead before I get off the boat and you know it. The Committee is out there, and they don't bother with due process."

A chill rocketed through her. "Then we'll have to get you out of here," she said in a decisive voice.

Billy's laugh was without humor. "Good old Sissy, always ready to save the world. There's nothing you can do . . ."

She heard the hand on the doorknob, but Billy was even faster, diving behind a huge desk that took up most of the small room. Jenny tried to pull herself together in time to face the man who pushed open the door.

She knew it would be him, of course. The tall man with a gun even bigger than Billy's, looking at her out of cold and dangerous eyes. "Who the hell are you?" he demanded roughly, and that gun was pointed at her chest.

She didn't make the mistake of moving. She could feel the tension in the air, and everything narrowed down into one thing. She had to get this man and his gun away from her brother. It didn't matter what Billy had done, he was still her baby brother, and she knew he hadn't understood what he'd been doing. She certainly wasn't going to watch him be gunned down in front of her eyes.

"I'm Jennifer Parker," she said in as calm a voice as she could muster, trying to ignore the gun. "I'm a lawyer and a victims' rights advocate. I get called in on cases like these."

"Who called you?"

Shit. Should she lie? No, he was clearly the kind of man who checked the details. "No one. I heard the news on the police band on my car radio and decided I should show up and offer my help."

"Alone in an empty cabin?" His voice was derisive. "So why did I get the impression that you were hiding out from someone?"

She glanced over at the desk and suddenly realized that Billy had left his damned cell phone on it. She strolled over, trying to look casual as she picked up the phone and shoved it in her pocket. She perched on the desk, trying to look natural, and swung her leg, ignoring her brother crouched down just behind her, with that lethal gun in his hand.

"You looked like you were going to shoot first and ask questions later," she said, trying to appear at ease. "I'm here for the victims, not the enforcers."

"You're right, I would have." He reached out and yanked her off the desk, ungently. "There are too many damned civilians here already, but since you're here you may as well make yourself useful. They found one more victim hiding in the sick bay. You can talk to her and tell her we mean her no harm."

"Is that true?"

"If she's innocent. She's not the one I'm looking for. I don't expect you saw a young man in his early twenties around here?" The question came off as casual, but Jenny wasn't fooled. She looked at the gun in his hand, then up into his face, and for a moment she froze, staring at him.

He was . . . mesmerizing. He was a tall man, six feet or so, with the kind of lean build that was deceptive in its strength. She didn't for one moment underestimate just how dangerous he could be. His eyes were blue, not the bright blue of an innocent, but a steely feral blue, like a cold flame, and they should have been a warning. He wore his dark hair too long, as if he never had time to get it cut; he hadn't bothered to shave in a couple of days, and his high cheekbones suggested some kind of exotic ancestry. With any other man she might find herself attracted to him, but not this man, not this threat to her brother. Not a man who would shoot first and ask questions later.

"I haven't seen anyone." The lie was instinctive, necessary, shameful.

"Then why were you skulking around?"

"I've seen three dead men since I came aboard, and you were standing there with a very large gun in your hand," she said, keeping her expression blank. "I hadn't seen anything to fill me with trust."

"You shouldn't be here."

She couldn't agree more. "You're right. Why don't you take me to see this woman you've found, and I'll see what I can do to help her. She must be shattered." She had to get him out of this room, away from Billy.

He shrugged. "That's not my worry. Jim Long can take you to where she's waiting."

Relief washed through her. "I know Jim—I've worked with him before. And you are . . . ?"

"None of your damned business," he said succinctly, opening the door for her.

She didn't hesitate. He must be part of the Committee that her brother had mentioned. She needed to give Billy a chance to escape. "I didn't see Jim out there."

"I'll take you to him."

"Perfect," she said, meaning it.

The man shot her a sharp look, but she simply gave him a cool nod and walked out the door, listening as he closed it behind them. If there was any chance Billy had really known what he was doing, then she'd protected the worst kind of criminal, and she was going to have to live with that. She just had to believe in him, and in her own instincts. Anyway, it was too late now, and if she told this unnamed man the truth he would probably shoot Billy, or the other way around, and she couldn't bear the thought of any more dead bodies. She let the man lead the way, putting everything out of her mind but the young woman who needed her help. She'd done what she could to help her brother. Whether she'd made the right choice or not remained to be seen.

An hour later she found herself bringing Soledad to the bus for the refugees, her brother forgotten in the chaos. The exquisitely beautiful young woman was in some kind of shock, unable to produce more than a word or two, despite Jenny's excellent Spanish, but she came along obediently enough, though Jenny could sense her distrust. Who could blame the girl? She'd been kidnapped from her home in Calliveria, locked inside a freight container with as many women and children they could fit, and then endured the grueling voyage up to New Orleans. It was lucky she wasn't comatose.

The little ones bounced back more easily. When she climbed into the bus behind Soledad, she heard the buzz of noise, and the sudden, relieved laughter of a young child. She turned, needing the solace of it, only to see the man who'd seemed so threatening less than an hour ago squatting down beside a particularly grubby child, talking to him in calm, liquid Spanish. She couldn't hear his words, but she could see the child's reaction—gleeful and mesmerized. Maybe the man just had that effect on people, she thought for a moment. And then he rose and saw her, and his face went cool and blank, like a killer's face.

She knew what a killer's face looked like, thanks to her father. She knew this man had been responsible for some, if not all, of the dead men on board. *Danger, Will Robinson!* flashed in her mind.

"You can go home now," he said to her.

She couldn't resist. "Oh, may I?" she said, her voice heavy with sarcasm. "How kind of you to dismiss me."

"If it were up to me you'd be answering a lot more questions, Ms. Parker," he said. "But my friends on the police force tell me you're untouchable. How much do you pay for that privilege?"

She bit back her instinctive reply. In fact, their hands-off approach with her came more from the work she did and the help she gave rather than her father's generous payoffs, but the guilt that had been pushed to the back of her mind surged forward again, and he looked at her sharply, as if reading her mind.

"Nothing at all, John Doe," she snapped. "The good I do outweighs any possible infringement on policy."

He cocked his head to one side. "They might believe it. I don't. And the name's Ryder. Matthew Ryder. You're going to be hearing it again." It was a clear threat—the farthest thing from flirtation she could imagine—but she simply smiled at him.

"I'm looking forward to it." And she realized with slightly horrified amazement that she actually was.

Chapter Two

"What the fuck?" Six weeks later Matthew Ryder was sitting in the inner office of the American Committee for the Preservation of Democracy, nursing a glass of scotch that he shouldn't have been drinking before noon, when the sound of the front doorbell of the old mansion in the Garden District shot through his head like a spike. Of course he had a hangover, so even the wind in the live oak trees surrounding the house would feel like the universe crashing down around him, but he'd been counting on a peaceful day all to himself. Granted, it was just past eleven, but it was a Sunday, and the Crescent City seemed to have two things on its mind on Sundays—football and drinking. He was holding up his end on the drinking part, but he didn't give a crap about football. In fact, he didn't give a crap about anything but being left alone, and yet standing outside the broad double doors of the recently refurbished mansion was Ms. Jennifer Gauthier Parker, Esquire, one of the last people he wanted to see on a very long list of people he wanted to avoid.

Ms. Parker was, of course, a member of the ancient Gauthier family, one of the oldest in New Orleans, wielding more power than any other comparable family, and in the Big Easy, power was even more corrupting than in Washington, DC. The Gauthiers were as dirty as they came, except, presumably, for the saintly Ms. Parker, who had left the family business for the virtuous life of a pro bono immigration lawyer.

He stared at the high-definition screen that was a far cry from most surveillance systems, into the impatient, ridiculously pure face of his current nemesis. Parker looked to be in her late twenties, with a head of reddish brown curls, a stubborn mouth, opaque eyes, and the kind of rounded figure he particularly liked. Too bad she was such a major pain in the ass. She had one of her stray waifs beside her, a small, slight female figure with a bowed head of thick black hair. He didn't give a shit about her either. He just wanted to drink in peace.

Speaking of pain in the ass, Ms. Jennifer Parker was still ringing his doorbell, and he rose, kicking the wastebasket across the room. It was empty, of course—any paper that they used, and they used damned little, was shredded and burned—but the clanging noise expressed his bad temper perfectly. It also rocketed through his head, and he wanted to groan. Too bad he had no reason to sock Parker in the nose—though if he did she'd probably shriek and make his splitting head even worse.

The hair of the dog was supposed to cure his hangover—all it did was make him feel like dog hair. And Ms. Parker, Esq. wasn't going anywhere no matter how determined he was to ignore her. Might as well face the music and get it over with.

He almost wished he were drunk, but he'd barely had time to settle down with his too-early drink when Ms. Goddamn Parker began ringing the doorbell. He slammed the door behind him, winced, slid the concealing wall across the space, and made his way down the wide, curving staircase at a leisurely pace.

She'd be getting really pissed off by now, and the thought made him slightly more cheerful. He'd never been big on martyrs and do-gooders, and Parker was just a bit too saintly for his tastes, despite the fact that she was absolutely delicious, with her mop of curly hair, her warm brown eyes, and that very fine body she disguised with too-proper clothing. Which was fine with him—she hated him even more than he disliked her. She wouldn't be any happier showing up on his doorstep on a Sunday afternoon than he was.

At least he could cherish that thought.

Jenny was standing outside the huge old house in the Garden District of New Orleans, the bright winter sun beating down on her and her companion, and she would have given ten years of her life to be anywhere else. "Don't worry, Soledad," she told the slender young woman beside her. "I'm sure Mr. Ryder is here—he just takes his time when it isn't normal business hours." The thought was depressing—she couldn't count on another reprieve, and she had to face him sooner or later.

"But I do not understand," Soledad said in her softly accented voice, her gorgeous brown eyes downcast. "Why are we coming to see him?"

"Because his organization is responsible for stopping the criminals who kidnapped you and so many others and brought you to this country," she said firmly, leaning on the doorbell. "It's their job to clean up the mess, and we need his help. I wish we didn't—the man is a distrustful pain in the ass, but beggars can't be choosers."

"I would have thought . . ." she hesitated, her English momentarily failing her, "just stopping those terrible men was enough. Really, Miss Parker, you do not need to do this. I can find work on my own—I do not need any help."

"You'd be an illegal alien," Jenny said. "And the Committee knows how to pull strings to get you your green card."

"What is this . . . Committee?"

Jenny shrugged, shoving a hand through her unruly hair. "No one really knows, and I'm not about to ask. I just know they were responsible for your release from that container ship, and they're so secretive they must have a huge amount of power. That was one thing I learned from my family," she added wryly. "The more mysterious the organization, the more influential it is. Besides, they took care of the paperwork for the other women and children—if you hadn't been sick, you would already have your papers as well." Jenny suspected that if Soledad hadn't gotten sick, she would have taken off before the papers arrived, but that was neither here nor there. She couldn't blame the girl for being distrustful, especially after all she and her fellow captives had been through at the hands of the traffickers. At the hands, innocent though they'd been, of her brother. Had she been in the same position, she wouldn't have trusted anyone either. "It was a good thing the police searched the ship thoroughly and found you in the sick bay. Otherwise you might have gotten towed out to impound and no one would have found you."

Soledad gave her that sweet smile that had captivated everyone at the small, street-corner office that held Jenny's practice. "Yes, I am very lucky," she said in a tranquil voice. "We will have to hope that this Mr. . . . Strider will be as wonderfully helpful as everyone else has been."

"Ryder," Jenny corrected. "I've met him before, and he's not likely to be wonderfully anything except an asshole. But he's going to make sure you can either stay here or go back home, whichever you prefer . . ."

"Stay here," Soledad said quickly. "It is too dangerous for me to go back to Calliveria."

"Then you'll stay here, and Ryder will see to it." Jenny straightened her shoulders as she heard the footsteps beyond the closed door. If she'd had any choice she would have gone to someone else, but the various agencies had run through their allotment for illegal immigrants, and she had no choice but to see if the secretive Committee could do better. She braced herself for another confrontation, and the last thing she was about to do was show weakness in front of someone so desperately in need of a champion, even if her stomach knotted and her fisted hand trembled slightly as she raised it to pound on the door once more. Because like it or not, Matthew Ryder had a very powerful, very unwelcome effect on her and her previously dormant libido.

It was a good thing she had excellent reflexes or she would have ended up pounding on Matthew Ryder's face, and he wouldn't have liked that one bit. She'd been around dangerous men all her life, her father, her uncles, her brothers, and she knew a wolf when she saw one. It was a wolf who opened the door and stood staring at her, an unpromising expression on his face.

"Well, look who's here," he said, though she suspected he had known perfectly well what awaited him on the other side of the door. "What brings you out on such a bright Sunday afternoon, Ms. Parker?"

She straightened her already-stiff spine and gave him an equally stiff smile. "Good afternoon, Mr. Ryder. I see you've been enjoying your weekend."

If she'd managed to annoy him, and she'd been trying to, he didn't show it. He was clearly hungover—she knew that much about men as well. He was scruffier than usual—he was one of those men who had to know he looked sexier when he didn't shave, and he was wearing faded jeans and a wrinkled linen shirt with the sleeves rolled up. His feet were bare, and he had a glass of whiskey in his hand. She looked at it disapprovingly.

He saw where her eyes went. "You have a problem with my drinking, Ms. Parker?"

"Not if you don't," she replied in a determinedly pleasant tone of voice.

"None at all, as long as no one interrupts me. So what do you expect me to do for this girl that your own damned family can't accomplish?"

Bastard, Jenny thought, ignoring the frisson of nerves that attacked her stomach. She'd only seen him once since their first encounter on the container ship, and by that time he seemed to know everything there was to know about her, including her background, her family, and probably the profit and loss statements, mainly loss, for her small law office. He'd been about as unhelpful as he could be, but she was getting used to this man and his suspicions, though she had no idea exactly what he suspected. Since then she'd done her best to avoid any other chance encounters as they both dealt with the refugees.

"I haven't had anything to with any member of my family in years," she lied easily enough. "I don't involve my family in my business. I prefer to keep them as separate as possible, given their quasi-legal proclivities."

His cynical laugh didn't improve her mood. "Their quasi-legal proclivities have them working with the wealthiest law partnership in the city, while it does appear that your career path hasn't been quite as successful."

She swallowed her instinctive retort. She needed a favor from him, and it wouldn't help matters if she went out of her way to annoy him. She already seemed to have irritated him enough, and she didn't want him looking at her too closely.

"So what is it you want me to do with your current waif?" he said, when she didn't come up with a response.

At that Soledad lifted her head slightly to give him the full benefit of her huge brown eyes, and Jenny waited for him to melt just as every other male had. He barely blinked, turning his attention back to Jenny without the slightest show of interest.

She tried not to show her surprise. "Papers," she said after a moment's hesitation. "A job, and a place to stay. And counseling," she added as an afterthought. "She's been through a lot."

Ryder's cynical smile wasn't meant to put her at ease, and she could feel her palms begin to sweat. *Nerves,* she reminded herself. What was it about this man who sparked such odd reactions from her?

"What about a rich husband as well?" he drawled, taking another sip of his whiskey.

"If you can dig one up that would be a nice bonus," she said in a smooth voice. "Now why don't you invite us in out of the midday sun instead of letting all that lovely air-conditioning out? Because I'm not going away and I expect you know it."

He muttered something beneath his breath so shocking she would have slapped him if she'd been absolutely certain what he'd said. She couldn't be, and she wasn't about to wait. She took the slender hand of the young woman beside her. "Come with me, Soledad," she said. "I think Mr. Ryder's bark is worse than his bite."

"Don't count on it," he said softly as she took a deep breath and started forward. For a moment she was afraid he wasn't going to move out of the way. She really, really didn't want to touch him, not when she had this inexplicable reaction to him. He stood in the doorway watching her, and at the last minute stepped back just enough so that she nearly brushed against him when she thought she'd been clear. It was only the lightest of touches, barely more than the sleeve of her silk suit brushing against his rumpled linen shirt, but heat shot through her body. Damn the man.

As she and Soledad entered the darkened hallway, she thought she could hear his soft laugh and her irritation rose even higher. Unfortunately it wasn't enough to drive away the feelings that filled her when she saw him, and nothing—not common sense, not experience, not Matthew Ryder's own annoying behavior—could obliterate this strange thread of attraction. At least, thank God, he had no idea that she seemed to have developed a crush the size of Texas on him. He closed the door behind them, plunging the already-shadowy area into darkness, and Jenny blinked, trying to get accustomed to the gloom. She turned back to him, a bland smile on her face to meet his equally bland expression.

His mouth was pure sex. It was that mouth, she decided. If she could just avoid looking at it maybe she could avoid the sexual upheaval she was going through. Her brothers would tell her she needed to get laid. That was probably true, but Matthew Ryder was the last man she was going anywhere near.

"On the left," he said, and Jenny turned into the large room, half dragging Soledad with her.

Whoever had been in charge of the restoration of the house on Magazine Street had done an amazing job. The room, with its floor-to-ceiling windows, was the right blend of business and social, and the comfortable furniture still felt in keeping with the original style of the place. Pulling her reluctant client along with her, Jenny sank down on one of the plush sofas, leaned back, and crossed her legs.

Which was in fact a major mistake. Ryder sat down opposite her and her movement immediately brought his gaze to those legs, and she felt oddly exposed. She was depressingly average and she figured she was probably ten pounds past her goal weight, but her legs were definitely her best feature, long and shapely, and for some reason she didn't want him looking at them. Not that he seemed the slightest bit interested—he was simply, dispassionately taking her inventory. She sat forward and needlessly tugged her skirt down to cover more, which caught his attention, and a faint smile appeared on his usually expressionless face.

"So exactly what is it you want from me?" he said. "I can write you a check . . ."

"Money doesn't solve everything, Mr. Ryder," Jenny said, and then could have kicked herself—she sounded like a prim old lady. He was giving her an easy out—she ought to take it. "For now Soledad can stay with me, though my house is a little small and I'm in the midst of renovating it. I need a green card for her, I need a job for her, and in fact, I need someone to oversee her well-being."

"That's all well and good, Ms. Parker, but what does she want?" Jenny could feel herself flush again, and she glanced at Soledad. "It's what she wants too."

Ryder turned those cool blue eyes on Soledad. "Why aren't you letting her speak for herself?"

"Of course it is what I want," said Soledad. "It is the American dream, is it not?"

Ryder shrugged. "If you say so." He turned back to Jenny. "What's wrong with you overseeing her welfare?"

Jenny found she was nervously picking at the hem of her skirt and she quickly released it. She hated the way he made her feel—all edgy and itchy inside. She couldn't rid herself of the feeling that he could see right through her. "I have other clients, Mr. Ryder," she said with admirable calm. She'd also run out of favors, but she wouldn't admit that to this man. If she'd had a viable choice other than coming here she would have used it, but for some reason she'd hit a brick wall every time she tried to make arrangements for Soledad.

"And you think I'm just sitting around with my thumb up my ass?"

"I think you have a larger staff and a much larger financial war chest than I do. You have connections all over the world. It would take a phone call from you to see her safely settled."

"Ms. Parker, you must have a very high opinion of me. I don't work miracles and I'm not omnipotent. Arranging for your little waif's future requires more than a simple phone call."

Jenny looked at him, her expression impassive. She had learned early on that silence was the best way to get what she wanted. Pleading was a waste of time, logic got her nowhere, but men hated a vacuum, even dangerous, inhumanly controlled men, and if she just sat there long enough, quietly enough, he'd come up with an answer.

It took longer than she expected, but then Ryder was no ordinary man. She was about to give in and say something when he finally spoke.

"So what is it you expect me to do?" He was sounding more irascible, and he hadn't touched his drink. If he really was a drunk, he'd be wanting to get rid of her so he could get back to his bottle, and she was in the catbird seat. She had less to fear from a drunk, no matter how well he covered it up.

But she didn't think he was. There was a bright-burning intensity about him that unsettled her, and it wasn't simply a matter of her guilty conscience. There was no way he could know what she'd done—Billy was long gone, out of harm's way, and even if Ryder suspected something he'd have no way to prove it. Then again, he struck her as a man who didn't need hard-and-fast proof before he acted, and he wouldn't be the forgiving type.

"What are you blushing for?" he demanded suddenly.

"I'm not," she said defensively.

"Is it your temper? I've always heard that redheads have a hell of a temper."

"I'm not a redhead," she snapped. "My hair is brown."

"If you say so. That looks like russet to me. And you've got the freckles to go along with it. In fact, if you had a better personality you'd be downright cute."

Jenny made a low growling noise in the back of her throat. "I'm not interested in your opinion of my physical attractions," she said, and could have kicked herself. *Cute*, she thought. What a revolting image. She needed to keep her mouth shut, though, because once again she was sounding like a repressed virgin.

"Of course you're not," he drawled, and she couldn't tell whether he was being sarcastic or not. Surely he couldn't have any idea about her shameful crush on him? After all, she'd seen him only one other time besides their initial meeting, when she'd run into him at the DA's office, and he'd done everything he could to annoy her and drive her away. Unfortunately it hadn't worked.

"Too bad I'm not interested in playing your games, Ryder," she said. "Just tell me whether you're going to help me or not and I'll leave you alone."

"You almost convince me."

She ignored him, plowing on valiantly. "I need an apartment for Soledad as soon as possible. She needs a job, and I wouldn't mind if she had a bodyguard for the first few weeks, just until I'm sure she's not in any danger."

If she wasn't so preternaturally aware of him she might not have noticed the sudden sharpening in his cool blue eyes. "Why should she be in danger?"

"She's made enemies in her home country," Jenny said. "And I don't think they counted on her escaping her fate. You know she was hiding in the infirmary when your men raided the ship, and she was so terrified that you were there to kill her that you almost didn't find her."

"Not me, lady. I don't do a job halfway. So what has your innocent little darling done to make enemies—she hardly looks old enough to have annoyed anyone."

Jenny glanced at Soledad. She couldn't understand his hostility when every other man who'd come near the young woman had been smitten. Maybe she'd been wrong all this time, and he was batting for the wrong team.

No, she always had a sixth sense about these things. Matthew Ryder liked women all right—he just didn't seem to like her, a fact that filled her with almost nothing but gratitude.

He didn't appear to be any too enamored of Soledad either. "She worked with the resistance back in Calliveria," Jenny continued, "which didn't make the government and the police force very happy. If she goes back there she'll be arrested, tortured, and probably murdered."

He was singularly unimpressed. "You do have a flair for the dramatic, don't you, Ms. Parker? So let me get this straight: we need one apartment, one job, and one bodyguard, and you expect us to pay for it?"

"Your organization was the one who pulled her off that ship. When you save a life, you're responsible for that life."

His expression was jaded, cynical. "Then it's lucky that saving lives isn't usually in my job description. I'm usually the one taking them."

It was a good thing she was unable to come up with a fake laugh at his joke because a moment later she knew he wasn't kidding. She'd seen him with that gun in his hand, seen the bodies on the ship. She swallowed. "Are you going to help me, or not?"

He watched her closely for a long moment. "I'm going to help you," he said finally, "simply because I want to know what you're hiding."

She felt like she'd been punched in the stomach, but she kept her face impassive. If she weren't careful she would look guilty as sin, and she couldn't give this man any more reason to distrust her.

She summoned up her coolest voice. "Why would you think I was hiding something from you? What would I possibly have to hide?"

"I'd say 'you tell me,' but I think it would be a waste of time. You're not about to give up your secrets until someone makes you."

She felt cold now, frozen. "That someone being you?"

"Maybe. It depends on just what you're hiding and how much I need to find out. Don't worry—for now I think it's something stupid that has nothing to do with the human trafficking and the slime responsible for it. You're too nice a girl to know people messed up in something like that. Unless it's your family."

Jenny wanted to throw up. She jerked her face up to look directly into his dangerous blue eyes. There was no expression in them—he was playing with her, though she wasn't quite sure why.

Their eyes caught and held for a long, tense moment, and she didn't dare back down. Finally he leaned back. "However, even your family steers clear of child prostitution and sex trafficking, at least as far as I've been able to discover. Even if you're closer to them than you pretend, they're unlikely to have been involved. So that rules out one possibility."

It wasn't the most reassuring thing he could have said, and she hid the shiver that went down her back at his prosaic words. Before she could say anything he rose, clearly dismissing them. "All right," he said, bored, "you told me what you want—I'll do my best to get it as long as you promise to leave me the fuck alone."

She could feel Soledad's faint tremor at the sound of the word. The girl knew that word, and knew it meant anger, danger, and trouble. "Watch your language," Jenny said.

"Or what?" He eyed her coolly. "I don't think you have much leverage in the situation. You can't tell my mommy on me."

She wanted to tell him what an asshole he was. She didn't trust him, didn't like him. She knew the negative feelings were mutual, but he was the only one she could go to for help. Her only solace was that there was no way he could find out what she had done that day on the freighter—only she and Billy knew.

She turned to Soledad, trying to ignore him. "I'll take you back to my place for the time being—I'm sure Mr. Ryder will do his best to get you settled as soon as possible." She turned and gave Ryder an even glance. "You will, won't you." It wasn't a question—Ryder was someone who would use any uncertainties to his advantage.

"Your wish is my command," he said, moving toward the door. He stood there waiting for them to precede him into the hall. At least that mama she couldn't tattle to had taught him good manners.

They walked in silence down the darkened hall, with Jenny reaching the front door first. It had an array of locks and safety measures that looked as if it belonged in a nuclear facility, and she waited for him to start unfastening them. He did so quickly and efficiently, pushing open the door into the bright, hot midday sun of New Orleans.

"Have a good day, Ms. Parker," he said, and she knew he was mentally saying don't let the door hit you in the ass on the way out. She could feel relief and regret pulsing through her.

"I have every intention of doing so. I'll call you first thing tomorrow morning to see what the plans are."

"It depends what you consider first thing. I don't get up before ten o'clock."

She didn't believe him, but she was hardly going to say so. "I'll call at eight." Moving past him, she stepped out onto the marble entranceway when something whizzed past her and a piece of stone went flying. For a moment she froze, looking back in confusion, and then the sound came again, like some crazed bumblebee had decided to attack. It stung the side of her head and she put her hand up when suddenly Ryder grabbed her, yanking her back into the darkened house so quickly she stumbled and went sprawling on the hardwood floor. He slammed the door behind them and Soledad quickly knelt at her side, her soft small hands touching Jenny's face, a look of worry in her beautiful dark eyes.

And then it was Ryder's face looming over her, looking both disgusted and inpatient. "Just how big a fucking idiot are you?" he demanded. "Don't you know when you're being shot at?"

Chapter Three

"Shot at?" Jenny echoed dizzily. "Why would anyone shoot at me?" She reached up to touch the stinging spot on the side of her head, and her fingers came away wet and sticky. She didn't have to look at her hand to know it was covered with blood, and she gulped. She'd never been good with blood, particularly her own.

"You tell me," he said. "And it may be your little friend they were after. Whoever they were, they were a piss-poor shot. If it had been me, your head would have been blown apart with the first bullet."

Jenny wasn't sure which was worse, her nausea at his gruesome image or his calmly stated expertise. "Thrilled to know you're so accomplished," she muttered.

The bastard actually smiled. "You have no idea how talented I am," he said. Before she realized what he was doing, he slid his arm behind her back and helped her into a sitting position. She didn't want him touching her, but she wasn't strong enough to sit by herself—not with a ridiculous amount of blood pouring down the side of her face.

"Am I dying?" She realized too late that it gave him the perfect opening. He was probably going to respond with "I should be so lucky."

Once again he surprised her. "No, though you might have a hell of a headache. Head wounds bleed like crazy." She felt the pressure against her waist as he slowly helped her to her feet. "Come on, let's get you cleaned up."

She really wanted to stand on her own two feet, but the feel of the blood sliding down her skin and Soledad's horrified little squeaks only added to her dizziness. She started to sink back, and Matthew Ryder simply did the unthinkable and picked her up in his arms.

"Put me down," she gasped.

"Don't be an even bigger pain in my ass than you've been already," he said tersely, starting up the curving front stairs with Soledad keeping pace with them. "Once you get cleaned up you'll feel a lot better."

If she didn't throw up first. The thought of vomiting all over him filled her with mixed emotions. On the one hand, it would be completely embarrassing, and on the other, it would be perfect revenge for his lack of sympathy. In the scheme of things she didn't like vomiting, so she did her best to swallow her bile, despite the slight bounce as he carried her up the long flight of stairs. She just wanted to go home and go to bed, but Ryder seemed to have other ideas.

"Press your head against my chest." His voice was matter-of-fact.

"Why should I?" The last thing Jenny wanted to do was cuddle up against him. She could already feel the beating of his heart and the warmth of his skin against hers as he mounted the stairs, and it disturbed her. She didn't want to think of him as a living, breathing man—he was too tempting when she was much better off thinking of him as the enemy.

"Because otherwise you'll bleed all over the goddamn carpet." His rough voice was heartless. "We just had this place decorated, and I don't need your blood leaving a trail up to the bedrooms."

"Why, how thoughtful of you. I'll do my best not to bleed on you as well." Her voice was admirably cool.

"Too late for that."

Having someone carry her was a strange sensation, she thought. It made her feel safe, protected, wiping out her instinctive feelings of distrust. He was so strong and warm that she wanted to burrow against him, looking for comfort, but she did her best to simply press her bloody head against his shoulder without rubbing against him. "You're probably used to people bleeding all over you."

"Not really. I usually shoot them from a distance."

That left her speechless. Soledad was with them, a worried expression in her big eyes, and Jenny leaned forward, wanting to reassure her, when Ryder simply pushed her back against his shoulder, holding her there as he reached the top of the landing. "Worry about yourself, not your little waif."

"Is there something I need to worry about?" She couldn't keep the edge from her voice. "I thought this was just a graze." Suddenly she began imagining all sorts of things: her head split open, her bleeding to death in his arms.

"It is. It won't take more than a few minutes to get you cleaned up and bandaged, and nothing's going to happen to your protégé while I take care of it." He turned and looked back at Soledad. "Why don't you go on ahead into the room on the left? There's a TV in there, and if you look hard enough you'll find the Spanish-language channels."

"Don't be a racist!" Jenny said fiercely. "Soledad's English is excellent."

"I was being practical, not a racist. She can watch PBS or soap operas for all I care. You're more than enough to deal with right now—I don't have the time or patience to put up with her."

Jenny sucked in her breath, ready to tear into him when a sharp stabbing pain hit her right between the eyes, and she let out a pathetic whimper. She was going to die after all.

"I thought the headache would hit sooner or later," he said smugly. "Don't worry, it's only normal when you have a bullet graze the side of your head. I'll clean you up, wash away the blood, and find some ibuprofen for you. Unless you want something stronger— I can get you that too."

"Ibuprofen will be just fine. As soon as it kicks in, Soledad and I will leave you in peace and head back home."

"I don't think so."

"I beg your pardon?" Her eyes flew open in dismay.

"You're not going anywhere until I find out who the hell shot at you."

She ground her teeth. "I didn't know you cared."

"I don't. I just don't like people shooting holes in my house. That ridiculous historical committee is going to pitch a fit."

"Knowing New Orleans, I expect most of these houses have had their share of bullet holes," Jenny pointed out.

"True enough." He carried her into one of the rooms, angling her body so she didn't whack her head on the doorway, and Soledad had disappeared. Jenny closed her eyes again, the sight of the room swinging around making her dizzy, and she didn't open them again until he'd set her down.

It was a bathroom the size of a bedroom. The giant marble tub opposite her must have been original to the house—they didn't make bathtubs that size anymore. She was sitting on the commode, and Ryder was rustling through the drug cabinet, pulling out bottles and bandages and littering the marble vanity.

It was then she realized that he was going to have to put his hands on her—on her face. There was something unbearably intimate about it—the touching of one's face was a gesture reserved for lovers and parents. Ryder was neither.

"I can handle it," she said quickly, trying to dismiss him.

Ryder simply ignored her. "You won't be able to see the extent of the wound, particularly with all that blood. Don't be a baby, Parker.

I know how to treat gunshot wounds and you don't. Unless you've been more involved in the family business than I realized."

She was past feeling fear. He didn't know anything, he couldn't, and if she'd felt better she would have snarled at him. Instead, she pulled herself together as best she could. "I believe my family outsources all its violence," she said icily.

She didn't like the cool smile on his face. "Of course you do. I expect you think the tooth fairy is real as well."

"Don't trust everything you hear about the Gauthiers. I won't deny that my family is politically corrupt, but so is everyone else in this city. It's part of its charm." She didn't bother to hide her sarcasm.

"For some reason I don't find them that charming."

"You're a fine one to talk. No one seems to know anything about who and what you and your organization are, but you've made it more than clear you aren't above using lethal force."

If a wolf could smile he would have looked like Ryder. "You don't need to worry about it. Unless you're not exactly what you say you are."

A cold chill slid down her back. "I'm a lawyer who takes on too many pro bono cases for my own good. What else do you think I am?"

"I make it a habit never to trust anyone, counselor. Not even good little girls like you."

Don't let them know you're afraid. She couldn't remember where she'd heard that, but it made perfect sense. She was so busy being pissed off at him that she didn't realize he was already moving his fingers through her blood-matted hair, and then it was too late to do more than freeze.

If he noticed, he didn't say anything. "You're a lucky girl, Parker. A fraction of an inch closer and we wouldn't be having this conversation."

"That's too high a price to pay no matter how obnoxious this conversation is. Ouch!" He'd managed to pull her hair, not by accident, she decided, and her desire to snarl at him increased.

"I knew you'd think so," he said, daubing at a tender place on her skull. She tried to think of him as a nameless, faceless EMT cleaning up her wound. She glanced down at her pale peach suit— the one she'd chosen as proper for church and lawyerly things, a well-tailored piece of armor against the bastard with his hips at her eye level, giving her a perfect view of the contours of . . .

She jerked her head away, and Ryder swore. "Hold still or you're going to end up a platinum blond."

Instinctively she reached up to touch her hair, coming in contact with his hand. He brushed hers away with clear annoyance. "What are you doing to me?" she demanded.

"Cleaning your wound with hydrogen peroxide. It's not bad enough to need anything more powerful."

"I don't want . . ." She began in panic, thinking of her slightly drab but perfectly acceptable plain brown hair that was not, repeat *not*, russet or any other exotic color.

"I don't give a fuck what you want. You've bled all over the carpets and all over me, and right now I own your ass. We'll do this my way, and if your hair gets screwed up we can play girls' sleepover and do each other's hair. I'm sure there's plenty more peroxide around."

She looked up at his too-long hair dispassionately. "What do I do with you—give you a perm so you can look like Bradley Cooper in *American Hustle*?"

"Cancel that. You're not touching me."

"Don't trust me, Ryder?" she taunted. As long as she didn't let him know how unnerved she was by him, she stood a chance.

"No." His voice was flat.

She didn't flinch. "Besides, a sleepover with you is the absolute last thing in my schedule. Ouch!" she added as he washed the wound. It burned, and she could probably blame his overzealous use of peroxide for that.

"Think again, Parker." There was something about the way he drawled her name that got on her last nerve—she'd already shattered all the other nerves in her body. "You're not going anywhere. Not when someone wants to kill you or your little protégé."

"How do you know they weren't shooting at you?" she countered. "This is your place, not mine, and I'm sure you've made a lot more enemies than I have."

"Is that so? I don't know if I'd take your word for that."

She looked up at him from behind the strands of her wet, blood-soaked hair. "The only person who seems to consider me an enemy is you, Ryder."

Once more that grim mouth showed just the trace of a smile. "You have no idea what I think of you."

She couldn't come up with an answer to that. "I'm not staying here," she said firmly.

"You wanted a place for Soledad to stay. This place is huge. Just stay out of the rooms that are off-limits and we should get along fine."

"Don't . . . Ouch! Are you deliberately hurting me every time we have a disagreement?" She eyed him suspiciously. Her head had continued to throb, the beginnings of a pounding migraine, and she was looking forward to the ibuprofen.

"Yes." He leaned back and looked at her, and for a moment she stared up into his dark, expressionless eyes. "Where's your waif?"

"Stop calling her that! She's twenty years old!" she said at the same time Soledad spoke up from the doorway.

"I am here, Mr. Ryder."

"Help Ms. Parker clean herself up," he said curtly, "unless you think you can't handle it. I can wash her hair—cleaning around a cut like that can be tricky . . ."

"I have a great deal of experience helping people who have been shot or tortured," Soledad said in her liquid, tranquil voice.

He raised an eyebrow at that. Jenny had never seen anyone who could do that, and for a moment she was distracted.

"Do you indeed?" he answered Soledad, and Jenny was temporarily forgotten. "You'll have to tell me all about it at a later time."

"Of course, Mr. Ryder," Soledad said politely, her accent barely noticeable.

He turned his attention back to Jenny. "You," he said in a peremptory voice, "behave yourself and do what she tells you. I'm leaving you in her hands, and I expect you to look halfway human when she's done with you. I'll find you some clothes, and see what our surveillance cameras picked up. In the meantime it might be worth your while to think of anyone you might have pissed off with your dulcet ways."

"Apart from you?"

"Well, I've got an alibi, remember? I'll find something clean for you to wear—you look like a cast member of *The Walking Dead.*"

"I believe the rotting flesh is the major fashion statement," she said.

"Not if they just had a snack." He rose, all fluid grace, and turned back to Soledad, who'd been following all this with a bewildered expression on her face. "Make sure she doesn't do anything foolish."

He started out the door, and Jenny called after him, incensed. "I didn't do anything foolish! I just opened your goddamn door." But he was already gone.

"The Walking Dead?" Soledad echoed, looking perplexed.

"A television show," Jenny said briefly. She was hardly going to explain to Soledad about the gory TV show that had been her obsession from the first episode.

Funny that Ryder happened to mention it, but then it was a part of popular culture by this time. She turned to look at the massive bathtub that graced the huge room. Ryder and his organization certainly had spared no expense in the renovation of this old house. They could fit a family of four in that bathtub.

"I will draw you a bath," Soledad said in the mellifluous English that she'd said was compliments of the good sisters who'd lived and died as missionaries in Calliveria. "It will calm and relax you."

"I'm perfectly calm and relaxed." Her defensive voice was pitched just a bit too high.

Soledad smiled sweetly as she turned on the taps. Instant hot water responded with a blast of steam. She turned back. "May I help you undress? Your pretty clothes—I do not know if I will ever be able to get them clean."

"I told you before, Soledad, you don't have to do things like that! I could send the suit to the dry cleaners but I don't think I ever want to see that thing again."

She began unbuttoning the stained silk jacket, then stared down at her bloody hands. Shuddering, she looked away.

"We may have to go back to the house to find me some clean clothes. I don't trust Ryder—he'll probably find a Mardi Gras costume or something equally disturbing for me to wear."

"I think Mr. Ryder will be taking very good care of you, Ms. Parker."

There was a faintly teasing note in Soledad's voice, one Jenny chose to ignore. Soledad's English might be flawless, but that didn't mean she understood the nuances. "I doubt it," she said wearily. Ryder disliked and distrusted her, for all his decent attempts at taking care of her. Once she got Soledad settled she'd have no more reason to see him, which was a very good thing. He was far too suspicious for her peace of mind, and she suspected he wasn't the type to let anything go. She needed to get as far away from him as she could.

She had no doubt at all the bullet that had hardly grazed her scalp had been meant for him. After all, he was the one who dealt with terrorists and international criminals—she was simply an immigration lawyer, and a pro bono one at that.

She felt strange stripping off her ruined clothes in his house, stepping into his deep bathtub. She might as well enjoy it while she could—her narrow shotgun house had only a rusty stall shower, and the luxury of a bath like this was not to be taken lightly. With a sigh of decadent delight, she slid down into the warm, faintly scented water and closed her eyes.

Chapter Four

Ryder stared at the computer screen, scrolling through the images impatiently. There was no angle surrounding the house that wasn't covered by surveillance cameras, and it had taken Jack, the best hacker in the business, no more than fifteen minutes to isolate the car driving by, the shadowy passenger in the hoodie, the almost imperceptible circle of a gun barrel pointed at the old house. A gun that size shouldn't have been able to reach the front door, the first and possibly most important conundrum, the second being the identity of the shooter. It hadn't taken Jack any longer to trace the anonymous late-model sedan to a stolen car report, and he had little doubt it was already abandoned on the edge of the Ninth Ward.

Ms. Jenny Parker, Esquire, could have been right and the bullet was meant for him. After all, no matter how discreet they'd been, the underworld would become aware of their location sooner rather than later, and he had enough murderous enemies to fill a 747.

But his instincts, the ones that had kept him alive to the ripe old age of thirty-seven in the most dangerous life imaginable, told him that the bullet was meant for one of his visitors. The question was, which one? And why?

"So you've finally got Parker in your clutches," Jack drawled from his spot in front of the bank of computer screens. Jack Abbott was one of the Committee's greatest assets, though he seldom left the computer room. "You figured out whether she's involved or not?"

"If I had proof she was part of the sex trafficking, she'd already be dead." Ryder's voice was matter-of-fact. "I just know she isn't who and what she says she is. She acts twitchy around me."

"Anyone with any sense will act twitchy around you, Ryder," Jack said dryly. "You're a lethal weapon and maybe she's smart enough to see that. I would have thought you would have managed to get a read on her by now."

Ryder frowned. "Easier said than done. She was trying to get the last girl from the boat into our household, and now she's wormed her way in here as well. Good thinking for an enemy."

"She said she wants to be here?"

"She's too smart for that. I'm thinking that bullet wasn't meant for anyone. I think it was just an excuse to get us to keep them here, where they think they can find out what we know. Hell, maybe Parker plans to murder us in our sleep."

"Doesn't seem the type. Doesn't seem the type to be involved in an international sex-trafficking ring either."

"You forget she comes from a family of gangsters," Ryder said grimly. "We've got a complete background on her, down to the tiniest of details."

"True enough," Jack said. "But as far as I can see there isn't any connection between them and the Corsini family or their front man, His Eminence. We cleared up that nest of spiders, and the shipload of human cargo brought up from Calliveria was probably just the tail end of the Corsinis' operation. And there's no connection with Jenny Parker at all. Apparently she's a perfect Mother Teresa."

"Except that she's been there from the beginning, making certain the hostages got taken care of, sent off someplace safe where no one could ask any questions. She's done a great job of covering up, whether she meant to or not."

"Well, don't kill her until you're sure she meant to," Jack warned him. "And what about the girl who's with her? If she's one of the bad guys, why would she bring a possible witness in with her?" Jack spun around his chair, ignoring the screens for the moment.

Ryder considered it. "Maybe Soledad is part of the whole mess as well. Just because she looks like a Madonna doesn't mean she's not evil."

"You don't trust anyone, do you?" Jack said.

"No. Not if I have even the slightest reason to doubt them. And Parker's been just a little too busy with the refugees to satisfy me. We know there's at least one person at this end that we haven't caught yet. It may or may not be Parker, and I'm not giving up on her until I'm sure."

"And if you find out she's the local connection . . . ?"

"I suppose it depends what Peter Madsen says. He can make the hard decisions—it comes with the territory. The smart thing to do would be to get rid of her," he said coolly. He could do it, of course, if ordered to. It wouldn't matter that he didn't want to.

Jack shook his head. "How do you think her family would take to that?"

"You think I don't know how to make people disappear? I've never been squeamish about any of the less savory parts of my job, and that's not about to change," he said quietly. "Either Ms. Jenny Parker is a bleeding-heart liberal who enjoys throwing her time and money into a lost cause, or she's a member of a ruthless cartel that traffics in women and children. All she has to do is slip up, just for a moment, and I'll clean up the mess."

Jack shook his head. "She doesn't give off that kind of vibe."

"You haven't even met her face-to-face. I have and I still can't read her."

Jack watched him out of quiet eyes. "You ever made a mistake?"

Ryder froze. "What kind of mistake?"

"You ever killed an innocent?"

"No one's innocent," he said flatly. "If she's the target then someone had a reason to shoot at her, so she must have pissed someone off, big-time. Apart from me."

"You gonna tell me why she pisses you off?" Jack said, spinning back to look at his computer screens full of data.

"What the fuck do you mean by that?"

"I think there's more going on than you're aware of, and I don't want you jumping to conclusions just because she makes you feel uncomfortable."

"If I were the type to jump to conclusions, she'd be out somewhere in the bayou, served up as alligator food."

"You're a sick bastard, Ryder. You know that, don't you?"

"Yup," he said.

Jack punched in a few numbers on the computer before turning back. "Look at it this way: the Gauthier family has enough enemies—she might just be the target of a mob war. Taking out a relatively innocent member of the family could always deliver a crippling blow."

"Maybe. The big-eyed waif with the mysterious background might have been the target as well. After all, Parker's looking for protection for her, so there must be an interesting story behind that Madonna expression and passive demeanor. Either way, with the two of them in the house I'll figure out what's going on. If it turns out she's innocent, I can push her off to Remy or even one of the junior operatives—it's a simple enough issue compared to what I usually deal with. Speaking of which, where is Remy?"

"On his way back from Oklahoma City," Jack said briefly. "Weapons transport."

As usual the information was succinct, without any human interaction. As far as Ryder was concerned, Jack was part machine himself, no emotions, no social niceties. It made work more efficient—right then Ryder thought he'd be happy if all his coworkers were the efficient, deadly machines Jack was.

"Emery, Johnson, and Duvall?" Ryder demanded of his favorite machine.

"Emery's downstairs in reception, Johnson's awaiting orders, Duvall's with his wife."

Ryder made a muffled sound of disapproval. "Why the fuck did he have to go and get married? Women are nothing but a complication."

"So are men," Jack pointed out absently, typing something into one of his many keyboards.

"Call Emery, will you?" Ryder demanded. "I've got a job for her."

That was enough to make Jack turn around, and once more Ryder was startled by his face. Jack was almost unnaturally beautiful, with long straight black hair, and an Asian tilt to eyes of an impossibly blue color—some trick of genetics Mendel would be hard put to explain. He had long lashes that could effectively hide his expression, high cheekbones, and a mouth he'd been told by Emery was luscious. With a face like that he'd be excellent at undercover work, particularly in third-world countries where his mixed-race beauty would blend in, but so far he'd been much more valuable gathering intel on anything and anybody.

"Something I can do? I'm just running facial recognition and that takes time."

It took forever, even with Jack at the helm, and Ryder knew it. He also knew what had prompted Jack to make the offer. He didn't like having anyone up on his floors, near his computers, if he could help it, and that seemed to go double for Emery.

"Secure the third-floor work areas and show Ms. Parker's little waif to one of the guest rooms while I take our lawyer friend home. And look a little deeper into the Gauthiers. Just because we haven't found anything so far doesn't mean they're clean in this deal. The trafficking run by the Corsini family had to have been public knowledge among the criminals in the city, which includes the Gauthiers. Check again to make sure none of them was involved. There are three brothers besides the old man, aren't there?"

"Maurice runs their shady law firm, Tonino is involved in shipping, and the youngest one, Billy, just graduated from college and is off in Europe," Jack rattled off instantly.

"Tonino is the obvious one, if he's connected with shipping. Shipping what?"

"Cheap souvenirs from China, with stolen artwork and drugs on the side, though they've been raided a couple of times and nothing was ever found."

"A couple of times? Someone's making hefty payoffs."

"That's how business works in New Orleans," Jack said cynically. "You think that bullet was meant for Parker and not the Madonna?"

"Why not me? There sure the hell are enough people who hate me."

"You're hard to kill," Jack said. "So why are you thinking Parker's the target?"

Ryder shrugged. "Instinct, and those instincts are why it's so hard to kill me. She's hiding something, and I intend to find out what." Jack had already turned his back on Ryder, staring at the screens, dismissing their conversation from his consciousness. "Keep checking," he said.

Jack didn't respond, his straight back a reproach to such an unnecessary order, and Ryder turned to deal with the lying Parker.

He shoved the door shut behind him, closing Jack into his domain, and slid the bookcases across the entrance, camouflaging it from any nosy visitors. He turned and almost slammed into his quarry.

She was watching him with no more than casual interest. "That seems awfully low-tech for a super spy agency."

"We're not a super spy agency," he said irritably, taking in her appearance. When he'd seen her before, she'd worn her short hair in a professional sweep across her forehead. Now it was a rumpled mess, a halo of curls around her face, curls she'd always manage to keep under strict control, and he found himself wondering what else she kept under strict control.

She was wearing the clothes he'd left out for her. His jeans fit her—she filled them out much better than he ever had. Not that he gave a damn, but he couldn't help but notice she had a delectable butt. He immediately put it out of his mind.

His old T-shirt clung to her, and a bloody stain was spreading from her bra into the white fabric. For some reason he'd had no idea how curvy she was beneath those businesslike suits she wore like Southern armor. He had a hard time dealing with Southern women—the charm seemed to cover a deadly determination, though in most cases it was simply a lethal determination to get their own way.

The woman in front of him had succeeded, as she presumably knew she would. He made a noncommittal sound. "That's why we don't like having guests. But don't worry, Parker," he said, his use of her name deceptively friendly, "you've won this round. We'll keep the two of you here for the time being until we ascertain whom that shot was meant for. In the meantime your little one is already settled in"—at least he hoped she was—"and I'm taking you home to get your things."

She bristled immediately. "I don't need anyone to take me home, Mr. Ryder. I'm perfectly capable of taking care of it myself. And you're mistaken—I'm not staying here. I have a perfectly good house, and there's no reason why anyone would have shot at me."

"Yeah, that's what the bullet graze on the side of your head is saying."

"No one wants to hurt me. It's Soledad they're after, not me. I told you she needed protection. I'd rather have your resources spent on her than wasting your time with me."

"And what makes you think I give a shit about your preferences?" he said.

She gave him something just short of a glare. "Then surely you can send someone else home with me if you're suddenly smitten with concern for my welfare."

"No one else is available," he said with a blatant disregard for the truth. "Your waif is under lock and key, and the sooner you can get your things, the sooner I can dump you and get back to my work."

"I'm fine on my own," she said, and he controlled his instinctive snort of exasperation. Of course she'd be convinced she was safe, no matter what she was hiding. Her old man, Fabrizio, would make certain she was protected at all times. So much for turning her back on the family business, which was all well and good until she needed protection or a favor.

They wouldn't provide protection from him. There was something going on with her, something inexplicable. The tension between them was palpable, but it wasn't simply a matter of dislike. More women than he could remember despised him—some he'd wanted, some he hadn't—but there was a hidden thread of . . . something between them, something he didn't want to look at too closely. There was definitely more to her than met the eye. For all she looked like an auburn-haired pixie, he wasn't fooled into thinking the surface had anything to do with the real woman inside. She had secrets, and he never trusted a woman with secrets. Especially not the daughter of one of the most corrupt political families he'd ever seen.

He didn't have time to waste on her. She probably wasn't a major player, and the sooner he could clear her, the sooner he could get back to business.

Giving her a deliberately impatient look, he started forward. "You coming?"

"What makes you think it's safe to walk out the front door? Your enemies might still be out there."

He mentally counted to ten. "We haven't decided whether they were shooting at me or you or your supposedly endangered waif, which is why we're holding on to both of you. Once we know she's safe we'll get her settled in some anonymous city, and she can go on to live the American dream. In the meantime our computer hacker is checking the surveillance tapes in the live feed. The facial-recognition software should give us an answer sooner or later, and in the meantime Jack will let us know if the coast is clear."

"Isn't that rather a lot for one man?" she said caustically.

"You haven't met Jack. And you're not about to, either. And that's the last question I'm answering. Where are your bloody clothes?"

"I tossed them," she said. "Soledad told me it was impossible to get blood from silk."

Ryder paused. "What bothers me," he said meditatively, "isn't that she knew about field dressings and bloodstains, but why the hell should she know about silk? Hardly your common jungle wear in Calliveria."

There was only the faintest movement of her long eyelashes, but he realized the same thing had occurred to her. No dummy was his Miss Parker.

Not his, and he sure the hell didn't want her. He just wanted her sorted out and gone.

"If I have to be escorted home, couldn't your computer guy take me?" she said.

"He's busy." Not a complete lie, but he'd sent Jack off on diddly-shit missions like this before. He could have taken care of this one with no difficulty, but Jenny Parker was his job, not Jack's. "Look, if it makes you happy we'll go out through the basement."

Ms. Parker made a long-suffering sigh. "Let's just get it over with. My head is killing me, and all I want to do is lie down in a darkened room and sleep."

He frowned. "You think you might have a concussion?"

"No! It was just a graze, and I certainly don't need someone hovering at my bedside, waking me up every few hours."

"I wasn't offering."

She gave him that haughty look she'd perfected. Usually he liked cold women who were completely secure with who and what they were. Not Ms. Parker, but then, her self-assurance was only skin-deep. "Good," she snapped. "Your job is to take care of Soledad, my job is to take care of myself, which involves a long nap in my own house."

"Dream on." He put his hands on her when she headed for the front door, and apart from yanking her arm away from him and glaring at him, she didn't let out a peep. She didn't even remember her waif until he'd shepherded her next to one of the sleek, low-slung cars in the basement garage.

"I didn't say good-bye to Soledad."

"That's all right, one of my people will explain everything."

"But I need . . ." She started back toward the stairs, but he simply caught her and swung her around back to the Audi.

"You don't need anything. Everything will be explained to her, and you don't have to worry your pretty little head about it again."

She made a low, warning sound, like a jungle cat about to strike. "Don't you fucking patronize me!"

"Then don't act like a baby. You wanted to dump her on me—consider her dumped. You just come along as the booby prize. We need to find out who shot at you. Once we do, you can go home and we'll get her settled with the job and an apartment and a new name if necessary. What more do you want?"

It almost seemed as if she were going to tell him. "To see the last of you," she said finally.

He wasn't sure whether to believe her or not. She was lying about something, and he still couldn't tell what. "The feeling's mutual," he said. The sooner she was permanently out of his life, the better. "Now get in the fucking car."

Chapter Five

Jenny prided herself on the fact that she was practical, levelheaded, and unemotional. At that moment she found herself unaccountably close to tears. She wrapped her arms around her body—the loose T-shirt wasn't enough in the icy blast of the air conditioner as he drove the Audi too fast through the tourist-jammed streets of New Orleans, but she said nothing. She had no intention of uttering a single word to him. If she needed to follow up on Soledad, she'd have Daisy, her paralegal, make the call. She certainly wasn't going to give up her house for even a day. Soledad would be safe on Magazine Street, and she'd be safe in her tumbledown shotgun cottage.

Except that Daisy was a wuss, and she'd likely crumble before a bully like Ryder. And that's exactly what he was, a big, mean, beautiful, scary bully, with gentle hands when it came to bullet grazes . . .

Shit, she was going to have to talk to him after all. "Shouldn't we report the shooting to the police?"

"No."

"What if my wound gets infected and I end up having to go to the hospital? They'll be asking all sorts of questions—you're supposed to report gunshot wounds."

"Doctors are supposed to report them, not the people who get shot. And you won't need a hospital or any kind of follow-up unless you're the biggest hypochondriac in the world. It was a small graze. I cleaned it thoroughly, and the only aftereffect you're going to suffer is a headache."

"Oh, really? I thought that was you."

"Funny." His voice was flat.

Okay, now she could shut up. Snapping back at him gained too much attention—she needed to be soft and quiet and polite so he didn't look too closely. Even though she was still burning with questions, she wasn't going to ask him a thing. He'd just blow her off.

Could someone really have been shooting at her? Granted, Billy was upset that she wouldn't return the cell phone that was right now resting in her pocket, but Billy would never hurt her. That cell phone had been part and parcel of the trouble Billy had gotten into, and he was going to need to convince her that there was nothing incriminating on it before she'd even consider returning it, and so far he'd done nothing.

So if they weren't shooting at her, and her instincts told her Ryder wasn't the target either, then that left Soledad, making her safety an even more important concern.

"Will you tell me if you identified the shooter?" she blurted out, then could have bit her tongue.

To her surprise he answered her. "Depends who he is. Since at first glance you're the least likely target, I'll probably deal with it myself. Maybe you were just in the wrong place at the wrong time. Which you seem to make a habit of doing, if I remember correctly."

Bastard, she thought silently, fuming. With luck she would keep her damned mouth shut until they reached her house.

And then she realized he was heading in the wrong direction, toward the mansions on the edge of the French Quarter. "Where do you think you're going?"

"I'm taking you home. What's the address?"

"Now you ask," she said grumpily. "I don't live in the French Quarter."

He turned to look at her, cold blue eyes full of something she couldn't quite define.

"I did a complete background check on you, lady, right after you showed up on the container ship. You live in the French Quarter."

"I haven't lived there in four months. I live at the edge of the Ninth Ward."

She managed to shock a reaction out of him. "You live where?"

"How the hell did you think I could afford a house?"

"People who wear Louboutin shoes can afford a house anywhere they want."

He certainly knew which buttons to push. "Those were a hand-me-down from my sister-in-law—they were too big for her. And despite your narrow-minded assumptions, I'm a far cry from wealthy. I own a run-down house which I'm gradually fixing up, and I'm very proud of it."

"I bet those shoes are real handy when you're pulling nails," he drawled.

She gave him a slow, considering look. "Did I run over your dog? Insult your mama? Cast aspersions on your manhood? Why do you always do your best to piss me off?"

He laughed then, but it wasn't a warming sound. "'Cast aspersions'? Who the hell talks like that? And trust me, my manhood can stand up to any aspersions you care to cast, if you'll pardon the expression."

It only took her a moment to get his pun, and she growled low in her throat, turning her face toward the window.

"Did I embarrass you, Parker? I knew you were a prude, but I didn't know it was that bad."

She realized belatedly that he thought she was upset about his manhood standing up, and her ire rose. "What in God's name makes you think I'm a prude? I was born and bred in New Orleans—no one could come from the Big Easy and remain a prude. I've seen enough things to shock a hardened criminal." *Hardened.* Good God, how had she managed to come up with that? Everything was now sounding obscene to her.

His grin made it clear he hadn't missed the double meaning, but thankfully he didn't comment on it. "Yeah, but you went away to school in the North from the time you were ten years old. I'm guessing your family didn't want their darling only daughter to be tainted by their shady business dealings."

"Not exactly. My mother died when I was ten, and my father didn't want to be bothered raising a little girl. I was always the odd one out in my family." Her and Billy, she thought, but she wasn't about to even mention his name out loud. "And what makes you think everyone who spent time in the North is a prude? I assume that would include you, since you clearly don't belong in the South. You're the very antithesis of a Southern gentleman."

"No sipping mint juleps on the front porch or whupping slaves in the back forty. No, Parker, I'm no gentleman at all, least of all a Southern one. I grew up in Idaho."

"I bet there are just as many prudes in Idaho. And I'm not a goddamn prude!" she added belatedly.

"Would you like me to tell you what a prude you are?" His voice was silky with a kind of menace. "You wouldn't imagine the kinds of things I know about you. What you like, what you don't like. What you're willing to do, what you refuse to do. I know the name of every lover you've ever had."

Ha! She could call his bluff on that one. The only lover she'd had, apart from her husband, Greg, was the fumbling college student who'd taken her virginity one unpleasant night up north, and even she had blanked on his name. He made it sound like he thought there were dozens.

"Name them all," she taunted him, secure in her bluff. "Don't leave out a single one of them."

"That would be hard to do." There was just the fainted caress of the word *hard*, and she ground her teeth. "Gregory Parker and Ricky Turnbull, who died in a car accident about five years ago, by the way. I realize you two had lost touch."

She could feel the color drain away from her face. *Stupid, stupid, stupid!* She knew his mysterious organization had some of the most advanced intel-gathering abilities in the world. Of course he could find out anything he wanted to know. The question was, why did he want to know it?

The last thing she was going to do was ask him. She'd dug herself into a very uncomfortable hole, and she wasn't going to make it worse. "Turn left up ahead," she said abruptly. A thought struck her, and she decided, what was another foot or two? "How come you know all about my absolutely useless sexual history, and you don't know where I live?"

"It's your past I check on. Remy had already vetted your present, and I wasn't particularly interested in the details."

No, another foot or two in that hole was worse. "Then you can find the house on your own," she said stubbornly, leaning back, prepared to ignore him. "Ask your friend Remy for the address."

"Already got it."

She wanted to beat her head against the dashboard in frustration, but she managed to keep her expression distant and stony. "Then we have nothing more to say to each other."

"Nothing more," he agreed.

Damn, her head hurt. She needed to get away from him, grab a couple of Tylenol to beef up the ibuprofen, and then retire to her dark bedroom with an ice pack. Assuming she could find her way to the bed without breaking her neck on the pile of lumber she had stacked in the hallway in preparation for reframing the back porch. So he knew she was lousy at sex and came from a family of criminals. Did he know she could frame a wall, tape and spackle drywall, do simple electricity and plumbing, and even manage a bit of finish carpentry? Of course not—he just wanted to know all the bad, stupid things about her.

Well, fine. The only bad, stupid thing she knew about him was that he was a royal bastard, and that was enough. As long as she kept away from him she'd be fine. There was only one problem with that plan. She didn't want to.

It took her a moment to realize he'd already pulled up in front of the small house that was her pride and joy. He'd even turned off the car, and he was watching her out of hooded eyes. "You just going to sit there?" he said. "Or were you waiting for me to open your door for you? I thought we established I wasn't a gentleman."

"I never had any doubts," she said, reaching for the door handle. To her horror he climbed out as well, slamming the door behind him, and she stared at him across the top of the Audi. "What are you doing?"

"Seeing you to your door."

"Oh, good God," she said crossly. "I'm home, I'm safe. Just go away—you're making my headache worse."

"My heart's breaking for you," he said, moving ahead of her up the front stairs that led to the narrow porch. New lumber gleamed from the places where she'd already replaced rotting floorboards, but he didn't bother to look down and admire her work. Of course he didn't. "I doubt that anyone was gunning for you today, but just in case, I intend to check over the place before we leave here."

"For Christ's sake," she said, pushing ahead of him and opening the door. "How many times do I have to tell you I'm not coming back to Super Spy Central?"

"You have any idea how annoying that is?" he said, shouldering past her, and she found herself shrinking away from him, skittish as always. He stalked down the center of her house, his eyes sweeping each room as he went. She waited a moment, and then followed him, nervous with him in her precious house. It was like having a tiger loose in a bedroom.

"I love shotgun cottages," she said, knowing she was babbling. "The way one room leads into another makes it feel like my own hobbit home." *Hobbit home? What a stupid fucking thing to say!*

Fortunately he seemed to be ignoring her, searching through her front parlor, looking behind the curtains she'd hung to shut out some of the midday sun, then the unfinished kitchen, the microwave and hot plate and dorm-size refrigerator the sum total of her current culinary abilities. He scouted around the functional bathroom, into the first bedroom, and on into the second, with her unmade bed, her clothes on the floor.

She needed him out of her half-renovated house. He was too big, too intense, too *there*. If she had any white sage she would have burned it after he left, because she had a sense she was going to feel his presence here long after he was gone.

"What's out back?" He jerked his head toward the flimsy back door that she had yet to replace. "Because if you're relying on that door to keep you safe from predators, you're even more naïve than I thought."

"I'm not the slightest bit naïve." *And that was a lie*, she thought. "I was born in this city, remember? There's a tall, locked fence all around the backyard. Besides, there are some advantages to being a Gauthier. People think twice about interfering with Fabrizio Gauthier's only daughter."

He surveyed her coolly. "I would guess they would. In that case I'll let you get . . ." He froze midsentence, and all affect dropped away from him.

Her stomach clenched in sudden fear. It was like seeing a man turn into a machine, the look of a serial killer when he finally dropped his surface charm. Had he seen something that implicated her? "What's wrong?"

He moved so fast he was a blur of energy, grabbing her and running toward the back door. She tried to shriek at him, to demand what the hell he was doing, when he pulled her into his arms and threw them both through the broken back door, the remaining wood splintering around them, as the world exploded in a maelstrom of fire and heat and noise.

They landed hard on the packed dirt behind her house, his body beneath hers, and then he turned and pulled her under him, as the sky rained hell and damnation.

Chapter Six

Jenny was deaf, she was blind, she couldn't breathe as his body crushed her into the hardscrabble earth as she fought for air. A roaring filled her ears, a blast of heat practically blistering her, and everything was sharp and painful.

Her breath came back with a shocking whoosh, letting her take in thick, greasy smoke, and she began to choke, squashed beneath his weight, stones digging into her back, the fires of hell all around her.

He was up, pulling her with him, but her leg collapsed under her, and she saw with shock there was a jagged piece of wood sticking into her calf. With a muttered curse he scooped her up and began running, leaving her with only jumbled impressions.

Her house was gone. In its place was a roaring fire, billowing, ugly smoke rising in the Sunday-afternoon air. The walls were gone, and half of the empty house beside hers was gone as well.

Her gates had been blown off their moorings, and he climbed over them, cursing, out into the street where a crowd had begun to gather. The Audi was engulfed in flames as well, but Ryder didn't slow down, didn't hesitate, taking a narrow alley away from the conflagration, moving until he saw a small parking lot. It was closed, the gate chained across the front, but there were still cars in the yard.

He set her down carefully. "This is our best bet," he said, half to himself, and pulled out a set of lock picks. It took him less than thirty seconds to open the big lock, and then he slid the chains free before scooping her up again.

"I can walk," she tried to say, but it came out with a spasm of coughing.

"Shut up."

So much for comforting small talk. He went straight for an older-model sedan, used the same picks to unlock the passenger side and push her inside. He slid in behind the wheel before she even realized he'd closed the car door, and a moment later the engine roared to life.

"Were you a car thief when you were young?" The words came out in a croak that sounded foreign to her ears, but at least it was understandable.

"Yes," he said, and tore out of the parking lot, heading away from the remnants of her beloved house.

Jenny fastened her seat belt with shaky fingers, and her hands were black with smoke and dirt. They didn't hurt, and while she could see some blood beneath the soot, she didn't think they'd been burned. She flexed them tentatively, then leaned back as the stolen car careened through the streets of the Ninth Ward. The car smelled like singed fur, which made no sense, since it had been two blocks away from the blast. Sudden realization hit her, and she looked down at her blackened clothes. The shard of wood was still sticking in her calf, and she reached down to pull it free when his hand stopped her.

"Leave it."

He hadn't taken his eyes off the road and she couldn't figure out how he'd known she was reaching for it. "It doesn't hurt," she said, surprised.

"You're in shock."

"I am not," she said, stupidly incensed.

"Don't argue with me. I'll remove it when we get back to the house."

"The house? I want an emergency room."

"Wuss."

"I want the police."

"This is New Orleans, remember? The police aren't going to be doing us any good, and it would give them a license to search the big house. I'm not letting any curious eyes in there. Bad enough I had to let you in."

"My house . . ." The words choked in her mouth and her already-raw throat.

"I'll find out who blew up your house, and Parker, I promise, I'll even turn him over to your family. There's a fate worse than death."

There was almost a note of kindness in his voice, and for a moment she wanted to cry, but her eyes were dry and scratchy.

She tried to pull herself together. She wasn't in shock—just because she couldn't cry and apparently couldn't feel pain didn't mean she was such a frail creature. She drew herself up in the seat. "How do you think they knew you'd be there?"

"What?" He took a corner at a reckless speed, but all four tires hugged the road, and he seemed to have a preternatural ability to avoid the police.

"Why else would anyone bomb the place? No one would want to hurt me. You're the one involved in international . . . whatever." Words failed her. She wasn't sure exactly what he did. "They must have been following you . . ."

"Sorry, sweetheart, but that bomb was set ahead of time. There was no way anyone would guess when I'd be there. It was meant for you or your little waif, just as that bullet was."

Her conscious mind immediately rejected it, just as it rejected the fact that the house she'd loved and worked so hard on was gone in a matter of seconds. "But why?"

"You tell me. You're the one who insisted Soledad was in danger. Maybe you were right after all. Or maybe there's something you haven't been telling me."

Jenny's stomach knotted. This couldn't have anything to do with the cell phone lodged safely in her front pocket—no one but Billy knew she had it, and she wasn't giving it back until she was convinced there was nothing incriminating on it. She could always destroy it, but right now it was the only hold she had over him. As long as she had it, he couldn't be tempted to get mixed up in that disgusting business again.

"Why bother shooting at us if they were just going to blow us up a few hours later?" she said stubbornly.

He slanted a glance at her. "Maybe you're not in shock after all. It's a good question. Maybe they wanted to shoot you and then blow up any incriminating stuff left behind."

"You saw my house—do you think there was anything incriminating in that chaos?"

He ignored her question. "Or maybe they needed time to set the charges, and shooting at you kept you away from the house for a while."

"Two inches closer and I'd be dead."

"Two inches farther and it would have been just a scare. It would have been a hard shot to make. You piss anyone off in the past few weeks?"

"Besides you and my father?" *And my brother*, she added silently. "I don't think so."

"Great company. You got any enemies? Disgruntled boyfriends?"

"You already said you knew my entire history."

"Yeah, both of them would be disgruntled," he drawled, and instinctively she hit him in the side, no more than an angry jab. She was shocked at his flinch and the sudden outpouring of very impressive cursing. "Hit me again and you'll regret it," he growled.

"That was nothing," she said righteously.

"Usually."

He was wearing black. A black T-shirt and black jeans, and the side of the shirt was shiny. With blood.

"You've been hurt," she said flatly, guilt and shame swamping her. This man had saved her life and she'd only made things worse.

"Don't worry about it. It's nothing. Just don't punch me."

"I'm sorry," she said, stricken. "You carried me even though you were hurt, even though I probably could have limped along."

"I told you, you were in shock."

She looked out the window, biting her lip. They weren't anywhere near the Garden District, and she turned to look back at him. "Where are you taking me? The house is in the opposite direction."

"I changed my mind. We're going to see a doctor friend to get patched up. Don't worry, she's got her license."

Jenny felt unaccountably defeated when she should have been relieved. The less time she was alone with Matthew Ryder and his suspicions, the better. "Good," she said. "And then I can go . . ." She suddenly realized she couldn't go home. There was no home anywhere. No clothes, no photographs, no favorite paperbacks piled by her narrow bed, no jar of Sumatran coffee pods by her fancy coffee maker. No makeup or expensive hyacinth-scented shampoo, no shoes, damn it. She took a deep breath of despair, and then the physical reaction set in, so that she was rocked by a spasm of coughing.

The coughing was so violent it brought tears to her eyes, but she fought them back.

"You're coming back to headquarters," he said flatly. "Once we get patched up we'll head back to my place. In case you hadn't noticed, someone wants to kill you or your protégé. How many people knew she was staying with you?"

"No one knew," she said wearily. "In fact, she hadn't even moved in yet. You saw my place—it's in the midst of . . . It was in the midst of a major renovation. I was going to put her on a fold-out bed in the front parlor."

"Really?" he said, sounding no more than casually interested. "Where had Soledad been staying?"

"I had her in a motel room in the French Quarter with round-the-clock protection, but I was running out of money."

"Bullshit. You're a Gauthier—you don't run out of money."

"Fuck you. I don't take money from my father. I have a small inheritance from my mother but I used most of it to buy my house." Her voice didn't falter this time, she noticed with pride. "And my law practice is mostly pro bono—I take only enough paying cases to cover the bills, and they always need to be for something or someone I believe in, like Soledad."

"Well, aren't you the little saint," he drawled. "You insure the house?"

"Of course I did!"

"Then stop bitching."

Fury swept through her. "I wasn't bitching!"

"You were about to, or cry, and I can't stand women who cry."

"I bet you have a lot of experience with them," she said. "How much longer to your doctor friend?"

"Fifteen minutes, depending on the traffic. She's outside of the city. Your leg bothering you?"

"No."

"You're still in shock, then."

"Fuck you."

"Stop offering."

"What?" she shrieked.

57

"Don't worry about it, counselor. Close your eyes and take deep breaths. You know how to meditate? Who am I kidding—of course you do. Lean back and meditate. Just put me and everything unimportant out of your mind."

"Gladly," she said, resisting the temptation to lie and tell him she knew nothing about meditation. She hated to be so predictable. She closed her eyes and began her breathing, focusing on each part of her body and forcing it to relax. Her leg was beginning to throb, she thought in triumph. So much for being in shock. She began to count backward, traveling down the staircase she always pictured, but this time it resembled the one in the American Committee headquarters.

She was gone.

Ryder glanced over at her as her breathing evened out. She was a mess, but she'd been too freaked out to realize it. Her face was covered in soot and dirt, her red-brown hair was singed on one side and bloodstained on the other, and that stick of wood was going to be a bitch to remove. He could always ask Doc Gentry to come to the mansion, but he needed to get Jenny away from Soledad long enough to question her. Her protégé had the unfortunate habit of sticking like glue, and Ryder didn't trust either of them. If Parker was the innocent she seemed to be, then no one would have a reason to kill her. Of course it was just as likely Soledad was the target. His instincts had been on full alert from the moment Ms. Parker interrupted his little pity party that afternoon. Something about the entire situation didn't feel right, but he was damned if he was going to jump to any conclusions without thinking it through. Conclusions were something you couldn't back away from, and he was surprisingly reluctant to condemn Parker without proof positive.

Doc Gentry was across the river, in a hidden little delta just outside the city, and as he pulled up to her deceptively ramshackle building, he felt Jenny begin to stir beside him, and the tension in the car began to rise. His fault as much as hers—he couldn't keep from baiting her. Given that his back was killing him, and he could feel the blood soaking through his shirt into the cloth upholstery of the old POS, it was lucky he could even come up with a civil word. He pulled up to the small, roughly built house and yanked the hot wires apart, effectively turning off the car.

"This is it?" Jenny said in tones of deep distrust as she surveyed the run-down building.

"This is it." He climbed out of the car, hiding his instinctive grimace of pain, and went around to extract her. For a Southern woman she was fast getting out on her own, but she was leaning heavily on the open door, there were beads of sweat on her soot-stained forehead, and he knew her leg wouldn't support her.

"I don't suppose this place comes with something as mundane as a pair of crutches . . . What are you doing? Oh, for God's sake, put me down!" she cried.

"Stop struggling and you'll make this easier for both of us," he said, the searing pain in his back not helping his mood.

Dr. Gentry appeared on the rickety front porch, drying her capable brown hands on a dishtowel. "What you doing here, boy, and who is it you brought me?" she demanded, not moving from the porch.

"Had a bit of trouble, Doc," he said. "Building blew up."

"Not that big-ass fancy place in the Garden District?"

"No, ma'am. This one's a house."

"Put me the fuck down," Jenny whispered fiercely.

"You watch your language, girly, or I'll wash your mouth out with soap while I'm cleaning your wound," Doc said.

"Doc doesn't like cussing," Ryder advised her. He looked back to the old woman. "Can we come in? I'd rather not take her to some-place public."

"You don't look any too good yourself, Ryder. Bring that girl in and I'll see what I can do for the both of you."

He expected more of an argument from Jenny, but she'd stopped fighting, and he carried her into the shack and straight into the small surgery Doc had set up, placing her on the examining table with great care. She immediately tried to scramble off.

"You've been hurt too," she said as he calmly placed her back on the table and held her there.

"Then stop making things worse by fighting me. If Dr. Gentry thought I needed to be seen to first she'd tell you. Now sit still and shut up."

"I was never very good at that."

"Your father should have whipped your ass when you were young."

"He did," she said in a flat voice, one that hinted at troubles that were none of his business.

Doc came into the room before he had time to respond. "Now let's see here what's going on with that leg," the old woman said, wearing a spotless white apron. "Matthew, honey, get that girl a pil-low for her head. You just lie back, and let Doc Gentry take care of you and you'll be right as rain."

The old woman's voice was soft and crooning, almost hypnotic, working her magic, and it was no surprise that Parker lay back on the examining table, a pillow tucked beneath her head, as Doc began to cut away at the jeans. She started to protest, then she must have remembered they weren't her jeans, and she closed her eyes.

"That's right, baby," Doc crooned. "Just relax. I know just how to take care of you."

Ryder had every intention of keeping out of Parker's way, pain in the butt that she was, but apparently Dr. Gentry had other ideas. "Come and hold her hands, Matthew. Make yourself useful."

"I don't . . ." Jenny began.

"I'll tell you what you need," Doc said sternly, and Jenny subsided.

Ryder came forward and took her unwilling hands in his. He knew he must look just as battered and soot-stained as she was. Her hands were small in his big paws, he thought grimly, but he had no doubt hers could be lethal. He'd learned long ago never to underestimate women. His side still hurt from her pulled punch.

He turned his attention to Doc. "Can you take a look at her head when you're finished with her leg? She caught a bullet graze a few hours ago, and I cleaned it up as best I could, but it could use your expert eyes."

"Don't waste your flattery on me, boy. I can see that piss-poor bandage. I'll get to it after I've seen to you."

"I'm fine," he said in a flat voice, his hands tightening on Jenny's.

"Don't you be telling me my business!" she snapped, though her hands were gentle on Jenny's leg. "Now hold on tight, baby, and it'll all be over in a minute."

Jenny obediently shut her eyes, though she made no effort to let go of his hands, and he had no intention of releasing her. He had his back to Doc, focusing on Jenny's pale face, trying to distract himself. She looked like she was in pain.

He heard the beginning of a rip, could feel the tug as it shuddered through her entire body, and Doc pulled out the shard of wood with a sound of triumph. Parker let out a shriek, tears of pain filling her eyes without warning. She quickly blinked them away. For a moment their eyes met, held.

It took him a moment to realize he was rubbing his thumbs across the backs of her hands in an unconscious, soothing gesture.

She tried to let go of him, not needing any crutch, in particular the help of her worst enemy, but she couldn't seem to let go. And he couldn't seem to release her.

"Ouch!" she said weakly.

"Won't be much more," the old woman said in a soft voice. "I just have to make sure I got all the splinters out of the wound before I dress it. Out of my way, boy." She elbowed Ryder to one side. He released Jenny's hand, one of them, but she clung to the other. He made no attempt to pull it free.

"Now let's have a look at that head wound," Dr. Gentry said. "Woo-hoo, that was one close call! I take it the bullet was meant for you?" She turned to Ryder.

"I don't think so. Somebody blew up her house a few hours later. That's why we're here."

"You don't say," Doc mused. "I'll change the dressing after I look after you."

"I'm fine . . ."

"Cut it out, Ryder. I got eyes—I know when someone's hurting," Doc said briefly. She leaned over Parker. "You think you can sit up? I got you stitched up all nice and clean but I can't give you anything for the pain until I check your head, and I have to make sure Ryder isn't going to drop dead on me."

Jenny pushed herself up to a seated position, still looking slightly dazed. "Oh, I'm fine," she protested.

"I've never seen so many 'fine' people show up in my infirmary," Doc Gentry said sarcastically. "Ryder, help her into the wicker rocking chair. She can watch while I deal with you, and that way I can keep an eye on the both of you."

The last thing he wanted was Jenny's watchful eyes, but then he didn't really have a choice. He scooped her up, trying not to flinch as she struggled against his left side, and dumped her into the ancient chair by the table, a chair that had held countless worried mothers over the decades.

"That's right. Now take off your clothes and get up on that gurney."

He gave Doc Gentry a stern look. "You know I'm not going to do that."

"Never seen you worried about modesty before. You don't have anything I haven't seen before, though I do admit you're a sight prettier than most."

"Never had an audience before," he said in a cool, low voice that must have carried straight to Jenny's ears. He glanced at her, but her eyes were closed, and perversely he snapped out her name. "Parker!"

Her eyes flew open, and she looked blessedly cranky beneath the soot and blood. "What?"

"Don't fall asleep. We haven't ruled out a concussion."

"You probably would have left me alone in my house if it hadn't exploded." Her voice was querulous. "Where was the worry about my concussion then?"

"Who said I was going to leave you?"

That shut her up. She slouched into the protesting rocker, for all the world like a grumpy teenager, and the relief that filled him was out of proportion. He didn't bother to examine it too closely. He didn't want her hurt on his watch. Not anymore. Not until he had his answers.

Chapter Seven

She really didn't want to be here, Jenny thought, keeping her eyes determinedly open. She'd been hoping to avoid watching her nemesis take off his shirt, so now she was simply going to have to hope he was pale and flabby, or covered with a thick pelt, because there was no denying that Matthew Ryder, super spy, was one hell of a good-looking man. Even a possible concussion and the loss of her house couldn't dull that knowledge, and she didn't need that kind of distraction.

Maybe she just needed to think about something else. Damn it, she wasn't in shock, but just a hint of denial, and if looking at Ryder would distract her, then she'd damn well look. And fantasize if she felt like it. It wasn't as if he'd ever know. He disliked and distrusted her, and as far as he knew the feeling was mutual. There was nothing dangerous in taking inventory of a good-looking sex object.

He was starting to peel off his bloodstained T-shirt, and she got a flash of tanned, flat stomach. She braced herself.

"Oh, for mercy's sake," the old woman snapped. "Let go of it and I'll cut it off."

"No, thank you." He was still struggling to get the shirt off, and the more stomach she saw the more bothered she felt, until she saw the blood. How badly was he hurt? "I don't intend to go home shirtless," he grumbled.

"And what makes you think I'm too old to have gentlemen callers who might leave clothes behind?" Dr. Gentry demanded, affronted.

"Doc, you have no use for gentlemen," he said. "You like bad boys."

"Which is why I put up with you," she said, advancing on him with a pair of blunt-tipped scissors, and Jenny could tell by the blood on them that they'd been used to cut off her pant leg to expose her wounded calf. For some reason her stomach lurched, but she controlled it, determined to appear unmoved.

In a moment the ruins of the black T-shirt were on the floor and Jenny's errant lust had vanished. To hell with his chiseled abs and golden skin—he had a long gash across his back that was oozing blood and ugly bruises on his shoulders.

"My, my, you two are a pair," the doctor said. "What happened—a house fall on you?"

"So to speak," Ryder said in an even voice, as if he weren't having a nasty wound across his back being cleaned with the same incredibly painful stuff Doctor Gentry had used on her. He didn't even blink. "I told you her house blew up."

"And she escaped with a piece of wood stuck in her leg while your back looks like it landed directly on you."

"Like the Wicked Witch of the West," Ryder said dryly. "I'm sure that's what Ms. Parker was thinking."

Heat flooded Jenny's face. That was exactly what she'd been thinking. "Of course not," she protested weakly.

"What'd you do—throw yourself over her body to protect her?" Dr. Gentry scrubbed at his back with a little more energy, and finally he winced. She shook her head. "Of course you did. Always got to be the hero." She stepped back to survey the wound, which was still oozing blood. "I've got some Krazy glue to fix that."

"Krazy glue?" Jenny echoed, horrified.

"She's talking about surgical glue," Ryder said irritably. "Don't take her at face value—she was top of her class at . . ."

"Long time ago," Dr. Gentry said, her leathery brown face creased with amusement as she turned to Jenny. "And then I'll perform a voodoo rite. You can spare some of your blood, can't you?"

Jenny froze in horror for a nanosecond, then realized she was being teased. She leaned back again in the creaking chair. "Want a piece of my brain too?"

"Depends on how much you got to spare."

"Stop teasing her, Doc," Ryder said, holding very still while she applied the ointment. "You don't want to offend a member of the Gauthier clan."

Dr. Gentry looked unimpressed as she glanced back at Jenny. "What's your name, child?"

"Jenny Parker."

"Jennifer Parker, Esquire, née Gauthier. She doesn't take after her brothers or her father. She is a hopeless do-gooder. She's the one who wants to be a hero." Ryder's voice was a lazy drawl, and Jenny did her best to keep her expression blank. He knew about her brothers—of course he did. But did he know exactly what they did? Exactly what Billy had done, and how she had covered for him?

"I'm surprised she didn't wrestle you to be on top, then," the old woman said. "Get down and get yourself an ice pack for those shoulders. I want to look at your girlfriend's head wound."

"I'm not his girlfriend!"

"She's not . . . !"

The protests came out simultaneously and vigorously, and Dr. Gentry ignore them both. "Why is it"—she inquired of no one in particular—"that young people are so stupid?"

"Neither of us is young, Doc," Ryder said, sliding down from the table with his pantherlike grace. "She's twenty-eight and I'm a hell of a lot older."

"You're thirty-seven, boy. And I notice you don't deny you're stupid."

Ryder stalked from the room without a backward glance, and Jenny started to rise from the chair until Doc's strong, capable hands stopped her. "You don't need to move. I can see just fine from here."

She was surprisingly gentle as she poked at Jenny's scalp, making clucking noises as she asked her all the questions about blurred vision and sleepiness.

"You're good," the old lady said finally. "Don't worry about feeling tired—just hearing about what you went through makes me want to take a nap."

"I think," Jenny said hesitantly, "that I might be in shock, maybe just a little bit. I can't even cry over my house being gone, but all I want to do is curl up in a bed with the covers over my head. But don't tell Ryder that."

"That boy? Of course I won't. He seems to think he knows everything about everything. You'll be right as rain in a little while. Old Dr. Gentry's been around a long time, and that little tap on your head isn't going to do anything. If you've survived being shot, having your house blown up, and being flattened by Ryder, then you're going to be just fine."

"What are you telling her about me?" Ryder's disapproving voice came from the doorway, and instinctively Jenny turned to look, then regretted it.

Somehow in that short time he'd managed to take a shower, and water still glistened on his bare chest.

"Where are the ice packs?" Dr. Gentry demanded.

"Screw the ice packs. What are you telling her about me?"

"Not a God Almighty thing except that you must've crushed her."

Jenny was surprised Doc even bothered to answer his rough question. "Don't be rude," Jenny snapped at him. "I already know who you are and exactly what you do."

"I doubt that. You need another bath but Doc only has a shower. If Doc is finished with you I can help you get clean."

"I'll help her," Doc said sternly.

"To paraphrase your elegant words, she doesn't have anything I haven't already seen."

"I don't give a damn what you have or haven't seen. The woman deserves her modesty."

"I thought you had somewhere to be," he said with a meaningful undertone.

"I don't leave my patients until they're ready. Now get those damned ice packs, or you won't be able to move your shoulders by tomorrow."

He gave her a disbelieving glance. "You really think so?"

"All right, you're Superman. Make things easier on yourself for once and use the ice packs."

Ryder made a disgruntled growl as Dr. Gentry helped Jenny to her feet. "You just come along with me," she said. "You'll feel a sight better after you're cleaned up."

The woman was right. Half an hour later Jenny was coming to the conclusion that Dr. Gentry was always right. She even managed to shampoo the dried blood from her hair with a minimum of discomfort to her lacerated scalp, but when they were done Jenny was shaking with exhaustion.

Dr. Gentry toweled her off with capable, impersonal hands, found her an ancient dressing gown that came to her ankles and looked like it had once belonged in Storyville, that notorious center for prostitution in old New Orleans. *Great*, she thought. As if she weren't already feeling vulnerable and uncomfortably sexual for no good reason. At least there was a pocket for Billy's cell phone. She'd had every intention of leaving it at her house, and now it was about the only thing she had left, useless as it was to her.

The bathroom was off a tiny bedroom with a sagging, tarnished brass bed taking up most of the space. "What you need most now is sleep," said Doc.

"I want to go . . ." She'd been about to say "home" when she realized she had no home. Sudden tears filled her eyes.

"Now don't be worrying about anything right now. Things will sort themselves out—you'll see. You just climb into bed—that's right—and I'll tell Ryder to leave you alone."

The sheets were wonderful—like heavy linen—and the bed was soft and comforting. She blinked away her tears, patted the phone in her pocket, and a moment later she was sound asleep.

Chapter Eight

Soledad looked around her large room in the headquarters of the American Committee for the Preservation of Democracy and sniffed disapprovingly. It was filled with old furniture, like the rest of the house, with old rugs on the polished floors, marble in the bathroom, and heavy curtains to block out the sunlight. She had watched a great many shows on American television and she knew this was not what a rich house should look like. It should have stainless-steel appliances and granite countertops for fat American women who never cooked. All this old furniture belonged in a dump, she thought contemptuously.

It was getting late, and it seemed as if the house was empty. There was no sign of her jailer, the saintly Ms. Parker, or the bad-tempered man who'd let them in. She'd done a preliminary canvass of the place and found nothing suspicious—not a computer in sight, not even a telephone, not anyone to question why she was snooping around, but she knew she was far from alone. She'd already identified one hidden camera in the bedroom, three in the hallway, and she had no doubt the place was littered with them. She kept her stupid sheep expression on her face. Even the most innocent of women would be curious about a place like this, especially someone who supposedly grew up a sheltered innocent in a third-world country.

There were no innocents in third-world countries, but Americans were too stupid to know that.

It was getting very late. Ms. Parker wasn't the kind of woman to spend the night in the arms of a man like Ryder, though Soledad would have been tempted if he weren't the enemy, but then Ms. Parker didn't know how to enjoy life. She was so caught up in being good, trying to prove she had nothing to do with her rich family. If Soledad had had a family like her jailer's, she would have made full use of it.

Right now, though, Soledad was better off depending on herself. If the house really were empty, then she needed to use her time wisely, find out where the hell Parker had hidden the cell phone. Once she found it she could be long gone, no longer at the mercy of her saintly lawyer. God, but that woman annoyed her! It was no wonder someone had shot at her.

Soledad didn't know who had fired the gun and she didn't care. It had come nowhere near her, and she had the kind of enemies who didn't miss.

She slipped out the door, heading down the hall, the saccharine smile on her face. She knew she could pass for a teenager, when in fact, she was twenty-five in years and ancient in experience. She had yet to find one person she couldn't fool.

She knew better than to look at the cameras stationed around the hallway. She was on the second floor, and she suspected that's where the heart of the operation kept itself. She couldn't very well tap the walls, looking for a hollow sound, but she could keep her chastely lowered eyes glued to the doors, looking for a trace of light escaping from beneath the heavy wood. *Ugly*, she thought to herself. She would have torn down the whole place.

"Well, aren't you a pretty little thing?" a voice came from behind her, slow and lazy with the New Orleans accent she was getting used to, the one Ms. Parker seemed to be missing, and she jumped, cursing herself for being so jittery.

She turned to find a man watching her. He was tall, lean, with a charming smile on a too-handsome face. *Child's play*, she thought. He would be so used to women falling at his feet that he would assume she would do the same.

She put a fluttering hand to her chest, surreptitiously tugging the ridiculous peasant top down a bit to accentuate her breasts. Men were stupid to begin with, but breasts seemed to render them witless. "You frightened me," she said in a breathy voice, her shy smile hiding the instinctive curl of her lip. "I didn't know anyone was around."

"I realize that," he said, and with someone else it might have almost sounded cynical. Not this man, though. "I'm Remy Vartain, at your service. Ryder put me in charge of you once I arrived back. You don't happen to know where he is, do you?"

"I have no idea, *señor*," she said, wondering if she was laying it on a bit too thick.

But no, his smile just broadened. "Call me Remy," he said. "So Ryder's run away with the lawyer, has he? That's no surprise."

"But why would he? They hate each other," Soledad said, honestly perplexed. Ms. Parker couldn't mention the man without fuming, and from what little she'd seen the feelings were mutual.

"Sure they do," Remy drawled. "Just how young are you, sugar?"

"Twenty."

"That's what I would have guessed," he murmured. "Except you have old eyes."

And Remy Vartain was more observant than she had thought. "That's because I've seen many, many bad things in my life," she said with great dignity.

"I'm sure you have. In the meantime, why don't you get your sweet self back to bed before you see anything else that you shouldn't?"

She arranged her face in worried lines. "There is something here I shouldn't see?"

"There are always things young girls shouldn't see. Just go back to bed and I promise I won't let the bad guys get you."

He wouldn't notice the grim edge to her smile. "I find it hard to trust these days."

"You can trust me. I make it a habit to keep innocent young girls safe from harm."

She lowered her eyes sweetly. "Thank you, *Señor* Vartain."

"Just Remy."

"Thank you, Remy," she said. He was a fool to trust anyone he'd just met, a fool to think she'd trust him. She'd cut his throat before she left this place, and she'd make sure he saw her after she did it.

Everyone needed to be taught a lesson on occasion.

———

Jenny awoke in darkness, sleepy, disoriented, and for a moment she didn't want to move. The bed was a soft cushion beneath her and she was wrapped in a cocoon of safety. She was someone who liked a rock-hard mattress and the lightest of covers, no matter how high the air-conditioning was set, but right now all she wanted to do was snuggle down closer into the blankets as unwanted memories hit her.

She'd let a criminal escape. Billy had been so remorseful for the hideous trade he'd been involved in, and she'd covered for him, saved him.

But Ryder would have killed him. She had no doubt of that—Billy had had a gun and he'd never been one to back down from a dare. If she hadn't lied they might all three be dead in a hail of bullets.

Instead they were alive, all three of them, with Matthew Ryder viewing her with the deep distrust she deserved. He was intense and tenacious—sooner or later he was going to find Billy's connection to that freighter filled with women and children, and then, for all she knew, he might shoot her for lying to him.

If Billy stayed away long enough, stayed out of trouble, then he had a fighting chance. He was only twenty-two, for God's sake. It had to be the first time he'd gotten involved in something so foul that not even her father would touch it. He must have learned his lesson. Please, God, let him have learned his lesson.

Her only contact with him had been that brief conversation when he'd begged her for his cell phone, and she'd felt like a cranky bitch for refusing him. If worse came to worst, if he slipped and got back into something as heinous as human trafficking, she could always use it as leverage to force him to quit, though whether he'd believe she'd actually turn him in was a moot point.

She hadn't bothered talking to the rest of her family. Her father wouldn't want to know what she'd done, and she refused to give him the satisfaction of knowing she'd helped a criminal, albeit an unwitting one, escape. It was none of their business, only hers.

She was paying for her own crimes already. She believed in karma, not in hell, and payback was a bitch. *Her house.* Gone, everything was gone—the pictures of her mother, her books, the few pieces of jewelry her mother had left her. The Limoges dinner set, the Tiffany pitcher . . .

She had to stop thinking about it, or it would make her crazy. She remembered more—being shaken awake time after time, only to grumble and fall back asleep again. It must have been Doc Gentry. That's where she was—she remembered now. In Dr. Gentry's shack by the water, but she had no idea what slow-moving river ran along the side of the place. It was too small for the Mississippi, and a bayou was more stagnant. Ryder must have gone back to the city and left her in Doc's capable hands.

She snuggled down further. Now that her eyes were accustomed to the darkness, she could make out a faint sliver of light behind the door and the muted sound of music from a computer or a CD player. Hell, in this place it might even be a record player. Dr. Gentry was pretty old school. Jenny recognized the music—it would be no other but the great Satchmo himself. The song was "Basin Street Blues," but she would know the tone and the sound of his trumpet anywhere. The slow, sad notes drew her, and she climbed out of bed, the old dressing gown rumpled around her, and headed toward the music.

It was coming from the back porch overlooking the river. There was a moon that night, shining down on the river, and she moved toward it without thinking, drawn to the music as it slowly picked up tempo.

At first she thought no one was out there. The chairs were empty, and the hammock that was strung along one side didn't move. She walked to the railing, looking out over the shining stillness of the slow-moving river as a fish leapt in the water, all grace and silver beauty, before it splashed back down again and was gone.

She sank into one of the chairs and put her feet up on the railing. The flimsy dress slipped past her knees, and there was a faint breeze off the water, cooling her. Where had Ryder gone? It shouldn't matter—she was safe now. The car was gone, he was someplace else, and for the time being no one was going to bother her. She was going to sit by the river, the soft music in the background, and try to figure out what she was going to do with her life without the distraction of Ryder.

"Couldn't sleep anymore?" Came his deep voice from the doorway, and Jenny's heart caught.

———

Ryder took a long, unemotional look at the woman who just might be an international terrorist and wondered if he was being way too suspicious. She looked rumpled, sleepy, and Doc had put her in some kind of nightgown or dress that gave him way too good a view of her body. Knowing Doc, she probably did it on purpose just to teach him a lesson.

"You think that little girl is a killer, Matthew?" she'd demanded over glasses of her excellent bourbon once Jenny had fallen asleep. "You've lost your touch. She's as innocent as a stray lamb."

"And I'm the big bad wolf?" he'd countered. "I don't think so. She's hiding something, I know it, and I don't give up until I know the answers."

Now, a few hours later, Jenny jumped at the sound of his voice, and she reached for the filmy shawl on the back of the chair, one that did very little for her modesty. Maybe she didn't realize how the moon illuminated every curve and shadow. Clearly she thought she'd been alone. That, or she thought he was stupid enough to be distracted by a half-naked woman. Not a chance.

"I thought you were gone!" she said in the edgy voice he'd gotten used to. "What happened to the car?"

Why was she so damned twitchy around him? Not that he went out of his way to be agreeable, but if she was who she said she was, then she was in no danger from him. "I got rid of it," he said, watching her. "Had someone take it north to Baton Rouge and leave it there. We don't want it leading anyone to us."

"Us?" she echoed.

"Afraid you've got me as your constant companion, at least until we find out who's so interested in trying to kill you. Consider me your new BFF."

"No one's trying to kill me," she said flatly. "It's impossible. I have no enemies, and not enough of a connection to my family to be a target of something like that. You must have made a mistake about the explosive device."

"Bomb," he corrected. "And I don't make mistakes—if I hadn't recognized it I wouldn't have gotten you out of there in time and the question would be irrelevant. No one gets shot and has their house blown up in the space of a few short hours without having some very bad people after her. What I want to know is, what have you done to make such a determined enemy?"

"Nothing! That's why it's so impossible—no one has any reason to hurt me. Maybe they've mistaken me for someone else."

"Maybe."

"I have other people who can protect me, you know." She pulled the shawl tighter around her and shivered despite the warm night air blowing off the river. "It's not your responsibility."

He shrugged. "I'll just drop you off at the family compound and you can leave it up to your brothers and your father's enforcers to keep you safe. And that might even work. For a while." He paused, waiting for the words to sink in. He suspected his self-sacrificing heroine would walk barefoot on Mardi Gras before she would go back home to her family, but he wasn't that much better an option in her eyes.

He continued in the face of her silence. "Of course, they don't have the connections or intel to find out who's trying to kill you, not unless it's one of their many enemies and they're targeting you as a hapless symbol of the Gauthier family. In which case going home is a very bad idea as well."

"Why?" She sounded perfectly controlled.

"Because attacking you would simply be the opening shot in an all-out war, and your father's house on Royal Street would be the obvious target, not our headquarters."

She turned to face him, putting the delicious bits of her body in shadow. What the fuck was he doing, lusting after Jenny Parker, Esquire? She was a major pain in his ass. Because lusting he was, and everyone knew it but her. It was a good reason for his cantankerous mood—you didn't fuck people of interest.

Maybe it'd been too long since he'd been gotten laid. He'd been too busy setting up the American Committee to bother, and his partner had been having enough sex for both of them. Not that Bishop ever slacked off on the job—he was a great multitasker, and Ryder actually liked his wife, Evangeline. He just needed things to settle down into some kind of normalcy, and that didn't include falling into the sack with a woman who could be as treacherous as a snake.

But Parker, oblivious to the convoluted direction his thoughts were taking, simply stood there. "What makes you think the house on Royal Street is his only residence? There are at least three other places that no one knows about . . ."

"The house in the Quarter, one in Lafayette, and the apartment in Atlanta," he rattled off, much to her obvious annoyance, "and I'm sure he could buy any number of bolt-holes for you, if you decided to ask him. I thought you made it a habit not to accept anything from your crooked family."

"That's easy enough to say when no one's trying to kill you," she muttered.

She looked like an unhappy little girl with her rumpled hair and troubled expression, at least, when he wasn't looking any lower than her face. It was almost comical, but Ryder wasn't amused. "You don't need to break your holy vow, Parker. No matter how much protection your father offers, it won't be enough."

"Why? I'm not worth anything to anyone. I'm not an international terrorist or a trafficker or even a very good lawyer. Scratch that—I'm a damned good lawyer, but not good enough that anyone would want to kill me. It doesn't make sense."

He could almost believe her. She really did seem confused, but there was still the faint trace of guilt to her. She was hiding something from him, and until he found out what it was, she was the enemy. "You're old enough to know life doesn't make sense." His voice was caustic.

"I suppose you've got an impregnable place somewhere that's just the thing to keep me safe?"

"The house in the Garden District. You'll stay there until we find out what's going on." He wasn't giving her a choice in the matter. "Whether you believe it or not, that place is impregnable."

"Unless I try to step out the front door."

"My point exactly."

He could see her frustration. "I believe you," she said finally. "I brought Soledad there, didn't I?"

"Speaking of whom, she's been wandering around the place when she was told to stay put. Remy isn't having any of it, and he can be an absolute bastard when he wants to be, and they've all had to be on high alert since they heard what happened to your home. We need you to keep her under control."

"Home?" she echoed dully, and he could see she was thinking about the bomb. Who the hell could have set it, and why? What was Ms. Parker mired in so deep that people were determined to take her out? He tended to be on the sides of the victims, but with Jenny Parker he wasn't sure which she was, an innocent or the devious target of a rival group of criminals. If she'd been involved in the trafficking, surely he would have come up with a trace of evidence by now—he'd been looking hard enough. All he had was circumstantial—her appearance just as they were raiding the ship, her speed in settling the victims so they couldn't answer questions. He hated liars, and Jenny Parker was lying to him.

"Don't think about it." There was no sympathy in his crisp voice. "Denial is more than a river in Egypt, and it can come in handy on occasion."

"You just don't want a crying female all over the place," Jenny said, sounding morose enough to be believable. Almost.

"You're right. I'm going to find out who's behind the attacks. I'm going to find out everything. And your cooperation would help."

"Like what?"

"Like telling me what you were really doing on the ship that day, and why that phone is totally different from the one I found when I searched your purse."

"You did what?" she said, outraged.

"Don't get your knickers in a twist. The purse and the cell phone are gone anyway. They blew up with your house."

"Nice of you to remind me."

"So why the different phone?"

It might have been a trick of the moonlight, but she looked a little sick. "I upgraded mine—is that a crime?"

"No. I just wouldn't have pegged you as such a devoted football fan."

She looked confused. Score one for him. "What do you mean?"

"The New Orleans Saints case on the old phone."

She let out a sigh. "Everyone who lives in New Orleans loves the Saints," she said. "So what? Exactly what are you accusing me of?"

"Not a damned thing. Not yet." She wouldn't be fooled by his almost affable tone. Ms. Parker was no fool.

"I'm worried about Soledad," she said, changing the subject.

"We'll head back when it gets light—even hired killers need to sleep, and it's the safest time."

"Since you've gotten rid of our stolen car, how do you intend to get us there?"

She wasn't arguing about coming back, he thought. He was expecting her to put up more of a fight. Again, suspicious behavior that had no explanation.

"Wilson will bring a car out to get us." He took a step closer, and she backed up, almost imperceptibly. He caught her arm. "Watch it! That railing is weak, and you don't need to go feed yourself to the gators to get away from me. Have I ever made a single pass at you?" Which had been easier when she wasn't wearing that filmy dress.

"No," she said warily. "You don't even like me."

He didn't bother to correct her. She was too close. He could smell Doc Gentry's herbal soap on her warm skin, feel the rapid increase in her pulse. She wasn't immune to him either, unless he simply frightened her. He was trying to, but it was more than that.

He could pull her closer to him, wrap his arm around that warm body with the mysterious curves and shadows, tilt her face up to his, and kiss her. He could strip that gown off her and take her against the rickety railing; he could get the truth out of her one way or another and he really wanted it to be this way.

In his experience women knew when a man wanted them, even if it was only subconscious, but he had no intention of giving her any proof.

"Sit down before you fall down," he said, releasing her arm, and she dropped back into the nearest rocker. "Stay put."

He turned back into the house to grab a blanket and another glass of whiskey. He draped the blanket around her, and she jumped, startled by his sudden presence. "Take this." He handed her the glass of dark bourbon.

She tried to push it back. "I don't like whiskey."

"Every good Southern girl drinks whiskey, especially those from New Orleans."

"Well, I'm about as much a good Southern girl as you are a Southern gentleman," she said.

"Well, amen to that," he drawled. "Drink the damned whiskey."

"My head . . ."

"Your head is fine. Doc Gentry said it was, but I've been waking you up every hour just to check on you. Drink the damned bourbon." She took a ladylike sip, and her tense shoulders relaxed slightly. He went in for the kill. "So who do you think is trying to kill you?" He dropped down in the seat beside her and put his bare feet on the railing in front.

She glared at him. "How many times do I have to tell you? No one would have any reason to kill me."

He hid his frustration at her obstinacy. "I've found that in this life there is always at least one person ready to kill you, no matter how blameless a life you lead. And you, lady, cannot be as innocent as you seem."

She stared at him for a long, thoughtful moment, so long he was starting to feel uncomfortable. "That is the saddest thing I've ever heard," she said finally.

"No, it isn't. If I'm to believe you, Soledad has led a life that's the stuff of *telenovelas*."

"*Telenovelas* aren't as brutal as Soledad's life. And don't distract me." She took another sip of her whiskey, and he realized she really wasn't used to drinking. She'd already dropped some of her usual defenses. "What kind of life have you lived that's made you so cynical? No, you're beyond cynical, you're nihilistic."

"What?"

"Nihilistic. It means that nothing matters to you . . ."

"I know what *nihilistic* means," he said irritably. "And I'm not. I'm just realistic."

For a moment she looked confused, and she took another sip. She was getting tipsy, and he had every intention of taking advantage of it. If, in fact, it wasn't just an act she was putting on. Everything about her could be an act, given the simple fact that she was hiding something.

"Tell me what you think you know about me, Ms. Parker. No, even better, I'll tell you what you think you know about me. I was a troubled kid from a broken home. My father beat me, my mother died young, and I got mixed up with street gangs early. I must've come from some inner city like DC—yes, we'll call it DC—and when I got caught stealing cars the judge gave me the choice of jail or the army. I chose the army, it made a man out of me, and I was recruited for the Committee from there. Does that sound about right? Poor, tragic street kid who found redemption in the killing of bad guys?"

She was staring at him in fascination. "How awful!" she said in a voice so concerned he almost felt guilty. Almost.

"Yup, it's a sad, sad story. The plot of many a bad TV show—it just doesn't happen to be true."

The softness left her eyes, and there was a flash of anger in them, something he was much more ready to believe. "You bastard," she said.

"Nope, not that either." He was enjoying himself. There was nothing he enjoyed more than pissing off Ms. Jenny Parker, Esquire. It kept her at arm's length.

"Then what is the truth?"

"None of your damn business." Growing up in Idaho with a single mother was far too dull, and he didn't want any of her damned bleeding-heart sympathy.

In response she threw the dregs of her whiskey glass at him, and he blinked in shock. She'd already finished most of it, so the effect was no more than if she'd spit in his eye, but she froze in horror, while he took the hem of his T-shirt and calmly wiped the whiskey off his face.

"I'm so sorry," she gasped. "I don't know what made me do that." She had leapt from a chair, staring at him like he was the lethal SOB he truly was, which just went to prove she had the good sense to recognize a threat when she saw one.

Whether he was a threat to her was yet to be determined. He rose lazily, draining his whiskey and setting the old juice jar he used as a glass down on the unsteady railing. He was going to have to send someone out to fix it for Dr. Gentry, or she'd just ignore it, he thought absently, staring at the woman. "Don't worry about it. I can be a real bastard sometimes."

The moon was bright overhead, and he moved closer, so close he was almost touching her. It was supposed to be an intimidating gesture, but it backfired. He'd told himself he wasn't going to touch her, kiss her, take her, but she was so damned tempting. He leaned closer, brushing against her, and took the glass from her limp hand.

Her swift intake of breath didn't help matters. He was scaring her, all right. But was it the danger he represented, or something else that ran between them on this lazy night by the river?

If it had been any other woman, he would have hauled her into his arms. She was sending out hidden signals that she was as turned on as he was—no, scratch that. He didn't think anyone could be as turned on as he was at that moment. His dick was rock hard in his jeans, painfully so, but he wasn't going to adjust himself in front of her. He wasn't going to show any sign of his reaction to her; it would complicate matters, not give him the answers he needed.

He hadn't gotten where he was by giving in to temptation, no matter how sweet and sultry it seemed. He had an iron-hard will, and nothing could break it—not torture, not lust, not mercy.

"The car's here," he said, and she blinked at his words, taking a belated step back from him. He might almost have thought she'd forgotten all about her secrets, but that guilty look was in her eyes again.

"How do you know?"

Score one for him. She'd been too caught up in the moment to hear the tires on the gravel road that ran up to Dr. Gentry's shack. He could even tell which car Wilson had brought—the anonymous gray Lincoln. Good choice.

"I listen," he said. "Why don't you go see if you can find a shirt or something to wear over that dress? Doc wouldn't mind."

"I don't want to wake her . . ."

"She's not here," Ryder said. "I think she was hoping we'd end up in bed. She's always telling me I'm too intense, that I need to get laid more often." There, he'd put it out there, just to see her reaction.

She turned pale, but her scoffing laugh was almost believable. "That's never going to happen. We don't even like each other."

"Who says liking each other has anything to do with sex?" He gave her a faint smile. "Find a shirt or a coat or something and let's go."

"I'm not cold," she said stubbornly.

"I can see your nipples and they're either hard for me or you're freezing. Or maybe both." He reached down and picked up the discarded shawl, dumping it around her shoulders, and for a moment he let his hands rest on her. She quivered under his touch, but he could feel her, soft, yielding.

Wilson was waiting, smart enough not to come in and interrupt something that wasn't happening. "Let's go," he said, releasing her, and headed out into the early morning.

He gave Wilson a nod of greeting, and the young man immediately went around to open the back door of the vehicle. He even kept his eyes averted from Parker's scantily clad figure, a rare feat for any red-blooded male.

She stepped into the back of the car, settling in, and Wilson gave him an inquiring look.

"No, I think Ms. Parker has had enough of my company for a while."

"Yes, sir," Wilson said, opening the passenger side door for him like the perfect chauffeur. On the way back around he popped the trunk, or whatever you did when the damned things were automatic, fetched something from the depths, and opened the back door, wrapping a rich-looking wool blanket around Jenny. He tucked it in with gentle hands, and for the first time Ryder saw Parker smile without the shadow of irritation and defensiveness, and he found the whole thing fascinating. Deeply annoying, but interesting. Clearly she didn't think she had anything to hide from Wilson, just him.

Well, Jenny Parker was his cross to bear, and Wilson was going to have to learn to keep his hands to himself. He should've been the one to wrap her in cashmere, damn it, if only to see her muffled fury at having to be grateful to him for anything.

Wilson slid behind the driver's seat and Ryder gave him a sour look. "Take us back to headquarters," he said briefly.

He should've known Ms. Parker wasn't down for the count. She'd snuggled into the thick, oversized blanket like a sleepy kitten, but her snippy voice emerged.

"Headquarters? You call that beautiful old house headquarters?"

"That beautiful old house, as you call it, is a state-of-the-art surveillance and intel-gathering operation, and an armed fortress besides. Which is exactly why you're going back there and staying there until I find out who's trying to kill you."

"Why do you care?" she murmured sleepily.

Good question. He shouldn't care, but he was damned curious. "They shot at you at my front door, they nearly killed me when they blew up your house. Let's just say I have a vested interest."

"But . . ."

"Go to sleep, Parker. I have to talk business with Wilson and I don't want you eavesdropping."

"Now I'm determined to stay awake," she responded, her eyes half closed.

"Sure you are. Go to sleep," he said again. "You'll have plenty of chances to eavesdrop in the future." He turned back to Wilson, resisting the urge to growl. "So what's been happening with our other unwilling houseguest?"

Chapter Nine

Jenny was asleep before she heard the answer, and by the time she woke up, Ryder was already carrying her up the broad front stairs. He must have felt her startle awake. He gripped her tighter and growled in her ear: "If you put up a fuss I'll drop you and let you roll down two flights of stairs. And while I might find the sight amusing and potentially interesting, I don't think you'd enjoy it."

"So instead we get to reenact *Gone with the Wind*?"

"You should be so lucky. I'm leaving you the moment I drop you on the bed."

"Lucky?" she fired back. "You do have a high opinion of yourself, don't you? I hate to tell you this but you're not exactly my type."

He said nothing, but she had the uneasy feeling he didn't believe her. He was the enemy, she reminded herself. Nothing more and nothing less.

He carried her all the way to the third floor, all without the slightest sign of effort, and Jenny found herself wishing she could make herself heavier. Anything to derail her damnable reaction to him. By the time he kicked open the door, she was so steaming mad she didn't bother to look around her. She was too busy thinking of biting things to say.

The problem was, none of her threats was viable. Her house was gone, and she'd never feel safe at a hotel. It didn't matter how many houses her father owned, how much muscle he could command, the fact was she wouldn't turn to him if she were dying. Especially after he'd gotten her involved in Billy's debacle.

She could feel the cell phone lying heavily in her pocket—thank God Ryder hadn't noticed. He'd paid far too much attention to the damned thing already. If he did she didn't know what she would say—her planned excuse was that she never went anywhere without her cell phone. There were hundreds of thousands of people with the same addiction—it was entirely reasonable, even if she didn't seem the type to have a New Orleans Saints case for it.

But she'd told him she'd replaced it. Big mistake, but she'd panicked. She should have said one was for business and one personal, but then he'd probably ask her something about the Saints and she'd be at a loss.

She hated the damned cell phone. Since the day she'd picked it up, she had spent every waking hour taking care of the kidnapped women and children, finding safe haven for them, trying to atone for her brother's sins, because sins they were, even if he hadn't realized what he'd gotten into. She had barely slept, eaten just enough to ensure she didn't lose the stubborn ten pounds that needed to be gone, and all her other clients had faded into the background. She needed her life back. Once she got Soledad settled she was going on a long vacation, and she would throw the damned phone into a volcano.

Ryder finally dropped her, and she landed hard on the bed, feeling herself settle into it, and she recognized the upscale mattress with appreciation. One thing in his favor.

He was already halfway to the door when she called after him: "You know how much I dislike you, don't you?" It was unnecessary, and she knew it. The depressing truth was that she was trying to convince herself, when more and more she was drawn to him.

Her words stopped him cold. He turned, and he looked almost brutal in the shadowy light of the bedroom. He came back toward her, his walk direct and purposeful, and she found she'd edged away from him, farther up the bed.

It wasn't far enough. He caught her chin in one hard hand, holding her still as his blue eyes blazed down into hers. "I'd be more than happy to demonstrate just how much you really hate me," he said, his mouth hovering over hers, and she felt her entire body freeze and then melt into nothing but pure desire. He was going to kiss her. This man, her enemy, was going to kiss her, and she wanted him to. Desperately.

His mouth moved close. She could feel his warm breath against her lips, and instinctively she parted them. He moved in, they were almost touching, and she closed her eyes, ready to take it all in. Her heart was in her throat.

"Your pulses are racing, Ms. Parker." His voice was silky. "Am I having an upsetting effect on you?" He didn't move any closer, he didn't move away. So close, and all her irritation abandoned her, so that all she could think of was how much she wanted him to kiss her, how much she wanted him to put his hands on her.

He moved closer, their lips almost touching, when she heard Soledad's bright voice from the shadows beyond. "Oh, Ms. Parker, I was so worried about you!"

Ryder moved away from her slowly, with no sign of being caught in a compromising position, but Jenny knew her cheeks had flushed a deep red and she must look just like a child found with her hand in the cookie jar. She scooted up the bed, out of his way, and she summoned her brightest smile.

"I'm fine, Soledad." She'd begged Soledad to call her Jenny a dozen times, but the young woman insisted on the tiresome Ms. Parker, making Jenny feel far older than her twenty-eight years. She'd given up trying, at least for now. Soledad had had a very sheltered upbringing, and certain formalities had been too deeply instilled. "Ryder got me out of the house before it blew up, and we've been at the doctor's place all this time. Surely someone here must have told you I was all right."

"They told me," Soledad said, her eyes wide and anxious. "But that does not mean I trust them. I find that men will lie quite easily. But what about this doctor? Who was he? Why did he not come to the house?"

Jenny opened her mouth to speak when Ryder turned, interrupting her. "We have a number of doctors on retainer. Did you need to see someone?" His voice was surprisingly short, without the drawling, infuriating caress he used when speaking with her. It made no sense, but Jenny couldn't rid herself of the notion that Ryder didn't want her talking about Doc Gentry and the shack by the river.

Soledad's expression made it clear that she considered Ryder one of those lying men. Her dislike was thinly veiled but genuine, which surprised Jenny. Even when he was being his most annoying self, Ryder was still an undeniably attractive man, with those piercing blue eyes, high cheekbones, and strong jaw. It was more than obvious that Soledad didn't agree, and for some reason it made Jenny happy. She'd seen man after man fall at Soledad's feet, and she'd prepared herself for Ryder to be equally besotted. Instead, their mutual antipathy was somehow cheering. If he could be wrong about Soledad, thinking the worst of her, then chances are he could be wrong about her.

Not that he was wrong. She just had to hope she could convince him that he was, or Billy would never be safe.

"There you are, my little dove!" A new voice murmured. "You keep running away from me."

"Do a better job, Remy," Ryder snapped, as one of the handsomest men Jenny had ever seen walked into the room. He was tall, with a sort of rumpled elegance and lazy stroll, with sun-streaked hair and the face of an angel.

She really must have a concussion, Jenny thought. This gorgeous man left her entirely unmoved, while the incalculable grump still sitting on the bed beside her made every inch of her body uncomfortably aware, her very skin tingling. If Ryder wasn't such a threat he would be dangerously attractive. Dangerous because she didn't want to be attracted to a man who solved things with guns. Dangerous because she suspected it was already too late. She'd wanted him to kiss her. She still wanted him to.

Remy ignored both the reprimand and Soledad as he came forward, a meltingly gorgeous smile on his face. "Pay no attention to him, Ms. Parker. Ryder's been in a bad mood for weeks now, and no one can figure out why."

She couldn't help but smile back at him while Ryder said nothing. "Afraid I can't help you," she said. "I only met him a few weeks ago."

"Exactly," Remy said obscurely. He turned back to Soledad, and there was a surprising note of steel beneath his charming voice. "Come along, chickadee. Your mentor has one hell of a headache, unless I miss my guess, and I think Ryder wants to be alone with her."

At that Ryder got off the bed, and Jenny wanted to protest. She'd liked the weight of him beside her, almost touching her on the big bed. She must be brain-damaged. He was nothing but trouble as far as she was concerned, and he needed to go away quickly, before her brain melted further.

"Parker needs to get some sleep," Ryder said. "I had to wake her up every hour to make sure she was all right. She must be exhausted."

ANNE STUART

"You must be just as tired," Jenny said fairly. "You should go to bed too."

The damned man looked at her, and then looked deliberately at the large bed she was in, at the empty space beside her. A moment later the look was gone, but it had left her strangely shaken.

"I've got things to do," Ryder said. "I'll be in the room across the hall—call me if you need anything. And you two," he addressed Remy and Soledad, "can make yourselves scarce. She doesn't need any more distractions."

"Aye, aye, captain," Remy purred. "Soledad is feeling housebound."

"I don't give a fuck how housebound she feels, she's not going anywhere."

"Just the Café Du Monde for some beignets," Remy said. "No one should come to New Orleans without sampling the beignets."

"No one should come to New Orleans and be subjected to the horror of chicory-flavored coffee," Jenny said in a grouchy voice. Caffeine would probably help her headache.

"Coffee snob," Ryder murmured.

"You too," she shot back, not sure how she knew that.

He didn't dispute it, and the man called Remy laughed. "She's got you there," he said. "You're the biggest coffee snob I know."

"We can discuss my gourmet tendencies after Ms. Parker gets more rest. And you're not taking Soledad anywhere!" Ryder was effectively shooing the others out of the room. He threw one last look her way, and the temporary warmth was gone, leaving the dangerous man she was too smart to want. "And you, stay put."

Right then Jenny didn't particularly feel like moving. The bed was comfortable, and she wasn't up to dealing with the complications that were Matthew Ryder, any more than she wanted to be responsible for Soledad at that moment. Any woman worth her salt would be so distracted by the man called Remy and his good looks that she wouldn't have time to get into trouble, unless, of course, it was with Remy, and Jenny's concerns weren't for Soledad's tender heart and no doubt virginal body. She could close her eyes and sleep in peace.

"But Ms. Parker is dressed like a *puta*," protested Soledad. "She needs something better to wear."

Ryder glanced back at her. "There are some clothes in the dresser. Help yourself."

And then she was finally alone. For a moment she was tempted just to stay where she was, until she remembered what Soledad had said about the flimsy outfit she was wearing. She dragged herself out of bed and picked the cell phone from her pocket, turning it on. It looked none the worse for wear, and belatedly she wondered why she hadn't just dropped it over the side of Doc Gentry's rickety railing. One problem neatly solved, and she'd missed her chance. She only needed it for leverage if she didn't completely trust him, and that was absurd.

On impulse she slid it under the mattress. She'd have to find a better hiding place, but that would do for now, particularly since no one in the house had any idea she was hiding it.

Looking in the massive chest of drawers, she wasn't impressed with her choices. She could wear old-fashioned men's pajamas or an oversized T-shirt and flannel boxers. Since that was closest to what she usually wore, she changed quickly and slid back beneath the silky sheets. She was so bone weary she could scarcely move, and her head was throbbing. She probably ought to ask for some Tylenol or something, but she couldn't bring herself to even lift her head from the pillow. At that point all she wanted was sleep.

"Where's our little waif?" Ryder said in a sour voice when Remy strolled into the hidden office on the second floor. "She didn't see you come in here, did she?"

"Ryder, please!" Remy said in tones of mock horror. "I wasn't born yesterday. Miss Soledad is pacing her room like a caged hamster, wanting to get back to our other houseguest and soothe her fevered brow. Speaking of which, what's up with all this? Since when did we become a halfway house for women in trouble? I thought you were convinced Parker was hiding something. Did you manage to clear her?"

"I wouldn't trust her farther than I could throw her," Ryder said flatly. "What better place to keep her than right under our noses? I was all set for a quiet afternoon yesterday when she and her protégé came tapping at the door. Since then I've been shot at and nearly blown up, all thanks to Ms. Parker. The question is, who's after her? If she's dirty, then it may be someone on our side. That, or a business rival who wants to take over the trafficking now that His Eminence is dead and the whole thing is in shambles."

"What about Soledad? I would think she'd be in more danger than some do-good lawyer—if they need someone to testify, Soledad would be perfect, and therefore a major liability."

"No one's testifying. The kingpin of the trafficking is dead, any of the surviving members of the Corsini family are long gone, and the ownership trail of the freighter filled with young women and children from South America is so convoluted even Jack couldn't find it. There's no reason for Soledad to be in any danger, despite what Parker thinks."

"Then why is she here?"

"Because Ms. Parker won't go anywhere without the damned woman. Maybe Soledad is some kind of hostage. That'll be up to you to find out. I get the sense she'd like nothing more than to get away from all of us, Parker included."

"Interesting idea. Parker doesn't look like she could hold anybody hostage, but I bow to your superior judgment. I get the feeling you're not that anxious to get rid of the woman, and I don't think it's just suspicion that's riding you."

Ryder growled. "Shut the hell up. The woman annoys the hell out of me."

"Exactly," Remy said.

"Almost as much as you annoy me. Someone takes a shot at you, they can have you," Ryder snapped.

"Oh, I can take care of myself. Why don't you send the woman who's sleeping in your bed home to her papa? The Gauthiers can keep her safe."

"I couldn't put her in any of the other rooms—I want to keep an eye on her, and I don't sleep much. I feel better with her in my bed."

"That's the truth," Remy drawled.

"Fuck you. And she refused to go home to her daddy. If I let her out of this place, she'll end up dead by the end of the day and I won't come any closer to having answers. There's at least one person still out there, and if it's not Parker then she knows who it is."

"Not your responsibility," Remy suggested. "If she's dead the case is closed." Ryder just gave him a look, and Remy shrugged. "I'm more pragmatic than you are. She's the wealthy daughter of one of the most corrupt families in this city, and if she's going to be so damned picky about who she'll accept help from, then she deserves what she gets."

"If someone kills her then the case isn't closed until we know who did it," Ryder said, part of his attention caught by the information scrolling by the computer. "I'd rather find out the truth about her first."

"Uh-huh. And exactly where will you be sleeping?"

"Go fuck yourself." Ryder didn't bother to look at him, focusing in on the computer screen.

"I'd rather have a partner, thank you. Too bad I'm the only one who will."

Ryder straightened suddenly, turning to glare at Remy. "You keep the hell away from Parker!"

Remy let out a long-suffering sigh. "Don't be an idiot. I can recognize when you've staked your claim, even if you can't."

Ryder decided to ignore that absurdity. As far as he knew she was the enemy and he meant to keep it that way. "Keep away from Soledad too. You're supposed to be looking out for her, not seducing her. You've never had any trouble getting women—just go outside and crook your finger. Don't mess with the women in this house."

"Not my style. I never was one for the virginal Madonna type. Parker, on the other hand . . ." His voice trailed off in a laugh as Ryder turned on him. "All right. You have no interest in her, you're just doing your job. You want me to keep away from her for some unfathomable reason, and I'm willing to do so. Does that make you happy?"

"No," Ryder growled. "Go away before I decide to throw you out a window."

"But think of the uproar that would cause. Just be glad you're not harboring some secret passion for the 'annoying' Ms. Parker. That would really complicate matters, and I know how you like things simple and straightforward."

"They seldom are," Ryder said, not moving his eyes from the computer screen.

"I'd remember that if I were you," Remy said, and took his leave before Ryder threw something at him.

It was ridiculous, Ryder thought, giving the computer screen only half his attention now that Remy had left. The life he led wasn't conducive to affairs, despite Remy's determination to prove otherwise. Finding a woman to fuck and forget wasn't as easy as one would think, even in a town as laissez-faire as New Orleans. Certainly he could do as Remy did—walk down St. Charles Street and find half a dozen beautiful women willing to come home with him.

But bringing women into the Garden District house was just too damned dangerous, and he didn't have an apartment like Remy had, far away from the business, to conduct his affairs.

It was easier to do without. He didn't trust anyone, and if he needed to, he could always make do with his hand. He wasn't a man who got lonely, who needed or felt affection, and if he really needed to get fucked he certainly wasn't going anywhere near a Gauthier with a martyr complex.

And he didn't need to be wasting his time thinking about her. There was too much on his plate already, and with his usual single-minded determination he dismissed the memory of Jenny Parker and that see-through outfit. He had work to do.

Chapter Ten

It was pitch black, and she was starving. Jenny woke with a start, disoriented, but after a moment she felt her heart rate slow to a reasonable pace. She knew where she was. Dressed in an oversized T-shirt and boxers, she was safely tucked up in Matthew Ryder's bed.

She knew it was his room, his bed, not because he'd left anything incriminating around. There was nothing personal—no photos, no knickknacks, no shaving kit or used toothbrush in the bathroom with the giant tub. Nevertheless, she knew it was his. She could almost imagine catching the scent of his skin on the soft sheets, though chances were if they'd stripped the bathroom for her, they'd probably changed the sheets. Nevertheless, she felt surrounded by him in the darkness, and for some reason her panic eased.

But not her hunger. She couldn't remember when she'd last eaten—sometime yesterday morning, and since then she'd been through more excitement than she had in most of her life. Growing up in the Gauthier family had been so restricted that she never had any sense of danger, of violence, even though it had surrounded her, and it wasn't until she had gone to school in the North that she discovered that real families didn't include bodyguards and armored cars.

Once she'd returned to New Orleans, she'd done her best to keep her distance from her disinterested family—everyone but Billy—and her father and two other brothers were content to let it be. Women weren't of much interest in the Gauthier family, and Jenny preferred to keep it that way. Her only hope was that Billy wouldn't be drawn into the convoluted world of power and crime that was her family's livelihood. She could face a little personal guilt if she could save him from that incontrovertible fall from grace.

Her stomach growled, wrenching her thoughts back. It was a good thing she hadn't eaten—she probably would have thrown up at least once.

Her head was hurting, her leg ached, but it was her stomach that was giving her fits. If she didn't eat something, and soon, she'd start in on Ryder's feather pillows, and he wouldn't like that.

She swung her legs over the side of the bed and slid down awkwardly. It was higher up than she'd imagined, and her sore leg gave way a little until she caught herself. For some reason she didn't want to turn on the light. She could see the outline of a window in the darkness, and she went and pulled up the shade, just enough to let in the streetlight and the faint glimmer of the moon overhead. It was cool and eerie and beautiful, a good night for gorgeous vampires to be roaming the streets of New Orleans in search of soul mates.

She laughed. If she weren't such a goddamn romantic, she wouldn't be in the state she was now. She wasn't used to finding men—particularly dangerous strangers—attractive. She must have deliberately chosen a husband who had only a marginal interest in sex—no, that wasn't true. He had plenty of interest in sex, but with someone else. He'd married her because she was a Gauthier, thinking the family business would set him up, and she'd married him because she was vulnerable and thought the only way to get past her lack of sexual interest was to get used to someone.

She never did.

And now Ryder of all people was stirring up odd feelings, sensitivities, emotions even, when all she should feel was wariness where he was concerned. She had everything to lose, and he wasn't the kind of man to understand or forgive. Besides, he disliked her as much as she ought to dislike him. And she did dislike him. Except when she thought he was going to kiss her.

Luckily it was simply a matter of stress that was making her so impractical. Whether she wanted him or not, Ryder was unattainable. Besides, he'd be a pain in the ass to deal with on a daily basis, no matter how pretty he was. Those cold blue eyes of his were enough to warn her off. You couldn't tame a wolf, and she didn't want to.

Once Soledad was settled she wouldn't have to see him again, and her common sense would return. She'd find some nice, safe man and forget all about Ryder. Growing up in her family had taught her to keep away from the dangerous ones, and it was a lesson she'd learned well. Which didn't explain her sudden vulnerability where Ryder was concerned.

Her stomach growled again, loud enough to distract her from her thoughts. Food was a necessity, and she wasn't about to wait any longer.

The hall was dark and quiet when she stepped out, her bare feet silent on the Oriental carpet. The other doors were closed, and she wondered if Ryder was asleep behind one of them. And she wasn't going to be thinking about Ryder in bed—the image was far too distracting.

The ancient stairs didn't even creak as she slipped down them, and once more she was astonished at the renovations this old place had gone through. The second floor was equally deserted, though there were fewer doors. She stopped and stared at the blank wall for a long moment, remembering the sliding bookcase. Was Ryder in there, holed up with a raft of computers?

After a moment she turned away, heading for the final flight of stairs, the broad curving flight that led to first floor. It was very dark down there, and for a moment she hesitated. These old places always came with rumors of ghosts—murdered lovers, abused slaves, Confederate traitors. She reached up and touched the burn mark on the side of her head from the bullet graze. There were a lot more dangerous things than the supernatural, no matter how much she'd like to believe otherwise.

She had no idea where the kitchen was, but logic told her the back of the house. In the old days it would be a separate building, but she doubted that whoever had done such a wonderful job of renovating this place had gone that far in the name of authenticity. All the doors were closed on this hallway as well, including the pocket doors to the main salon. She glanced at the door across the hall, then went over and tried the knob. Locked, of course. She put her ear to the door, listening to the omnipresent whirr of computer fans. What the hell was Ryder doing in this huge old house?

Her stomach rumbled, and she pushed away, starting across the darkened hallway to the back of the house. There had to be a kitchen there—otherwise she'd start eating the wallpaper. She was just moving when something came out of the dark, an arm around her neck, cutting off her breath.

She knew who it was immediately, and she stayed very still, waiting for him to release her. That, or she'd pass out, but she wasn't strong enough to fight him.

"What are you doing sneaking around here?" Ryder growled in her ear. "What do you think you'll find?" He gave her a little shake. "Answer me."

She considered kicking back at him, but she was barefoot and she could hardly do much damage against his shins. She couldn't make a sound with his strongly muscled arm pressed against her windpipe, and she was considering using her elbows, when the pressure loosened, and she was able to take in huge gulps of air.

"How am I supposed to answer if you're choking me?" she wheezed.

He released her, spinning her around to face him. The hallway was very dark, and she couldn't see his face, was only aware of him looming over her. His hands were on her shoulders, gripping tightly, and she'd probably have bruises tomorrow, she thought ruefully.

"Well?" he demanded.

"I was looking for something to eat, you idiot," she said in a hoarse voice, not particularly worried about calling a lethal weapon names. "I haven't had anything in more than twenty-four hours and I'm starving."

There was dead silence from the shadowy figure. Finally he spoke. "All right. Follow me."

That was the last thing she wanted to do. "Never mind. It can wait . . ."

"If you're telling the truth and all you came in search of was food, then you may as well eat."

"Do you remember when we last ate?" she said, her voice caustic. "Of course I'm really hungry."

He grunted, and she wanted to kick him. He wasn't giving her much choice though—he still had one iron hand clamped around her wrist and he was pulling her toward the back of the house, through what she should have realized was the logical kitchen door. Light flooded the room, and she blinked, momentarily blinded. And then she got a good look at Ryder.

He was shirtless. She hadn't noticed that in her uprush of fear when he'd first grabbed her, or she might have fought harder against accompanying him. Of course he was glorious without his shirt on, chiseled abs like some athlete-model. Except for the scars.

He still had a white bandage covering his side, where Doc Gentry had patched him up, but there were other marks as well, ones she hadn't noticed when he'd stripped off his T-shirt before. There was a long thin scar on his left side, the starburst of what was probably a bullet wound in his shoulder and his arm, and a half a dozen smaller marks.

"Jesus," she breathed, tactless as always. "Were you tortured or what?"

His eyes narrowed. "Interesting that you recognize the signs of torture," he said mildly enough, but she wasn't fooled. Once more she'd said too much, igniting his suspicions.

"I was kidding," she said, striving for dignity and failing. "You look like you were put through a meat grinder. Either you're really, really accident prone or . . ."

"Or I've been tortured. Shit happens." He'd released her arm, but now he took a step back toward her, and it took all her self-control not to back up. "Have you ever been tortured?"

He was frightening her. Then again, she always felt that frisson of nervousness when he was close to her, and she hadn't decided whether it was a justifiable fear or her ridiculous attraction to him.

"Fortunately the life I've lived hasn't been conducive to torture," she said primly, then hated the tone in her voice. "You said you were going to feed me?"

He watched her for a moment longer, as if he expected to catch her in a lie. But what lie? There was no way he could know what she'd done, and Billy was in Europe somewhere, well out of danger and the disgusting trade he'd accidentally dabbled in. "Peanut butter and jelly or peanut butter and jelly," he said, opening the refrigerator and pulling out a couple of jars.

"I can hardly decide. Maybe I'll have peanut butter and jelly," she drawled.

"Good choice." He shoved the jars at her. "Bread's over there"—he jerked his head in the direction—"and knives are in the drawer beside you. Dull knives," he added.

She opened the drawer. "Dull knives hurt more," she said.

Again that crazy suspicion on his part. Maybe paranoia was an important part of his makeup, but it was absurd when it came to her. "How do you know that? Experience?"

She gave him a long-suffering glance, accompanied by a world-weary sigh. "Didn't you ever see Robin Hood? The whole thing about cutting someone's heart out with a spoon?"

His dark face didn't lighten. "It's been done."

She just stared at him for a moment. "If you're trying to scare me you've succeeded. Now why don't you go away and let me get my sandwich without hearing about your paranoid fantasies?"

"And what's my paranoid fantasy?"

"That I'm your enemy, when in fact, whether you like it or not, we're colleagues." She began assembling her sandwich. She would have gladly forgone eating if she could get away from him, but he wasn't about to let that happen. If she could convince him she was no threat, had no secrets, then maybe he'd stop focusing all that intense energy on her and she'd be able to relax.

"Colleagues, are we?" He took the jar of peanut butter from her and proceeded to make his own sandwich. "What makes you think that?"

"We both want what's best for the victims of the Calliverian trafficking business. We both despise the filthy trade you and your colleagues broke up. We both want to help Soledad. Isn't that enough?"

"Depends. It's far from over with. We haven't cleared up the source of the victims in Calliveria. There's still at least one major player in all this, someone on this side of the world. You strike me as a woman with secrets. It was very convenient that you happened to show up at the ship just as we were taking down the final defenses. As far as I know there hadn't been any word out on the scanners. So are you telling me it's sheer luck that brought you there at the right time and place?"

She shrugged, pushing her guilt back. "I have friends in high places who make it their business to keep me well informed." She stopped as his words sunk in. "Don't tell me you think *I* have something to do with this wretched business! That you think *I* sold out women and children to be used abominably . . ." Her voice trailed off at the sudden sharpening of his expression.

He looked at her for long moment. "Interesting emphasis on the word *I*. If not you then someone else? Someone you know and are covering for?"

Stupid, stupid, stupid! She was going to get Billy killed with her own carelessness. She took a breath, thanking God it wasn't as shaky as she felt. "Don't be ridiculous. Anyone involved in human trafficking should be shot." The words came out instinctively, and she almost wished she could bite them back. Everyone should be shot but her baby brother, who had simply made a terrible mistake.

"I'm more for gutting them and letting them suffer, along with child molesters, but the end result is the same." He was still watching her carefully. "Are you going to eat your sandwich?"

She would choke on it. "I think I lost my appetite."

For a long moment he said nothing, and his dark blue eyes turned even deeper, almost black, in the shadowy kitchen. He set down his own plate and started toward her, and instinctively she tried to back up, only to come up hard against the kitchen island, the wooden countertop digging into her back. He put his hands on either side of her, trapping her inside the prison of his arms, and he was too damned close to her. She could feel the warmth of his skin, his soft breath on her hair, and she wondered if she stood any chance of shoving him away.

Not likely. She had to be calm, matter-of-fact, not let him know how much he unnerved her. "Would you back off?" she said caustically.

"No."

Damn, why was he so close? And why did she care? He was just a man, albeit a dangerous one, and if there was one thing she was certain of, it was that he had no sexual interest in her whatsoever. The threat of his barely clothed, masculine body had nothing to do with the peculiar heat that flooded her at his proximity. "What is it you want from me?" she said, her voice edgy with frustration.

"This," he said, and put his mouth on hers.

Chapter Eleven

She tasted like sin, and Ryder moved in closer, pressing his hips against her. He could feel the quiver that ran through her body when he kissed her, and he wondered whether it was fear or something else. It didn't really matter, as long as he could siphon the truth from her. Her mouth was soft beneath his, vulnerable, and he ran his tongue across her full lower lip before taking it in his teeth, tugging gently. He heard the surprised sound she made, and for a brief moment he forgot about prying secrets from her and concentrated on the ripe promise of her mouth.

He pushed his tongue past her teeth, and she shuddered in response. At some point her hands had come up from her sides and landed on his shoulders, but instead of pushing him away, which she no doubt would have wanted to do, she was digging her fingers in, pulling him closer to that delicious body of hers.

He wanted to fuck her. It would be easy enough to hoist her onto the butcher-block countertop, yank down that baggy pair of boxers, and thrust inside her. She'd like it—he'd make sure of that— but horny as he was, she wasn't worth the trouble it would bring.

And then she made a little moaning noise in the back of her throat, and he slid his hands down to her hips and lifted her up anyway, stepping between her legs so that he could push against her.

He deepened the kiss. He knew how to kiss—he'd long ago perfected the art, and he put all his expertise into it, coaxing her, inviting her, teasing her, so that she would forget where she was and whom she was with. She pushed against him, her arms sliding around his neck.

She was so soft, and she tasted so damned good that he knew a moment's regret. But this was a job, and he needed to remember that.

He pulled away, looking down into her slightly glazed eyes. They were a golden brown, somewhere between dark honey and amber, and he let his mouth quirk in a cool smile. "So are you ready to tell me what you're hiding?"

It was as effective as throwing a bucket of cold water over her. She shoved him, hard, but he wasn't about to go anywhere, and he gripped the counter on either side of her hips, imprisoning her there. "I don't buy your innocent act, and I don't believe a damned thing you've been saying. You're holding something back, something important, and I intend to find out what it is."

Fear flashed across those eyes, for just a moment, then was gone. "I don't know what you're talking about."

"Of course you don't," he said, and kissed her again.

She hit him then, but he caught her arms in his hands and held her still, and she wasn't putting up that much of a fight. She had every reason to despise him, and yet he felt her soften beneath him, and he wondered just how far he could justify going. Her hands were pushing at him but her mouth was kissing him back, and he could have sunk into the heat of their kiss.

Instead, he stepped back, releasing her, and she rubbed her mouth across her arm. "It won't be that easy," he said. "You can't wipe the taste of me away."

She slid off the counter, and if she stumbled for a moment she regained her footing before he could reach out to steady her. He found himself wondering if it was his kisses that made her so shaky, or the barely healing wound on her leg.

"Do you have any idea how much I hate you?" she said in a small, sharp voice.

"Why don't you tell me what you're hiding, and then I'll be glad to listen to a list of my failings as a human being."

"I don't think you are human." And then she took a nervous step back from his predatory smile. "Leave me the fuck alone."

She was trying not to cower. He suspected Jennifer Parker, Esquire, didn't cower easily. He watched her steadily, saying nothing, knowing his very stillness could rattle her. He could have his answers with just the right amount of pain, and it wouldn't take long, but for some reason he was loath to do it. It was a weakness of his—he didn't like hurting women. Then again, he didn't like hurting men; it was simply his job. When the task became pleasurable that would be the time to stop.

He waited, knowing she'd fill the uneasy silence. "I'm not hiding anything," she said finally. "I have no idea why you think I am, but there's nothing you can do to make me tell you something that doesn't exist. I don't know any more about human trafficking than you do."

Any temporary softness vanished. She was lying to him, and part of him was ready to force the truth from her.

But as far as he could tell, there was no hurry. She might know more than she admitted to, but the people responsible for the trafficking weren't fools, which was how they'd managed to elude the long reach of the Committee for years. There were signs, rumblings, that someone was still out there, and it would take time to hunt him down. There was no need to get that information right this minute. Not when he wasn't sure his motivations weren't a little too personal.

"Take your sandwich and go back to bed, Parker," he said wearily. "I don't like liars and I don't like people who aid other criminals and still think they're innocent."

It was a shot in the dark and it hit its target. She looked as if she might throw up. It wasn't her, then, but he'd never really thought it could be. She was covering up for someone, and with Remy searching her room and Jack looking into things from that angle, it wouldn't take long to isolate the person she cared enough about to risk her career and possibly her life. A lover, maybe, though for some reason he disliked that possibility. She didn't kiss like someone who had a lover.

"There's no one . . ." she began again, but he turned his back on her.

"Get the fuck out of here, Parker, unless you want to continue what we started."

She didn't take the sandwich. He wasn't going to take it up to her—he was on the razor's edge of good behavior and it wouldn't take much to tip him over. He simply covered it with a paper towel and headed back upstairs to the computer room. Remy should have had time to do a discreet toss of her room. It was time to find out what she'd been hiding.

———

There was no sign of Ryder when Jenny came downstairs the next morning. A man she didn't know was stationed in the front hallway, but he simply nodded to her as she headed back to the kitchen. It was empty, but someone had made a fresh pot of coffee, and she found bagels, pastries, and beignets under a domed lid.

The last thing she needed was a surfeit of sugar, but there were eggs in the massive refrigerator and frying pans by the stove. Half defiantly she made herself an omelet seasoned with filé powder and headed toward one of the stools set up at the counter, when the previous night came back full force. Jerking away, she moved to a far corner of the kitchen and propped herself against a row of cabinets. She didn't want to think about those few minutes in the kitchen, with his hard body between her legs, his erection pressing against her. And it had been an erection—there was no doubt about that. What she couldn't understand was why he had kissed her. No, scratch that, she knew why he'd kissed her. He'd done it simply to rattle her, to get her to tell him what he wanted to know. It hadn't been done because he was attracted to her but because he'd figured out she was attracted to him. He'd used sex as a weapon, and it had worked. At least enough to demoralize her, enough to wipe away her defenses so that she made the colossal error of kissing him back, of putting her arms around his sleek, warm skin, of clinging to him.

That was probably why he was hard—not in reaction to her, but the sheer triumph of winning. She knew as well as anyone that he had no sexual interest in her; he simply made a judgment as to what would break her the quickest, and he'd been right. If he'd kept on she would have spread her legs for him and told him anything he wanted to know. He was that good.

And she was that pathetically needy. It disgusted her—she'd decided after her disastrous marriage that she was going to do without men for as long as she could stand it, and that time shouldn't have been up. But it turned out she was only human after all, and the feel of a warm male body up against hers was irresistible, even if it was the very last man on Earth she should want.

Fortunately the moment he stepped back, sanity reared its ugly head. She shouldn't want him—he frankly terrified her. He was a man who killed, and she'd lied to him and tricked him. There was no guarantee that his need to exact revenge would be limited to her baby brother.

She'd lose her license if it came out. That was the least of her worries. She did a lot of good, trying to make up for her family's sins, but she could still accomplish a lot if she were disbarred. No, it was Billy she was afraid for, Billy with his innocent smile and his stupid impulsive mistakes. She knew that once he really understood what he'd been involved in he'd be as horrified as she was. He didn't deserve to die for one mistake, but she had no doubt Ryder would kill him. Because no Gauthier brother would ever allow himself to be taken into custody—again with the stupid male pride.

Her omelet was beginning to taste like sawdust, but she dutifully finished it, following it up with the peanut butter sandwich that lay neatly covered on the countertop. She would need fuel if she were going to hold out against Ryder, whether she liked it or not.

The sooner she got away from him, the better. In fact, there was no real reason why she had to be there—they could hardly force her to stay. She had friends who would always offer her a bed, and she had plenty of disposable income to afford a hotel until she could find some kind of apartment, but it was dirty money, family money, and she didn't want to touch it. At that point the very thought of putting her love and energy into another house was impossible.

When she'd first dressed she'd poked her head into Soledad's room, hoping she'd come downstairs with her and serve as some kind of buffer between her and Ryder, but Soledad had simply mumbled sleepily and turned over in bed. Could she dare leave Soledad behind, or should she take her with her? She didn't have the wherewithal to push a green card through, nor could she come up with the results the American Committee for the Preservation of Democracy could. But Ryder seemed to be the one man immune to Soledad's charms, and she wouldn't put it past him to use her as a way to get Jenny to tell him what he wanted to know.

He'd come so damned close last night! The thought that he might find out terrified her, but she seemed to be the only naïve idiot her father had raised. Billy, no matter how deluded he might be, wouldn't leave a trail of bread crumbs behind for Ryder to follow.

If Ryder decided she was covering up for a member of her family, there was still no way that he could prove which one it was, because all of them had been raised as world champion paranoids. "Leave no trace" didn't just refer to wilderness camping.

It was still early morning, but Jenny didn't feel like lingering around the kitchen until Ryder made an appearance. She couldn't even look at the counter where he'd placed her without feeling heat rise in her face, and she intended to do everything she could to make sure she wasn't caught alone with him again. Soledad would simply have to stir herself and keep her company.

Her progress on the stairs was slow and silent—she still had no shoes or clothing other than what she'd raided from the closet of mismatched clothes, and if she could have worn anything else she would have. It was unnerving to have his oversized flannel shirt around her—it was as if she were imprisoned in his arms. Or simply being held.

The landing was empty, and Jenny went straight to Soledad's room. "Wake up, sleepyhead," she called softly, opening the door a crack. "We're getting out of here." If the Committee declined to help Soledad, then she'd simply find someone who would. At this point she wasn't even against asking her father to pull a few strings.

There was no answering sound, and Jenny pushed the door open further, taking a step inside. The bed was empty, and Soledad was standing across the room, looking at her with an unreadable expression. "Soledad?" she said again, when she felt someone behind her. She was about to turn when pain and light exploded inside her head, and everything went black.

∿

Soledad looked down at the woman lying sprawled on the carpet, then up at Manolo. "Don't worry, you didn't kill her. Nothing can kill that bitch." She gave Jenny's body a vicious kick, but she didn't move. "I should have known she would come back for me too quickly."

"Maybe you played the part of the helpless victim a little too well," Manolo suggested.

Soledad shrugged. "Chances were she would have interrupted us anyway."

"She's not going to wake up anytime soon—I hit her hard enough to knock her out for a good long time."

"Do not be so cocky. She has got a head of iron, this one. I say we tie her up and put her in the closet so she won't interfere. I cannot find that fucking phone yet, and it is going to take time. I do not want to risk her waking up and causing a fuss."

"Are you sure we're not too late already? Maybe she turned it over to the Committee?"

Soledad gave Manolo a sour look. "She does not trust them and the feeling is mutual. She is not risking having anything happen to her baby brother, and we can use that, but it will only go so far. We have got to get the hell out of here and back to Calliveria before she can alert anyone. Chances are she will not admit to anything even after they find her, because she'll know it will be too late, but I do not take chances. We find the phone and get out of here before anyone notices she and I are gone. Fortunately Ryder dislikes her so much he will not make any special effort to come near her, and my bodyguard thinks I have a headache and am staying in bed. But I say we have only half an hour before we run the risk of getting caught. You go ahead into her room while I tie her up."

"Don't kill her," Manolo said dispassionately. "If she's that devoted to El Jefe then he might feel the same way about her."

Soledad laughed. "You're as stupid as she is. El Jefe doesn't care about anyone but himself. And, on rare occasions, me. After all, he was the one who told you to shoot at her and to set the charges at her house. There was a good chance she could have died in either incident. He knows how to take risks and accept collateral damage."

"*¿Qué?*" Manolo said.

"Move. I am going to enjoy doing a little damage to Miss Parker in return for her hovering over me."

She didn't bother to wait until Manolo had disappeared. Manolo might not be the sharpest of men, but he was thorough, and if the phone were anywhere hidden in Jenny's room, then he would find it. In the meantime Soledad took the duct tape and began wrapping it around Jenny's ankles and wrists, not caring how tight the bindings were. By the time she reached her head, she was swathing her eyes and mouth with the stuff, not paying much attention to whether she covered her nose or not. If Miss Jennifer Parker suffocated it would probably make everything easier, and no one would care enough to come after Soledad. No one would even guess she had done it—she'd set things up very neatly. It would look as if she'd been kidnapped, and in the long run they wouldn't consider her an important-enough hostage to go after. If they knew her real role she'd have half the police forces in the world on her tail, but men were always so stupid. They assumed a woman, particularly a pretty one, couldn't do such things. And Soledad knew she was very pretty indeed.

Hadn't it been her stock-in-trade her entire life, from the age of eight onward? Hadn't she led men around by their dicks, starting with her own father, since before she began to bleed? No, no one would guess what she'd done, and they wouldn't care enough to "save" her again. She would be considered one more victim of human trafficking, when instead she was the triumphant provider of merchandise.

She hooked her hands under the shirt Jenny was wearing and dragged her across the floor, banging her body against the solid bed Soledad had been sleeping in. Despite the fact that Jenny was a good four inches taller and twenty pounds heavier, Soledad had worked hard all her life, and she could lift many things that were heavier than she was. She grunted and shoved Jenny into the back of the closet, pulling her boring clothes in front of her limp body. That was another thing Soledad could blame Jenny for, and she gave her another hard kick. She'd taken Soledad out and paid for the most God-awful wardrobe, perfect for a cleaning woman or a grocery store clerk, or even a low-level secretary. Boring, ugly clothes that would cover up Soledad's beauty. She knew why too. Women were always jealous of her, and Parker wouldn't want men to look at Soledad with lust in their eyes, ignoring the lawyer. She shut the door and locked it, closing her away.

If they found her in time, so be it, but with luck everyone would assume the two of them had left together. Or been taken. By the time they found Jennifer, Soledad would be long gone, cell phone in hand, off to meet her lover.

It was about fucking time.

Chapter Twelve

"They're gone!" Remy broke into the room without his usual indolent grace.

Ryder sat up, moving slowly, with deliberate care as he set the newspaper back on the desk. "What are you talking about?"

Remy was looking harassed. "What do you think I mean? I went to pick up my little babysitting job and her room was empty. So is the room Jenny was staying in, and the place has been tossed."

Ryder wasn't a man to let fury take over, but it was coming close. He rose slowly. "Interesting. I assume they took the phone you found last night?"

"Of course. Though Parker would have known where she hid the thing, and I put it back in the exact same place after we dumped the information from it. There should be no reason for her to search the room. I've got Wilson and the others searching the house, but they're gone, man."

"Why didn't you keep a better eye on the girl? She was your responsibility."

"You should have let me sleep with her," Remy drawled. "Then we wouldn't have this problem."

Ryder made a dangerous noise in his throat. "Did they leave anything behind?"

"Not as far as I can see. Not that either of them had much. We need to find out where the hell they went and how long they've been gone."

"And what they're running away from," Ryder added grimly, heading toward the hall and the stairs to the third floor. He had a good idea what Parker was running away from. He'd tipped his hand, and he'd gotten way too close in his guesses. There was no way she could know they had found the phone, but she had good instincts, and she would have realized her time was about up. It still didn't explain why the room had been searched, but it didn't matter. She'd been so damned easy to read when he'd softened her up. Once he got her in bed she'd spill everything.

And where the hell had that idea come from? He wasn't getting her in bed—that hadn't been part of the plan. In fact, it would be a very bad idea, and he needed to remind himself of that fact. It wasn't as if the subject wouldn't come up—Parker and her little waif weren't going to be on their own for long. He would find her and drag her back kicking and screaming and, hell, chain her to the fucking bedpost if he had to.

His room was a shambles. The mattress had been torn off the bed, the pillows ripped open, drawers yanked out and dumped on the floor. He stared around him in fury. Why the hell would she think he was hiding something there? He certainly wouldn't have put her in a room with secrets.

Remy had followed him. "Do you think they left during the night?"

He shook his head. "Parker made herself breakfast this morning—we've got her on the security cameras."

"I don't suppose the ones on the third-floor bedrooms are working?" Remy said.

"They're for intel, not voyeurism. No, they weren't turned on. We should have feeds for the hallways, though." He grabbed his phone out of his pocket, pushed a number, and got Jack in the control room. A moment later he turned back to Remy. "Two people left an hour ago. Parker was bundled up in something, Soledad was looking pleased with herself, Jack says."

"Wasn't he supposed to be watching?"

"No, you were," Ryder said pointedly. "The question is, if Parker wanted to run off, and she has her reasons, why did she take Soledad when she wanted us to deal with her? Unless Soledad is in on it too."

"Do you hear that?" Remy demanded suddenly.

"Hear what?" A moment later the sound came. It was a muffled thudding noise from the direction of Soledad's room.

Remy was on his heels as he stalked back into the smaller bedroom. The thumping noise was coming from the closet door, and he swore, striding across the room to open it.

It was locked. The door splintered in one kick, and a body tumbled out onto the floor, trussed in duct tape and looking furious. Jenny Parker hadn't run off after all.

"Looks like your little waif isn't the helpless unfortunate you thought she was," he said, squatting down beside her. Her eyes were blazingly furious above the gag of silver tape, and he ripped it off, causing her to shriek with pain.

"You have to go after her. I think someone kidnapped her," Parker babbled, fury and clear embarrassment coloring her cheeks. "She was standing in the middle of the room, looking scared, and then someone hit me."

"Ma'am, you sure have had a lot of people beat up on you in the last three days," Remy murmured, and Ryder glared at him before turning his attention back to Parker. He wasn't in any hurry to release her from the rest of her bonds. "If you didn't have a concussion before, you probably have one now."

"I'm fine," she said in a panicky voice. "Get this stuff off of me so we can go after Soledad."

"Go after her?" Ryder echoed. "Why?"

"Because she's been kidnapped, you idiot," she said, squirming in her bonds.

He made no effort to release her. "She didn't look coerced in the video feed. She walked out with someone I thought was you. In fact, you're lucky you started making noise or you'd have been in that closet a lot longer."

"I'm so lucky," she said bitterly. "Will you please release me?"

Remy took a curious look at Ryder, then moved in front of him, the knife he always carried with him out and slicing through the tape before Ryder could stop him.

The moment she was free she tried to stand, but she staggered, and Ryder caught her as she fell against him, all warm femininity and fury. He held her a moment until she steadied herself, and then she yanked herself free a bit too enthusiastically, so that she almost fell again.

She managed to straighten up. "We need to go after her," she told Remy. "I warned you she was in danger, and now someone got past your defenses and took her. I would have thought this would be the safest place for her, but apparently someone just waltzed in with nobody noticing. You should make sure no one took anything."

"No one's touched the other rooms," Ryder said coolly. "Just yours. Someone had to let her 'kidnapper' in. Was it you?"

"Don't be ridiculous," she said bitterly. "If I had I wouldn't have ended up in a closet."

"Possibly," he said, eyeing her. She was still dressed in a pair of his boxers, a T-shirt, and one of his old flannel shirts, which came partway down her long thighs. She looked a hell of a lot better in his old clothes than he did, he thought, then banished the notion.

He wasn't going to be thinking about Ms. Jenny Parker's undeniable attributes. Not unless he needed to use them.

She was slowly pulling herself back together, and her gaze sharpened. "What do you mean, no one touched the other rooms?" she said. "Did someone . . . Did they . . ." Without another word she pushed past them, racing into the hall and into the trashed bedroom. She came to a halt, frozen in place, and a low wail came from her. "Oh, no!"

"Go downstairs, Remy," Ryder said suddenly.

"I can help . . ."

"Go back downstairs and help Jack with reconnaissance. No one's to come up here until I say so."

She turned to look at him then, and everything was stripped from her face but the truth: disaster and real fear swamped her.

He waited until Remy had gone. "You have every reason to look scared shitless," he said in a quiet voice, crowding her back into the bedroom and shutting the door behind them, closing them in. "What did they take?"

"Nothing." It wasn't even a good lie.

"Don't even try it," he said. He was going to make her tell him the truth by any means at his disposal. He kept his voice steady, low, but she had the sense to recognize danger when it stared her in the face. "What did they take, Parker? Who are you covering for?"

"No one. Nothing!" she cried, looking completely guilty and utterly miserable. "We have to find Soledad. They'll kill her . . ."

"If 'they'—whoever 'they' are—wanted to kill her, then we'd be finding her body and probably yours as well. You can count it your lucky day that they decided to simply truss you up like a turkey instead of slashing your throat. That would have been effective and quiet, and chances are we wouldn't have found you until you started to smell."

She looked at him in horror. "Is that what you would have done?"

"Yes. Which means your enemies aren't as smart as I am."

"Aren't you my enemy as well?" It was said in a small voice, devoid of hope, and he wasn't about to give her any.

"Yes," he said again. "Just how much danger you're in depends on how much you've lied. I'm going to ask you one more time—what did they take, and who are you protecting?"

"Nothing . . ." He cut off the word by shoving her up against a wall, his arm across her throat, his body trapping her smaller one. He wasn't using much pressure, but she wouldn't know that. To her, in her panicked state, it would feel like she was about to die.

"Tell me the truth. If you think Soledad was kidnapped, then we need to know why."

"I don't know why they took Soledad. She didn't even know I had the . . ." Her voice trailed off, and then she looked up at him defiantly. "The phone," she said.

Releasing his hold, he took a step back. She looked small and helpless for a moment, but he wasn't about to make that mistake. Jennifer Parker had more balls than half his men.

He moved away from her, shoving the mattress back onto the bed, kicking a gutted pillow out of the way before he turned back to her. He didn't worry that she'd try to run—he kept his body between her and the door at all times, and if she tried it, Remy or Wilson would catch her before she made the front door. They wouldn't like it, but they'd do their duty.

"You mean the phone you had on the boat," he said in a low, dangerous voice. It wasn't a question. "I thought you were using it to call your confederate. But it wasn't your phone, was it?"

She was watching him warily, not certain what to make of him, which was the first smart thing she'd done today. She'd probably never run into anyone as ruthless in her life, even with her family's criminal background. She didn't say anything.

"Was it?" he repeated, not raising his voice. He didn't need to. She shivered in reaction. He was one scary motherfucker when he wanted to be, and right then he wanted her scared shitless.

"No." Her voice was very quiet.

"Whose was it?" If she was going to keep giving him monosyllabic answers, he was going to have to shift this into high gear, and he didn't want to have to go there. But he would if necessary. He always did what was necessary.

She looked up at him with a sudden flash of defiance. "I'm not going to tell you."

"Wrong answer," he said, and a moment later he'd slammed her down on the bed. There was nothing sexual in it—he just needed her immobilized for what he had to do. "Who are you covering for?"

He twisted one arm behind her back, and he knew it had to hurt, but not nearly as badly as he was about to hurt her if she didn't give him the right answers.

"No one. It was nothing. I didn't . . ."

He knew interrogation techniques, and he knew when cold-hearted determination could get him what he wanted. He could have seduced her into telling him the truth, but it would take too long, and for some reason he didn't want to use sex as a weapon, effective as it could be. Not with this woman.

He knew how to hurt her, how to cause exquisite pain without leaving a mark, and he began to exert pressure on her other arm, enough that it cut off her words until she was panting with the effort not to cry out.

"You didn't what? Didn't traffic third-world children and women into a life of slavery? Do you know how long a child lives as a sexual slave? The average life expectancy is seven years. Seven years of hell."

"I didn't have anything to do with it!" she cried. He increased the pressure, and tears of pain started in her eyes. "It wasn't me."

"Then who was it?" He didn't give her a moment to consider it, twisting her arm. "Who?"

"He didn't know what he was doing," she said desperately. "He got in over his head—someone took advantage of him."

"Fuck your excuses," he said icily, twisting again, and she let out a low, keening wail of pain. "Who is it? What does the cell phone have to do with it?"

"Nothing . . ." She screamed then, but it didn't matter. If they heard her downstairs—and chances were they wouldn't, given the soundproofing in this place—they'd simply ignore it. "Stop," she begged him. "Please, God, stop . . ."

"Then tell me what I want to know. Who are you covering for? Whose phone is it?"

She bit her lip, a useless attempt to keep the words back, and he wondered if he was going to have to do some real damage in order to make her talk. She was more stubborn than he could even begin to guess.

"So Miss Goody-Two-Shoes isn't so good after all. Did you spend all your time helping the victims as a way to expiate your sins? Trust me, it doesn't work. You can't make up for what thousands upon thousands of women and children go through, and no one who's involved with it deserves a do-over. You understand me?" He shook her slightly, and she shuddered, staring up at him, her eyes glazed with fear and pain.

"I can't . . ." she began, and he'd had enough. He twisted again, and her high, keening wail made him want to throw up. He hated this, but nothing would show on his face but cold determination, no matter how much he hated this.

"You can and you will. Or you really won't like the consequences."

Her bitter laugh was thick was tears. "Unlike this torture? What are you going to do, rape me?"

"In case you haven't noticed, hurting you is not a turn on for me." He thrust his hips toward her, knowing arousal was the last thing on his mind. He released her hurt arm for a moment, only to catch her wrist with his other hand, holding the two together. "If you don't start talking I'm going to have to become creative, and those things leave marks and scars, and not just on your body. I think it's time you told me what's going on before we go to a place you'll never come back from." He put his hand on her throat, exerting pressure. "Tell me," he said, his voice low and vicious, devoid of humanity or mercy. "Tell me."

She broke, as he knew she would. "My brother," she gasped beneath the pain. "My brother Billy."

He released her throat immediately, knowing he wouldn't have to hurt her any more, knowing he shouldn't feel sick inside. "Tell me."

Tears were pouring down her face, tears of pain and shame. "He's my baby brother—he didn't know what he'd gotten himself into. He had a gun, and I knew you'd shoot him as you . . . you killed those other people on the boat."

He didn't disagree. "What did you do?"

"He was hiding under the desk when you came in. I just wanted to give him a second chance," she said brokenly. "Everyone makes mistakes in their lives," she said, a plea for understanding in her voice, one that left him entirely unmoved.

"You treacherous bitch," he said coldly. "What about the phone?"

"He wants it back. He said it contained names, information, and if it got into the wrong hands he'd go to jail."

"He'd be lucky if he made it as far as jail," Ryder snapped. "And you still think he's innocent? Next thing you'll be telling me he's a victim just like the people on that ship. I strongly suggest you don't. Where was the phone?"

"Under the mattress." Her voice crumbled, finally admitting the truth, and he wanted to curse, to shake her, yell at her.

He'd done enough to her. He levered himself off the bed, and she immediately curled into a fetal ball, hugging herself and her damaged arm, refusing to look at him.

Ryder was furious, with her for lying and making him hurt her, with himself for hurting her. And now there was a missing woman and the incriminating phone, and he had no choice but to go after both, when all he really wanted to do was get Ms. Goddamn Parker out of his life. When all he wanted to do was pull her shivering body into his arms and hold her.

No one hurt people like Jenny Parker on purpose like that, not the way he had. The sheer psychic shock of it was probably more debilitating than any pain he'd inflicted on her body. The pain was transitory, the disillusionment permanent. She now realized that people did such things to each other without a second thought, and it could happen again. She'd never feel safe.

"I'll have Emery bring you some clothes. You can't keep wearing my cast offs," he said in an expressionless voice.

She didn't lift her head. He could see only part of her tear-streaked face, and he kept his face impassive, feeling sick inside. "I'll be leaving tonight," he added in the same dead tone. "You'll stay put and behave yourself."

"No," she said, shocking him. He would have thought he'd stripped all the fight from her. "You're not going anywhere without me. You need me to find the cell phone."

"I don't think it'll be that hard to find a phone with the New Orleans Saints on it," he drawled.

"They get rid of the case, and then it will look like any other smartphone. I'm the only one who can be sure."

He looked at her in frustration. They'd been able to download most of the intel from the phone the night before, but the information still remained intact on the device itself. They couldn't allow it to get into the wrong hands.

"I don't trust you not to hurt Soledad." Her voice was barely audible, blurred as it was with tears and hatred.

"Don't be ridiculous. You'd only hold me back."

"If you want Soledad and the phone you'll need me with you. I'm the only one who can recognize his phone—it'll look like a hundred others to you. Besides, you're not going to do a thing to save Soledad unless I make you."

"Who says she needs saving?"

"I do. And I'm not going to let my brother be sentenced to execution without anyone speaking for him."

"And you're such a great judge of character," he said, sarcastic. "Believe it or not I don't shoot everyone who gets in my way. Your brother can rot in jail, just as he deserves. They don't treat child molesters very well in prison, and your brother's one step lower. He's a child pimp, and he deserves everything he gets." He headed for the door. "You can lie there and feel sorry for yourself for half an hour and no more. I could have done a lot worse. In a couple of days you'll be fine." Physically, it would be sooner than that—he knew exactly how much pressure to exert. Emotionally, it could take her a lot longer.

She slowly began to uncurl, and she was pulling herself back together, he realized with amazement. There was nothing she could do about her tear-streaked face, but the expression on it was cold and furious. "I won't help you destroy my brother."

"Your brother destroyed himself and you know it. And this isn't a democracy. If you want to come with me to find Soledad, then I won't stop you, but you're in for a rude awakening. Soledad's as dirty as your brother, and you're just too naïve to see it."

"She isn't!"

"I'll let you come because you're right—only you can identify the cell phone. You're the one who believes so strongly in Soledad's innocence—if it were up to me she could rot in Calliveria."

"You think that's where she is?"

"I have no doubt, but I'll have proof within the hour. If you're coming with me, then you have half an hour to get ready or I'll knock you out and carry you on board the plane. Don't make me do that—I don't happen to like hurting you."

Her derisive laugh wasn't quite tear-free, but it was impressive anyway. "Don't you think the flight attendants might notice?"

"Who says we're going on a commercial flight?" He shut the door quietly behind him. He could give her privacy to pull herself together—that was about all he could offer her. He could tell himself she'd survived the abuse a lot better than he would have guessed—she was already fighting back. It didn't help.

He headed down the stairs, refusing to glance at his reflection in a huge mirror on the landing. There were times when you couldn't look yourself in the eye, Ryder thought, and this was definitely one of them.

Jenny was freezing. She sat up on the bed, cradling her left arm with her right, trying to fight back the tears as her body shook. He'd kept telling her she was in shock yesterday. This was a lot closer to it.

How could he . . . No, she wasn't going to think about it. If she took slow, deep breaths, the lingering pain was bearable, and while her throat hurt from his grip, she wasn't going to give in. She needed to get out of here, away from him, away from a man who could do such a thing, could hurt her, could hurt someone he'd just kissed the night before. The sick bastard probably enjoyed it.

But then memory flooded her. He hadn't enjoyed it sexually—there'd been no hint of arousal in his flat, dark eyes or his body. He'd hurt her because he'd told himself he had to do it. And if he ever came near her again she would kill him with her bare hands.

She drew her knees up and pressed her forehead against them, letting the shudders wrack through her body. No one had hit her in over twenty years, when her mother put a stop to her father's lessons in corporal punishment. Her father's belt was probably worse than what Ryder had just done to her, she thought, trying to lift her arm. Pain seared through it, and she dropped it back down. Maybe not. Maybe he was even more of a monster than her father was. He was certainly more dangerous.

Would she have told him the truth any other way? Probably not. It didn't matter—he'd forced her to betray the one member of her family she still cared for. Her two older brothers were so deeply involved in their criminal lifestyle that they were practically strangers—they had no interest or time for the honest changeling in the Gauthier family, just as she had no interest in them. The less she knew about them, the better.

But her father had sent her to save Billy, and everything had gone to hell since then.

She took a deep, shaky breath, letting out the stress and tension, and realized in some small, dark way she was almost relieved that it was out in the open. She wasn't made for lying, and now she wouldn't have to worry about a slip of the tongue.

No, all she had to worry about was Matthew Ryder putting a bullet between Billy's eyes if he should find him.

But if they were going to Calliveria, he'd be safe. Billy didn't do third-world countries, and right now he'd be in Paris or Barcelona, conveniently forgetting everything he'd done or that his foolish sister had done for him.

Slowly she dragged herself off the bed, then glanced down at her arm. She was still wearing one of his flannel shirts, and she yanked it off her like it was made with poisoned nettles, dumping it on the floor.

She wasn't a redhead, despite what Ryder had said a lifetime ago, but she had pale skin, golden freckles around her brown eyes, and the tendency to bruise if someone even looked at her hard. The marks were starting to show on her arm, and she was tempted to walk around flashing those bruises, just to make him feel guilty. But Matthew Ryder wouldn't feel guilt—he did what he had to do, and the last thing she wanted was for other people to know what he'd done to her, alone in his bedroom.

He was a monster, and she hated him with the fiery passion of a thousand suns. Somehow, some way, she would pay him back for hurting her. He would have done the same with poor Soledad if he'd had the excuse, and Soledad had already been through too much brutality. At least Jenny was able to survive such punishment without turning into a basket case.

There was a mirror in the bathroom, and she walked in, checking out her reflection. The stain of tears was still on her face, so she splashed it with cold water, then looked back. A grim, satisfied smile curved her mouth. A few minutes ago she'd felt defeated, lost, shocked. Now she looked pissed as well. Her eyes were defiant, swimming with tears, her mouth stubborn, and if Matthew Ryder had any sense at all he'd be extremely wary around her. One thing was certain—he was never laying a finger on her again.

A long, thoughtful shower finished the job of cementing her cold fury, and when she came out there was a pile of clothes on the bare mattress, all with price tags still on. She wondered who had brought them, but she doubted it was Ryder. He was kept for strong-arm work, not deliveries.

She was good with numbers, and she mentally added up the cost of the new clothes as she went through them. Of course they were her size—she wouldn't have expected anything less from Ryder and his "Committee." Cargo pants, shorts, T-shirts and tank tops, sturdy walking shoes and sandals, and even a couple of sundresses, along with utilitarian underwear, plain white and boring. Her choice was to accept the new clothes or dress in Ryder's cast offs, and she'd walk around the house naked before she touched his clothes again.

The bruising on her arm was turning dark, and there were marks from his long fingers at the base of her neck. There was nothing she could do about that, but there were a couple of lightweight long-sleeve shirts among the clothing, and she pulled one on over the tank top and long pants. The less anyone saw of her skin, the better. She intended to make Ryder believe he hadn't hurt her, couldn't hurt her. She'd been so vulnerable when he'd touched her, and she was determined she would never be vulnerable again.

She ran into Remy on the second floor, and she braced herself for pity and even a joke. Instead he acted as if he knew nothing about what Ryder had done to her, greeting her in a casual voice. "Ryder's in the office, making final arrangements for the plane. I see you found the clothes Emery brought you. She's got good taste."

It was a relief to think a woman had chosen the plain white underwear. "I don't have a passport anymore," she said suddenly. "It was in my house."

"Oh, Ryder's seen to it. He's on top of everything."

Including me, when he hurt me, she thought, keeping her expression passive. "Good to know," she said. "Are you coming with us?" At least Remy would provide a buffer between them, something to keep her fierce hatred at bay.

He shook his head. "I'm afraid not. It's just the two of you— you'll have more luck in finding the little witch without bringing in an army."

"'Little witch'?" she echoed, surprised.

Remy's grin was wry. "Well, she either escaped or was kidnapped right out from under me—it's no wonder I'm a little pissed off at her."

"It was hardly her fault she was kidnapped," Jenny said sharply.

Remy shrugged, giving her his most charming smile. "If you say so." He started past her, then paused, and she knew he was going to address the elephant in the room. She didn't want him to, but she could think of no way to stop him.

"Did Ryder . . ." he began, all trace of a smile gone from his handsome face.

"I'm fine," she interrupted him. "I told him what he wanted to know."

Remy didn't look convinced. "He can be . . . determined when he needs to know something. I do know that he wouldn't have enjoyed what he did to you."

Her smile was brittle. "That's such a reassurance. Heaven knows Mr. Ryder's feelings are what's important."

"That bad, eh?" Remy murmured. "I'm sorry, *cher*."

"No worries," she said, almost convincing. "I've been shot and had a house blow up on me and been clubbed on the head. A little bullying on Ryder's part is child's play compared to that."

It wasn't, but he didn't know it. Remy looked relieved. "Well, don't let him get away with anything. He tends to think he knows best about everything, and he needs someone to set him straight."

He needed someone to stab him, she thought vengefully, but she wasn't going to be the one. "Not in my job description," she said lightly.

"What isn't?"

It was *his* voice, and she could feel her stomach knot, her entire body freeze. She willed herself to relax, and by the time she turned to look at him she knew she looked completely unruffled.

If she expected him to look guilty, she was doomed to disappointment. He looked as he always looked, not like someone who'd used well-refined torture to get her to betray the only member of her family she still cared about. She wasn't about to answer him, but Remy stepped in.

"I told her to keep you in line," he said. "You're an arrogant bastard when you've got something on your mind, and she doesn't need any extra grief from you."

"You mean apart from what I already gave her," he said, and it was all Jenny could do not to stare at him. He didn't have the slightest bit of shame or remorse, to bring up his abuse so casually. "I don't expect we'll have any problem in Calliveria. We both want the same thing, and she's smart enough to know that if she doesn't do exactly as I say she'll find herself in more trouble than she'd ever be with me."

Her small smile was icy. "I'll do what you tell me to do."

Ryder just looked at her out of his wolf's eyes, but she turned away, ignoring him. "I'm going to find something for lunch," she said, trying to come up with a casual excuse to leave his presence. She was shaken, and the last thing she wanted was for him to notice, even if the thought of food made her nauseous. "Just let me know when it's time to leave."

"That easy, is it? What if I told you I'd changed my mind and you couldn't come with me?" he taunted, and she wanted to slap him. How dare he hurt her and then mock her, pouring salt on her literal wounds.

"You said it yourself—we both have reasons to save Soledad, and frankly, I don't trust you to take proper care of her. She'll be in shock after being abducted again, and God knows what they'll do to her. She'll need me."

"Maybe," Ryder drawled.

"Leave her alone, Ryder," Remy protested. "Give the girl a break."

Ryder turned to look at him, his eyes flat and hard. "I don't remember asking for your opinion."

"Don't be a bigger asshole than you already are."

To Jenny's astonishment he actually laughed at that. "That's part of *my* job description," he said, before glancing back at Jenny. "We leave the house at five. Be ready."

She almost told him to fuck off. She opened her mouth to deliver the stinging response, then shut it again, sudden uneasiness filling her. God damn that man. There was just enough of her that was frightened of him. She could face down her father, bureaucrats, corrupt policemen, and hanging judges without flinching, but all Ryder had to do was deliberately cause her pain and something had broken inside of her. She hated it, and she hated him.

She couldn't give him a docile response either. She made do with a simple nod, walking away from him without a backwards glance. It wasn't until she reached the safety of the kitchen that she looked down and saw that her hands were trembling.

Chapter Thirteen

Ryder had almost hoped she'd be sulking. Not that she didn't have every right to—he'd hurt her, simply because he'd had no choice, and in the safe cocoon of the United States, most women weren't deliberately, passionlessly hurt. Thank God. With someone from Calliveria—Soledad, for instance—he'd have to do a lot worse to get her attention.

But Parker was acting calm and passionless. Granted, she had a stick up her ass, but he certainly couldn't blame her, and he treated her with distant courtesy, always the safest bet after the few minutes of cruelty.

She wasn't showing any sign of discomfort, but he noticed she was only using her right arm, which made sense. She'd be in pain for another day, and then the ache would begin to wear off. He could have done much worse, and he would have if she hadn't broken so quickly. There was always the chance that when she began to heal she'd start to trust him again.

Scratch that. That was never going to happen—he'd never be able to get near her again, which was definitely a good thing. He'd grown a little too fascinated with her recently, and not just because he suspected her of knowing something important. He'd liked watching her, liked her sassy attitude, liked her haughtiness.

She said nothing when she climbed aboard the expensive private jet that Peter Madsen had designated for their use. It was a hell of an expense, but it turned out to be a necessity. Even though they were stationed in New Orleans, the Committee was worldwide, and they needed the ability to get where they were needed at a moment's notice.

If Parker appreciated the comfortable leather seats and built-in flat-screen TV and bar, she didn't show it. She headed straight for the back of the plane, for the one seat that was usually reserved for a flight attendant, and buckled herself in, staring out the window in the darkness. He suspected she wouldn't look at him during the entire trip, though he was tempted to make her.

But he'd hurt enough people over the years, people who were basically innocent, and he knew she needed time to protect herself, to heal from the emotional shock of it. He could give her that much.

Once the jet reached cruising altitude he took off his seat belt and headed for the bar. He didn't tend to drink during an operation, but he'd been on edge ever since those few minutes with Parker, and a beer might take the edge off. The bar came equipped with his favorite craft beer, and he noticed a frozen margarita mix. According to the detailed background check, Parker had a weakness for margaritas. It wouldn't be much of a peace offering, and she'd probably throw it in his face, but he mixed it anyway, stalking toward the back of the plane and setting it on the table beside her.

She didn't look up or acknowledge his presence in any way, but she didn't throw the drink at him, which he figured was progress. When he stole a glance at her half an hour later, the glass was empty.

He slept, simply because God knew when he'd sleep again, and woke only when they touched down at the distant runway outside Calliveria's small city of Puerto Claro. She was already out of her seat belt by the time he rose, keeping just out of his reach, waiting for him like a docile, abused wife, and he wanted to snarl. Whether it was at her or himself, he wasn't quite sure.

The air in New Orleans had been warm and humid, but this place was practically liquid. Calliveria's geography went from rain forests up into the Andes, and Puerto Claro was down low in an area plagued with mosquitoes and disease. The sooner they were out of there, the better.

She wasn't going to like where they were going, but then, she wasn't going to like a damned thing about him ever again. "You ready?" he said unnecessarily, because the charged silence got on his nerves.

"I'm here, aren't I?" she said in a low voice, and his urge to snarl increased. He swallowed it and gave her a small, lazy smile that left her stonily unmoved.

"So you are. And you're going to do every damned thing I tell you to do, aren't you?"

"Will it save my brother?"

"I doubt it. But it might save Soledad." Whom he didn't trust one bit, but Ms. Parker was far too gullible when it came to people—people like her brothers.

"I'll do what you tell me to do," she said flatly. "Within reason."

"Reason has nothing to do with it."

"Then you should have left me behind in New Orleans."

"You didn't leave me much of a choice. You like being difficult, don't you?"

Again that shuttered look. The old Parker would have given him enough sass to amuse and infuriate him. The new Parker was muffled, faded, and it pissed him off. She'd given up fighting—she was a pale ghost of her former self, and it made him want to shake her.

"Come on," he said finally. "We can argue about it later."

"I have no intention of arguing with you," she said.

"Tough shit. I intend to argue with you."

He saw a flash of something in her eyes, and it could have been fear or anger. He hoped to God it was anger. He needed her to move past that slightly shell-shocked affect. She could be as pissed at him as she wanted, as long as she was alert and alive. Damn, he didn't hurt her that badly, did he?

The airstrip was miles outside of the town, a run-down field that had once been the staging ground for the last violent government overthrow. Nowadays Calliveria had a supposedly democratic president and congress, but the dissidents, the Guiding Light, were strong up in the mountains and a force near the rain forests. They no longer bothered with attacks on military installations—they spent their time kidnapping Westerners and holding them for ransom, in between their lucrative coca business. The question was, had their forays into capitalism included human trafficking? He wouldn't put it past them.

The ancient Buick was waiting for them, keys in the ignition, and Ryder headed straight for it, with Parker trailing along behind him. "What about the pilot?" she said when they arrived at the rusty vehicle.

"He's got his orders. It won't take him long to get back here if I decide to get rid of you."

"If you decide to get rid of me you could just slash my throat and leave me to rot," she said. "Why go to the trouble of sending me back if you're just going to kill me?"

"I'm not going to kill you," he said irritably. "For what it's worth I've decided you're basically innocent in all this. You may have let a felon escape, but he was your brother. I can't fault loyalty." It was as close to an apology as she was going to get, but she didn't look appeased.

"How generous of you," she said with a trace of bitterness, and he felt encouraged. If he could get her to fight back, then she'd start to make peace with what had happened to her. What he had done to her.

"Get in the fucking car," he said wearily. "If you're waiting for me to come and open the door for you then I suggest you think again. You're with me to find your brother's missing telephone, and we'd better do it damned fast before they're able to decode the damned thing."

"Decode it?" Her laugh was derisive as she climbed in and slammed the door, hard. "What do you think he has on it—state secrets?"

"Why do you think someone wants it so badly? And that someone was willing to break into what should have been one of the most secure buildings in the city just to get it?" He started the car. Fortunately the engine didn't meet the car's battered appearance, and it hummed happily.

"I was wondering about that," she said with a flicker of life. "You can't be nearly as good as you think you are when it comes to security."

"Someone had to have let him in. Since I know my people wouldn't, I'm putting my money on you or Soledad."

She immediately sprang to Soledad's defense. "She'd hardly let her own kidnapper into the house!"

"So then one has to assume that either she wasn't kidnapped, she went willingly. Or . . ."

"Or what?"

"Or that you let him in, that you've been holding on to Soledad for your own reasons, and you sent your man off with the phone so he could start up the shipments once more."

"Don't be an idiot," she said, showing more signs of life. "What good would the phone do?"

Christ, she really was an innocent, he thought. "If people want it back so desperately, if someone was willing to break into Committee headquarters in order to get it, then I expect it would do a great deal. At the very least it would provide contact information for people involved in the human trafficking. They lost their kingpin and the crime family that ran it, leaving the human highway from South America empty for someone to pick up the slack. I'm guessing your brother's smartphone will go a long way toward reestablishing the infrastructure."

"Next thing you'll tell is that it was my brother who took Soledad."

"I don't think anyone 'took' Soledad. But no, it wasn't your brother. He was my first guess, but the intruder was too short to be your beloved Billy, at least according to our intel. Any ideas?"

She said nothing, lapsing into the brooding silence again. God, women were a pain, he thought. The silent treatment was one of the most effective weapons he'd ever run across, at least with this one.

He tried a few more times, then gave up. By the time they reached the outskirts of the small city, his temper had begun to fray. He would have been better off not sleeping at all on the plane—he was better off powering through with effective five-minute catnaps than a deep six-hour sleep. He was lucky Parker hadn't stabbed him while he slept.

He glanced over at her as he pulled up to the small inn he'd chosen as their headquarters. Her face was averted, and shadows danced across her still expression. He was going to have to do something about it, he thought. Dragging an emotional zombie around Calliveria would attract too much attention, and that was one thing they couldn't afford. If he was to find the people who'd taken the phone and Soledad, they were going to have to fly beneath the radar, and Parker's stiff, touch-me-not demeanor would have everyone's attention, especially the men. The last thing he needed was to have people sniffing at Parker's heels, though he couldn't honestly blame them. There was something about Parker, some incandescent spark, that drew people to her. Just because he was thankfully immune didn't mean that everyone else was.

He put the car into park and turned it off. Time for Ms. Jennifer Parker, Esquire to come back to life.

They stopped outside an American-style hotel on the edge of whatever Calliverian town they had flown into, and Jenny surveyed their night's lodgings. The building was long and low, with doors leading from each room onto a veranda. It had seen better days—the paint was peeling and there was trash in the yard, but that bastard seemed to think it was the perfect place to spend the night.

He was already out of the car, clearly waiting for her. She didn't want to go inside with him—she didn't want to do anything with him—but she didn't have much choice. She'd insisted on coming this far, for Soledad's sake. No, it was more than that. If Ryder found her brother's phone, she had every intention of destroying it. She should never have held on to it—she'd thought it would give her some kind of leverage with Billy, but if she trusted his word she wouldn't need it. If Ryder didn't have it he couldn't send her brother to prison, without proof he couldn't kill him. Maybe. At that point she wouldn't put anything past Ryder's brutality.

She climbed out of the car and moved toward him, careful to keep her distance. She couldn't bring herself to look at him, really look at him, or she'd be reminded of the man who'd kissed her in the kitchen, the man whose hard, warm body had pressed up against hers with undeniable need. As long as she didn't look into his face she could pretend he was someone else, some brutal bully who didn't care who he hurt in his effort to get information. As long as he didn't touch her . . .

He put his hand on her arm and she panicked, trying to tear herself away, but she should have known it would be useless. He was much stronger than she was, and he simply hauled her against his body, wrapping one arm around her waist. "We're supposed to be a newly married couple on a really stupid honeymoon, and anything you do to make people think we're not is going to put us and everything you want to accomplish in danger. So chill."

Chill was the operative word. His hand was on her waist, she remembered the pain that hand had inflicted, and it chilled her to the bone. Her sore arm was trapped between their bodies, and she couldn't use it to push away. All she could do was stand still and try to disguise the fear that was leeching through her. She was trembling, and she bit her lip, trying to still the shaking, as he led her into the slightly run-down lobby of the hotel. He pulled her even closer, and for some unknown reason the heat of his body began to penetrate hers, and the tremors slowed.

"That's right," he murmured. "Just relax. I'm not going to hurt you."

She couldn't help it—she let out a small, derisive laugh. His hand tightened as a warning on her waist, but he still didn't hurt her. "Not again," he said simply. "Never again."

His Spanish was better than hers, and yet when he talked to the desk clerk, his speech was halting, tentative, as if he couldn't find the right word. *Turistas*, the man was obviously thinking, *and harmless*. Of course he had a room for the *norteamericano* and his *esposa*, and Jenny shivered again. One room. Of course it would only be one room if they were posing as husband and wife.

They were back outside in a matter of minutes, and Jenny immediately pulled away from him, ignoring the fact that she was suddenly so much colder in the warm, tropical night air. "I want my own room," she said stubbornly, knowing it was a lost cause.

"Be grateful you've got your own bed. I have no intention of letting you out of my sight now that we're down here. You'd probably take off looking for Soledad the first chance you got, and believe me, you don't have the intel to even start to find her."

He was wrong about that. She intended to wait until he came up with the intel, and then bash him over the head and escape. It worked in the movies, and it should work in real life. If she happened to kill him then she could live with that.

The room was small, bare, and thankfully neat. There were two double beds, a dresser, a small table, and two chairs in the beige room, and Ryder dumped her suitcase on the one farthest from the door. She didn't bother to protest—getting away from him wasn't going to be that easy. She'd have to wait until he went out to make her escape. But escape she would, no matter how determined he was to keep her prisoner.

She sat down on the bed, kicking off her shoes. The bed sagged slightly, and it was too soft, but she didn't give a damn. While he slept aboard the plane she'd been wide awake, trying to come up with a scheme that would lead her to Billy's missing phone before Ryder could get to it.

Finding Soledad seemed to be the only lead they had, and even in Calliveria, Soledad's dark, sloe-eyed beauty would stand out. If she had come through this port city, and chances were she had, someone would remember.

Ryder was watching her, but she leaned back on the bed and ignored him. If she could just get an idea of where Soledad was being held she could go after her. Ryder must have more than enough weapons on him that he could spare one. She'd learned to shoot years ago, at her father's insistence when one of his enemies was making a power play, and she was a relatively good markswoman. She didn't think she would hesitate when the time came, and if someone was threatening Soledad, after she'd already been through so much, then she'd shoot him without compunction.

She realized that Ryder was simply staring at her with an unreadable expression on his face. She could always shoot him, she thought dispassionately. He deserved it, and if she were close enough she could avoid anything fatal. Just something that would hurt him, very, very badly.

"Now that I've got your attention," he drawled, "maybe you could stop formulating plans for revenge and concentrate on the matter at hand."

She didn't want to talk to him, to pay any attention to him, but unbidden the words slipped out. "I was thinking I might shoot you."

"You could always try. If you had a gun, that is. Which do you prefer, a nine millimeter or a twenty-two?"

He was calling her bluff. Maybe he wasn't as smart as she thought he was. "Nine millimeter," she said instantly. With a full clip they were easier to reload.

To her astonishment he went to the travel-worn duffel bag he'd brought, opened it, and fished out a handgun, setting it down on the bed between them. She stared at it.

"Go ahead. Take it. You could even shoot me with it if you were so inclined," he said.

"I would have thought you'd be smart enough to know which you were in real danger of that happening," she said, eyeing the gun but not picking it up.

"You want me dead after what I did to you today. I get that. I also get that, unlike me, you wouldn't hurt or shoot anyone in cold blood no matter how much he deserved it. Pick it up."

"I'd watch it with the orders if I were you," she snapped. "Is that the same gun you had on board the container ship? The one you used to kill all those people? The one you would have used to kill my brother?"

"In fact, no. I'm keeping that one. It has a hair trigger and it would be too dangerous for someone not used to firearms."

"I'm used to firearms. My father insisted on it."

He looked skeptical. "And how many guns have you shot in the past ten years?"

None, but she wasn't going to tell him that. She picked up the gun, balancing the weight in one hand, and then pointed it directly at his chest. "I could always start again," she said silkily.

He didn't look the slightest bit perturbed. "Then you'd bring the local police down on your head. If you're determined to shoot me, then wait until we're out in the countryside and there are no witnesses. You could leave my body at the edge of the rain forest, and the scavengers would make short work of me."

She shuddered, suddenly horrified at the thought, and she tried to put the gun back down. Her hands were shaking too much. "You deserve to be shot," she said in a voice that sounded frankly sulky to her own critical ears.

"Many times over. Today was just one more blip in my life, nothing I haven't done before or would do again. But not to you."

She didn't believe him. "Why not me?"

"I could tell you that I'm too tenderhearted to hurt you like that again, but you'd know that was a lie. I have no heart, tender or otherwise. But I also know that I got everything I need from you—you weren't in a state to hold anything back. Therefore, you're safe from my methods of interrogation."

"Is that what you call it? I thought it was torture."

For a moment she thought she saw him wince, then decided it was her imagination.

"When it comes to torture, what I did to you was really quite tame. Trust me, you run up against anyone involved with the Corsinis and this morning would feel like a walk in the park." He tossed her small bag to her. "Get into your nightclothes. There's nothing more we can do tonight, but the sooner we get started tomorrow morning, the better."

"I'm not changing in front of you!"

"Suit yourself," he said, yanking the black T-shirt over his head. "Change in the bathroom, or under the sheets, or whatever uptight, prissy way you want to do it. Tell you what—I'll turn my back and you'll have my word that I won't watch."

His actions suited his words, and she got a view of his tall, strong back, and for a moment she forgot everything. Forgot that she hated him, forgot that he was a killer, forgot that he'd hurt her.

He had the body of a warrior. His beautiful golden skin was marred by scars, a testament to the abuse of a decade or more, and she felt a momentary softening of her rage. A man who had gone through that kind of physical torture would have very little hesitation in hurting someone else if he needed to.

"Are you going to change or am I going to turn around?" he said, his voice bored. She heard the snick of his zipper, and she let out a little shriek.

"You're not taking off all your clothes, are you?" she demanded.

"No, Parker. In deference to your maidenly modesty I'll leave my shorts on. But if you don't get moving . . ."

"I'm changing," she said abruptly, starting to pull the shirt over her head. Pain seared through her arm, freezing her, and against her will she let out a cry.

He immediately spun around, to see her sitting on the bed in a totally ignominious position, the T-shirt half over her head, her arms stuck inside.

"Go away!" she said between gritted teeth. "I can handle it."

She should have known she was wasting her breath. He took the hem of the T-shirt and slowly peeled it over her head, gently, relieving the pressure on her left arm as he did so. A moment later she was free, and she was sitting there in the plain-white cotton bra someone had bought for her, feeling totally exposed.

He wasn't looking at her breasts. He was looking at her arm, and she looked down to see the row of bruises his hands had left on her pale flesh. She almost opened her mouth to tell him that she bruised easily, then shut it in time. He deserved any guilt or remorse she could thrust on him.

He turned his back without another word, picked his T-shirt off the floor, zipped up his fly, and walked out the door, closing it behind him. She heard the sound of the lock, and she stared after him in astonishment.

She wasn't going to get away from him this quickly, and besides, she needed some sense of where she needed to go. She'd have to spend at least one more day with him. Stripping off her shorts, she slid down under the covers. Whoever had bought her clothes had failed to provide nightclothes, and she sure as hell wasn't going to sleep naked. The underwear would do.

She turned off the light between the beds, a pink ceramic monstrosity with writhing females all over it. He could find his own way back. She was tired, she was in pain, she was frightened, and she was mad. There were other emotions warring inside her, ones she didn't want to examine too closely, and she needed sleep. *Please God*, she prayed she wouldn't dream about Matthew Ryder.

Chapter Fourteen

Ryder walked out into the cool night, taking deep lungfuls of air. One look at Parker's bruised arm and he'd felt oddly claustrophobic, as if all the air had been sucked from the room.

He'd hurt people before. Innocent people, ones who just happened to be in the wrong place at the wrong time, and he'd never felt this way. He did what needed to be done, and he didn't waste his time second-guessing his actions. Parker had been holding something back, something important, and her time had run out. He'd needed an answer, fast, and he got it the only way he knew how.

She should count her blessings, he thought bitterly. He could have hurt her a lot more, gotten the answers even more quickly. Or he could have seduced her into telling him.

That possibility had been teasing him for days. He was past denying it—it was a simple fact of nature that he wanted her. There was something about her that drew him, and if he could figure out what it was, he'd have a better chance of fighting it. That, or give in to it.

He suspected she would have hated sexual coercion even more. Physical betrayal was bad enough. If he'd taken her to bed and forced the truth that way, she'd be in far worse shape than she was.

He wasn't squeamish—sex was as good a weapon as anything else, and he used it when he needed to. He'd had a very good reason not to fuck Parker into giving up her secrets. He'd wanted to.

He presented a cold, unemotional exterior to those around him, but some of the things he'd done for the Committee ranged from painful to despicable. If he'd taken Parker to bed in order to get her secrets, he'd have liked it too much, and the betrayal would have been too devastating. He knew full well how physical abuse could shatter someone's sense of self. She might not know it, but if he'd used sex, used pleasure instead of pain, she'd be in much worse shape.

But that didn't change the fact that he'd marked her! How the hell had that happened? He'd always been able to judge the amount of pressure, just how much to hurt someone to get the truth, never to go beyond that point. Somehow he'd miscalculated, hurt her worse than he'd planned, hurt her so badly she trembled when he touched her, shook when he was close. Ms. Jennifer Parker, Esquire, wasn't someone who broke easily—he, of all people, should know that. But he'd broken her. It was up to him to mend her.

He didn't dare go far from the seedy inn—there was no telling who was watching them. He wasn't naïve enough to think their arrival in Calliveria had gone unnoticed, and Parker would need protection whether she wanted it or not. She wanted to save Soledad, and he knew perfectly well she wanted to get hold of that cell phone and the secrets it held. It was his job to keep it out of her hands. In the end he didn't give a shit about her slimy brother. There was information on that smartphone that would help anyone who wanted to take the place of His Eminence and the Corsini family with their human-trafficking empire, and he couldn't allow such a volatile weapon to fall into the wrong hands. His job was to stop anyone before they got too solid a foothold in the filthy business, and he needed that smartphone.

All Parker could see was her baby brother, and he couldn't really fault her for that. She was seeing him with the eyes of an older sister, not impartially. She still clung to the pathetic belief that her brother hadn't known what he was doing.

Billy Gauthier had to have known exactly what kind of harm his actions had caused, and he didn't care. He'd continue, simply because he'd gotten away with it, and with the Gauthier connections the trafficking could soon become just as widespread as it had been with the Corsinis. Ryder wasn't going to let that happen, no matter what the cost.

And that cost was Parker, lying huddled and bruised in a bed in a cheap motel in a third-world country. She was terrified of him, and he had no idea how to get her past that, or if it was even possible. He only knew he had to try.

The room was dark and silent when he came back in an hour later, a bottle of cheap whiskey in one hand, compliments of the nearest cantina. He didn't dare get drunk—in fact he doubted he even could—but he needed something to take the edge off his self-loathing. What he should do was send Parker back home, have Remy keep watch over her while he did the dirty work.

But he didn't want the womanizing Remy anywhere near her. He didn't want her out of his sight. For all he knew she'd stumble into even more trouble in her desperation to save her brother from the consequences of his actions.

He set the bottle down on the table between the beds and kicked off his shoes. Yanking his T-shirt over his head, he stripped off his jeans, watching her body in the bed. He might almost believe she was asleep but for the faint tremor that shook the smooth surface of the covers.

He took another slug of whiskey, reached for the covers, and climbed into bed with her.

She erupted in panic, hitting at him, but he subdued her easily enough, wrapping his arms around to her to keep her from flailing, one of his legs keeping hers from kicking and kneeing him.

He'd been prepared to put his hand over her mouth, but she was smart enough not to scream. She just keep fighting, and he let her wear herself out as he held her, her desperate struggles weakening, then fading away into a quiet, panting watchfulness. At least she'd stopped shaking so badly.

"That's better," he said quietly.

That provoked another flurry of struggles, and by the time she fell back she was totally out of breath and absolutely furious. Excellent. She could either be mad at him or afraid of him, and he wanted mad.

"Are you done now?" he demanded.

"Get the fuck out of my bed," she said in a low, dangerous voice. "Get away from me, don't touch me, don't speak to me."

"Or what?"

In response she tried to knee him in the groin, but he was too fast for her, slamming her legs back down with his. "You know, that would really piss me off if you connected," he said mildly.

"Get away from me," she said.

"Not likely. We're not going to carry this off if you don't get used to me, and I figure the only way that's going to happen is a little aversion therapy. You may hate me, but you need to act like we're in love. You look like a terrified rabbit every time I come near you, and even in this backwards country where men rule the roost, your panic seems extreme. You can't be looking at me like I'm Jack the Ripper whenever you think no one will notice, and you can't shake like a leaf whenever I touch you."

A stray tremor ran over her body, but he simply held her tighter, careful not to hurt her bruised arm. She closed her eyes, looking exhausted and miserable. "Please," she said, "just leave me alone."

"I can't do that. It's just the two of us down here, and I need to know I can count on you. That you'll obey orders, that you'll use your impressive brain and stop acting with your heart. Yes, you want to save Soledad. Yes, you want to protect your brother. Yes, you're afraid of me . . ."

Her eyes flew open. "No, I'm not!" she protested, another shiver giving the lie to her words.

He allowed himself a wry smile. "Could have fooled me. I'm not going to hurt you again. I told you that."

"And you think I trust you?" She was relaxing more and more as they talked, his body warm against hers in the dark room. "You must be crazy."

"You trust me, at least a little bit, or you wouldn't have come with me."

"I trust you not to kill me, and that's about it. You weren't even in the equation when I insisted on coming to Calliveria. It's Soledad I care about."

"And your brother's cell phone," he reminded her.

She bit her lower lip, and he could feel himself getting hard. He hoped she didn't notice—she might think his attraction to her gave her some kind of power. It didn't.

"The cell phone is the least of my worries. I don't want Billy mixed up in trafficking any more than you do. I want it destroyed so it won't be of use to anyone."

"And I need it in one piece. One major bust won't get rid of human trafficking, but it's a start." He could feel her heart beat against him. It had begun to slow, not to a steady pace, but at least closer to normal.

"I promise I won't act skittish around you," she said in a low voice. "Just . . . please, get out of the bed."

"Sorry, Parker, but I'm sleeping here."

"What?" Her voice rose slightly in horrified protest.

"Don't worry—sex is the last thing on my mind," he said, a complete lie. Sex was all he could think about, but he wasn't going to do anything about it. "We're just going to sleep together, so you can get used to me."

"I can get used to you, I promise." She was sounding slightly panicked, but he simply shook his head.

"This will work better. You're just going to have to put up with it."

"Lie back and enjoy it?" she said bitterly.

"I told you, this isn't about sex. It's about familiarity."

He wanted to kiss her. She was looking at him with such distrust, and he wanted to quiet that distrust, to distract her, to take them both to that dark, dangerous place where everything fell away but the elemental connection between man and woman.

No, he reminded himself. *If you screw her she'll hate you even more*. Right now they had a job to do, and all his actions needed to be in service to that job. He turned her in his arms, tempering his strength with her reluctance, and then curved his body around hers, his leg still keeping her dangerous ones away from vulnerable parts.

She put up another fight, and she lay facing away from him, panting, furious. "I thought you said this wasn't about sex," she said after a long moment, and he knew she could feel his erection pressing up against her delectable butt.

"I said this wasn't about sex," he agreed. "I didn't say I didn't want you."

She froze, as if the idea were novel. "Dream on," she said finally.

"I intend to."

She was wearing her underwear, which left vast amounts of skin uncovered, and she felt cold to the touch. He wrapped himself tighter around her, and slowly her skin warmed, slowly her heart dropped back to a normal pace. "That's right, Parker," he murmured in the ear he really, really wanted to bite. "Accept the inevitable, and trust in the fact that I already hurt you enough today. I'm not about to follow through and use sex to get what I want. I promise."

"No sex and no violence?" she echoed with a trace of her old spark. "Now why don't I believe that?"

"You can trust my word?"

Her laugh was bitter. "Until you change your mind."

"No. No matter what happens, no matter how important it is, I promise you I won't hurt you again." It was an insane promise, one he couldn't possibly keep if the stakes were high enough, and yet he made it.

"What's to keep you from breaking your promise?"

"I make very few promises in this life," he said after a moment. "Those I make, I keep."

"You promise you won't hurt me or . . . or try to seduce me?" she said in a small voice, her warm, sleek body still stiff in his arms.

"That's not what I said and you know it. I said I wouldn't hurt you. As for the rest, we'll see what happens." He kept his hands where they were, holding her against him, when he wanted nothing more than to slide them up her sleek torso to that damnable bra and slip it off her. "When two people are as strongly attracted as we are, then chances are something's going to happen."

"I'm not attracted to you. I hate you."

"I believe you on the second. As for the first, I could prove you otherwise, but I'm too tired. Go to sleep, Parker. I'm not letting you go, so you're just going to have to get used to it."

"I hate you."

"Don't repeat yourself—it gets tiresome. Go to sleep, Parker. Or I just might change my mind."

He could feel reaction shoot through her body. Alarm, and something else that she refused to recognize. Getting her warm and wet and willing was going to be an uphill battle, but he had every confidence of winning. In the meantime, he just needed to sleep.

Ryder actually expected her to sleep like this, with his big strong body wrapped around her and long bare legs entwined with hers? He was insane.

Damn him. If it were up to her, she'd never let him anywhere near her again. But it wasn't up to her, and she realized with disgust that she was no longer trembling. Whether she wanted to believe him or not, apparently her body recognized when someone wasn't a threat, and her muscles were slowly relaxing back against him, too weary to fight any longer. Her arm hurt, but by chance he'd managed to keep from making it worse in their struggles . . .

No, it wasn't by chance. Ryder didn't do things by chance. He knew he'd hurt her, he'd done it deliberately, but she had the sense he was shocked by her bruises. Maybe the other times he'd tortured women he hadn't had to watch them undress afterward and see the results of his abuse.

No, scratch that. A man like Ryder could talk a ninety-year-old nun into bed, she had little doubt. There was an odd intimacy between them now, once they'd shared those moments of pain. It was sick, but it was the truth, and Jenny always believed in facing the truth head on. She wanted him to promise not to try to have sex with her, for the simple reason that sooner or later she'd give in. Even if her brain was screaming no, her body was molding itself to his in soft, animal acceptance.

His breathing had changed, and she knew he was asleep. She had to get away from him before she made a total fool of herself, and she tried to inch away, slowly and carefully so she wouldn't wake him up.

His arms tightened around her immediately. "I'm a very light sleeper," he murmured, "and I wake up crabby. Stay still and go to sleep."

"I can't!" she said. "I'm too uncomfortable." Her body seemed to fit back against his perfectly, but he wouldn't know that.

"Then just hold still. I'll know if you try to get away, and if you wake me up too many times you'll regret it."

"So much for your promise not to hurt me."

"I won't hurt you. That doesn't mean I won't tickle you until you promise to behave."

The idea was so ludicrous she would have laughed if she didn't already feel so vulnerable. "I hate being tickled."

"Then stay still."

To her astonishment his breathing slowed almost immediately, and she knew he was asleep once more. He was such a robot he'd probably trained his body to do exactly what he said. She had little doubt he slept just as lightly as he'd told her, and there was nothing she could do about her current position. She sighed, releasing some of the tension still inside her, and her body relaxed against his a little bit more. In fact, the bed wasn't that uncomfortable, and neither was Ryder. She might even be able to fall asleep after a few hours of frustration. She certainly was tired enough. The thought of sleeping in Matthew Ryder's arms was so absurd she wanted to laugh, but she simply moved closer, cursing herself as she did so, and tried to keep her eyes open, her anger hot.

She failed.

Chapter Fifteen

Skin. Warm, sleek, smooth skin beneath her mouth, her fingertips, the heat and hardness of him. Erotic dreams danced through her mind with elegant solemnity—every touch, every taste a climax waiting to happen. Every inch of her was sensitized, on fire, ready for him. She heard her quiet moan through the veils of sleep and knew she was on the verge of exploding. She could feel his heart beating against hers, a steady, solid counterpoint to her own rushed tempo, and she wanted more, so much more, from the stranger in her bed, the man she refused to recognize, the man she wanted with such fierce need she thought she might burn up.

His hand slid behind her neck, under her fall of hair, and she could feel the roughness of calluses, the strength in those long fingers as he tilted her face up to meet his, and she waited, ready to kiss him back, ready to take what she wanted with no excuse or justification.

"Parker, wake up," he whispered, his mouth a fraction of an inch away from hers.

She opened her eyes to the murky light, to the face of the man beneath her, to Ryder's eyes watching her steadily, to his mouth that was so close. She'd somehow managed to end up sprawled on top of him in her sleep, and he was warm and strong and hard beneath her. Very hard.

She didn't move, frozen, staring at the mouth that had done such wicked, wondrous things to her in her sleep, the mouth that had never touched her. "I'm sorry," she whispered, and tried to slide off him.

His other arm came up around her, holding her in place. "Who were you dreaming about, Parker?" His voice was low and sinuous. "You were making the most delicious noises."

She racked her brain, trying to come up with some ridiculous name, but she was too caught in a sensuous haze, and all she could think of was him. "I . . . No one," she stammered.

"It's warm in this bed, and your nipples are hard. Were you just reacting to me?"

Her entire body felt on fire. They were both practically nude— her stomach against his, her legs twined with his long ones, her hands clutching his shoulders, not letting go him.

Her brain wasn't working. Jet lag or lack of sleep or too much stress—all of them had taken their toll. She couldn't think, couldn't judge; she could only feel, only know what she wanted to feel, and that was Ryder's mouth on hers.

He stared up at her. A moment later he moved, turning her beneath him, half on top of her, holding her in place. "I can get up," he said quietly. "I can get in the other bed, right now, and leave you alone. That's the smart thing to do."

She said nothing. He was heavy, a good kind of heavy, on top of her, and he was between her legs, his erection pressing up against her insistently. "Tell me to be smart, Parker," he whispered, his mouth hovering above hers. "Because right now I think brains are highly overrated."

She opened her mouth to tell him to get off of her. She opened her mouth to tell him no. She opened her mouth to the man who'd hurt her, and she lifted up and pressed it against his.

His reaction was instantaneous. He cupped her face, holding her still, and slid his tongue between her teeth, an intimacy that startled her into even greater arousal. He kissed her with such thoroughness, his tongue dancing, tasting, teasing, and she heard her soft little whimper of response as her fingers tightened on his shoulders and she closed her eyes. She could go on like this forever, lost in the glory of his mouth, the feel of his teeth against her lower lip, tugging, then using his tongue to gentle it.

He moved his hand down her neck, a slow, sleek caress that caught the narrow strap of her bra and pulled it down her arm, and he moved his mouth to her jaw, to her wildly beating pulse, sucking at it, as he pulled her other bra strap down. She felt the faint sting of his teeth against her skin, and then he rolled her partway, and she felt the bra give way. He pulled it from her body, and she was lying beneath him in nothing more than the sensible white panties. She would have said something, would have tried to cover herself, but he slid his hands up over her, covering her breasts, his fingers on her nipples. Arching against him, she shivered in sensation as his mouth moved back up, first to kiss her again, a brief, claiming kiss, before he slid down and bit her ear, hard.

Reaction shot through her. She wanted his mouth on her breasts, between her legs, she wanted him *now*, before she could regain her caution and common sense. She wanted to be naked with him, wanted him inside her.

"Please," she whispered.

He was kissing his way down her neck, over the soft swell of her breast. "Please what, Parker? Please leave you alone?"

The words filled her with despair, and she shook her head wordlessly.

"Please put your mouth on my breasts and suck?" he suggested softly. "Is that what you want?"

"Yes." She couldn't believe it was her voice. "Please," she said again.

"Yes, please," he echoed with light mockery, and she felt his mouth at her breast as desire flooded her. He wasn't gentle, and she didn't want gentle. She wanted him to take her, to bite and suck and lick her, and when his teeth grazed one nipple when he pinched the other one she jerked in a swift, powerful reaction.

She hadn't even realized that he was taking her panties off until they were halfway down her legs, and he pulled them off before she could protest, would protest.

"I don't think . . ." she said, suddenly frightened of him once more, of his size, his strength, his hands.

"Good. Don't think," he said, his hands sliding up her calves to her thighs, and he put his mouth between her legs.

For a brief second it tore her from her erotic daze. No one had ever done this for her—no one had used his mouth, his hands—and the feel of his tongue was a shock, as he slid one long finger inside her, withdrew and slid two. She was tight around him, the invasion a surprise, but he caught one thigh with his hand, holding her still for him. She reached out to push him away, when the first wave of pleasure hit her, and instead she wound her fingers in his too-long hair, caressing him as he licked her, as thorough as he'd been with her breasts, pumping his fingers into her until she stiffened and cried out in unexpected climax, her hips arching off the bed.

He didn't stop. The second climax was even more powerful, shaking her to the core, and she let out a soft sob, her fingers digging into his scalp. He needed to stop—she couldn't take any more—but he kept on, and it went through her like a lightning bolt, her skin sizzling, her eyes blind, her entire body spasming in an orgasm that was almost painful in its intensity.

He slid up and over her, wiping his mouth on the sheet, and she realized he'd lost his shorts at some point, though she couldn't remember when. She should touch him, pleasure him, get him ready—the thoughts swirled through her brain—but then she felt him, rock hard against her, and his solid thrust went in deep, so deep, and she slid her arms around him, pulling him tight against her. Her nipples were so hard they hurt, pressed against the silky smoothness of his muscled chest as he moved, sliding his hands under her butt and lifting her up so he could go deeper still. He was huge, so big she wasn't sure she could take all of him, but he whispered in her ear, his tongue tracing her lobe, reading her fears. "You can take me. Just relax."

Relaxing was the last thing she felt like doing. Her entire body was rigid with the renewed onslaught of desire, and she lifted her knees, cradling him, pulling him deeper, so awash in sensation she couldn't speak, couldn't think. He was all around her, in her head, in her heart, in her cunt, and she wanted to devour him, own him, never let him go. His slow, steady thrusts made her gasp, getting her used to the size and power of him, stilling her apprehension, stoking her desire, as sweat slicked their bodies until they were slapping against each other, hard, fast, again, again, again.

Jenny cried out as she felt one last, sweet climax, and she wanted to hold him against her, hold him in her arms until he reached his own, but he wasn't finished with her. He slid his hands between their bodies, put his thumb on her clitoris, rubbing, and she exploded off the bed, just as she felt him go rigid in her arms, flooding her with his semen.

He was holding her, partway off the mattress as he slammed into her, and he lay her down carefully, gently. He pulled out, and she wanted to protest, but she was beyond words.

He looked down at her for a long moment and said succinctly, "God damn it to hell." A moment later he was gone.

What in God's name had she done? It was growing light in the room, when Jenny wanted nothing more than darkness to cover her. Shame washed through her, at war with the lingering incandescence of his possession, and she curled up into a ball, burying her face in her arms. He hadn't used a condom. For God's sake, she'd just had the best sex of her life with a man who'd hurt her to get information from her, a man who'd kill her baby brother if he got the chance, a man who was dangerous and heartless and cruel.

But there had been nothing cruel about his lovemaking. Should she call it that? No—it made it sound too pretty. They'd fucked, like rabbits, like animals in heat, like . . . She couldn't think of anything basic or shameful enough. And it had been her fault. He'd warned her, and instead of pushing him away she'd kissed him, invited him with her mouth, and there was no going back.

And she was lying to herself again. He would have stopped at any time—for some reason she knew that. He had the kind of self-control that he could have pulled away from her if she'd gained an ounce of intelligence and told him to. But she hadn't, and he hadn't, and now she was lying alone in a bed in a seedy hotel room with his semen between her legs, and she hated him and she hated herself.

She heard the shower, and for a brief moment she wondered whether she could slip into her clothes and simply disappear. The thought of facing him again, of the knowing smirk on his face was more than she could bear. How could she have been such an idiot? It was all the fault of her dreams, sabotaging her. It had been so long since she had slept with anyone, felt a strong, warm body entangled with hers when she was at her most vulnerable, that it was little wonder the dreams had come.

But she knew the difference between dreams and waking, and she'd known exactly what she'd been doing, even if she hadn't allowed herself to consider it too clearly. She had been warm and needy as she lay sprawled on top of him, and she would have done anything he wanted her to do.

Instead, she hadn't even touched him. She realized that with sudden shock—she'd lost count of how many orgasms she'd had, and yet she'd done nothing for him. He'd gone down on her, something no man had ever done for her, and expected nothing back.

She just needed to move, to get out of there before he came back in, get away . . .

The bathroom door opened, and Ryder walked out, unashamedly naked, ignoring her as he went to his duffel and grabbed some clothes. She immediately closed her eyes, keeping her head tucked down. Most people slept after sex—she was one of those few unfortunate ones who ended up feeling more energized.

She heard the creak of the other bed as he sat down on it, but she didn't move. *Go away,* she thought fiercely.

"I know you're awake, Parker." His voice was flat, cool. "I'm going out to see what I can find about Soledad. Don't even think of trying to disappear."

She turned her back on him, ignoring him, and she heard him sigh. "Don't be a baby, Parker. We fucked. Get over it. It wasn't like it was my idea."

Shame flooded her, and she blinked away sudden tears. "You really are a rat bastard, aren't you?" she said in a muffled voice, keeping her face turned.

"Did you just figure that out?" She heard the sound of his zipper, the clank of his belt, and then he rose. "Stay put. I'll bring back something for breakfast. In the meantime you can beat yourself up for your sins."

Enough was enough. She turned, her eyes narrowed to hide the brightness of tears. "Just tell me one thing, Ryder," she said in a deceptively cool voice, when she wanted to scream and weep. "Do you always go down on the people you torture? Is it your way of making up for it?"

She'd hoped to infuriate him. Instead he laughed, sounding almost lighthearted. "That's my girl," he said obscurely, and a moment later he was gone.

Chapter Sixteen

She was right, he really was a rat bastard, Ryder thought as he strode out into the early morning air. She'd been half asleep, groggy from whatever erotic dream she'd been having, and for all he knew she'd been fantasizing about having sex with some movie star, not him. Except when she looked at him all that slumberous arousal had been for him and no one else, and when she'd kissed him he'd stopped thinking. What was that line . . . God gave man a brain and a penis but only enough blood to run one at a time. He'd certainly been thinking with his cock last night.

If she just hadn't kissed him.

Hell, who was he kidding? He'd been looking for an excuse, any excuse, to take her in his arms. He'd wanted to be inside her so badly he hadn't stopped to think about the ramifications, and even if he had he still would have taken her.

Or maybe he would have given her more time to change her mind. Parker wasn't someone who lost her mind that easily—she'd been so aroused it hadn't take much to make her come, again and again, and if he really wanted to, he could have her on her back once more in a matter of moments.

He really wanted to, but he wanted to find Soledad and the smartphone first. With Parker all bets were off. In a better world he could spend days in bed with her, discovering her. But not right now, for God's sake, in a hostile country looking for a treacherous woman and a phone that could give someone the ability to start up the human trafficking all over again.

But God, she'd looked so pretty, lying there in his arms. She was a restless but heavy sleeper, and he was more than happy to have her end up half on top of him, breathing on his skin, the skimpy underwear no barrier to his imagination. His motives had been pure when he got into bed with her—he'd just needed her to get past her skittishness . . .

Who the fuck was he kidding? He'd wanted to lie in bed with her, wanted to hold her, and he wasn't quite sure why. Never in his life had he let his libido make decisions for him, and the older he got, the smarter he should have been. Fucking her had been a major mistake, and all he could do was move on from it.

In fact, it could all work out for the best. People who slept together gave off a certain tell, an intimacy that anyone with an ounce of perception could read. He would have known whether Parker was sleeping with someone, and for some reason the very thought pissed him off. He was feeling oddly possessive, when he'd never wanted to possess a woman in his life.

But right now he wanted Parker. Maybe it had to do with the dangerous situation they were in—he felt responsible for her, unaccountably guilty for what he'd had to do to her, and they were alone in a foreign country with very little backup. He wasn't a jealous man, but the fact that there'd been no man in her life for the past few years had pleased him, and he'd foolishly thought the lack of a condom would keep them apart.

Nothing could. She'd never admit it, but he knew she'd been wanting him just as much as he'd wanted her. He'd felt it in her body two nights earlier, when he'd kissed her. He'd felt it in her shocked betrayal when he'd climbed on the bed and hurt her. He'd felt it when he'd pulled her up against him, under duress, and her nipples had hardened in the warm darkness.

He'd turned a mess into a royal clusterfuck this morning. He couldn't afford to be thinking about the taste of her, the sweet hitch in her breath, the soft noises, her funny shock each time he brought her to orgasm. He was good in bed but she must have had particularly lousy lovers to be so startled by her own response.

He had to stop thinking about it. He had a job to do, and the first thing he needed was to find Tomás and see what he'd heard about a woman matching Soledad's description. He could only hope she still had the smartphone with her, but they couldn't afford to waste time.

He could moon over Parker later. For now they had work to do.

Jenny had showered and dressed by the time Ryder returned. She'd given in and wept in the shower, where no one could hear her, but enough time had passed that she was calm and clear-eyed, sitting on the bed, waiting for him.

Her nerves were strung so tight she jumped when he opened the door, a paper bag in his arms. He kicked it shut behind him, then turned to look at her in the shadowy room. She hadn't turned on the lamp, and daylight filtered in through the thick curtains, but she hadn't wanted people to be able to look in their window so she'd left them closed. The first thing he did after setting the bag on the table was open the drapes, flooding the dingy little room with light.

She wanted to hiss like a vampire confronted with sunlight, but she merely blinked, keeping her face stolid. "I brought you breakfast," he said, unpacking the bag. "A carton of orange juice, some lukewarm coffee, and some kind of egg sandwich. It's not good, but it's food." He dumped the purchases on the table.

"I'm not . . ." she began.

"Don't tell me you're not hungry, because I'm not in the mood to force-feed you. But I'd do it—I can't have you fainting with hunger. We've got a long day ahead of us." He took one more thing out of the bag and set it on the table. A box of condoms.

"I don't suppose you're on birth control," he said evenly.

Color flooded her face. "No."

"Where are you in your cycle?"

"Go fuck yourself."

"I'd rather fuck you. And that's why I'm asking. If it's a bad time of month I can get you a morning-after pill . . ."

"Please just stop talking about it," she begged, getting up and taking the cardboard cup of coffee. "It's not going to happen again."

"Then answer my questions."

"You're safe from impending fatherhood," she snapped, ignoring the heat in her face. She glanced at the condoms. "And you're not going to need those."

"I like to be prepared for emergencies. Hurry up and drink that coffee. We need to be on the road."

She looked up at him in surprise. "You've found something out? In that short period of time?"

"It doesn't take long when you have resources already in place. Finish your breakfast or bring it with you—I don't care which. We need to get on the road."

"And just how will we manage that?"

"I procured us a jeep. It doesn't look like much, but it will get us where we're going."

"And where are we going?"

"In the jeep," he ordered.

If the coffee had been hot she would have thrown it in his face. No she wouldn't—even cold, bad coffee was coffee, and she needed it quite badly. She drained it, then held it in her hand. "Should I bring this with us?"

He raised an eyebrow. "Why?"

She flushed. "I don't know. DNA or something?"

"I think we left plenty of DNA on the sheets, don't you? Leave the cup."

It was already hot and humid when they stepped outside the stuffy motel. Parker had lived most of her life in New Orleans, but this thick, sweltering heat felt even more oppressive.

The jeep had seen better days. It was mud-spattered, dented, and beaten up, the seats were held together by duct tape, and the windshield had a long crack in it. She didn't say a word, simply climbed in the front and fastened her seat belt. If he thought it would get them where they needed to be going, then she believed him. Asking questions led only to sharp answers, and she was beginning to think his nasty tongue was a more painful form of torture than what he'd done to her arm.

Which had stopped hurting. She glanced down at it and saw that the bruises were already yellowing. She was wearing a tank top and khaki shorts in deference to the hot weather, and she'd managed to braid her hair to keep it from flying into her face. He surveyed her critically.

"I don't know if that's enough to keep your hair under control." He climbed into the driver's seat and turned the engine on. It ran smoothly, which perversely disappointed her. She should have known he'd find a reliable vehicle, no matter what it looked like. "We're heading into the mountains," he said.

Sweat was already sliding down her spine, and she leaned back against the seat in relief. "At least it'll be cooler."

"Marginally," he said, putting the jeep in gear and heading down the road. "But the bugs could be worse."

"Great," she grumbled. "I don't suppose you feel like telling me where we're going."

"Someone with Soledad's description arrived in town twelve hours before we did and was met by members of the Guiding Light. Word has it they took her back to the mountain town that's their current stronghold."

She looked at him in astonishment. "The Guiding Light? The soap opera?"

He made a disgusted sound. "Don't you ever read the newspapers? La Luz is the rebel army around here. They like to think of themselves as freedom fighters but they're mainly into kidnapping, drugs, and extortion. And now it appears they've added human trafficking to their list of sins."

"And they have Soledad?" she demanded.

"And the smartphone."

"But what would they want with Soledad? There's no one who'd pay a ransom for her. Well, I would, but they don't know that . . ."

"Just how big an idiot are you? It's not what they want with Soledad, it's what she wants with them. She's no victim; she's involved in this whole stinking business."

"And you have proof of that?" she demanded coolly.

"No. Just instinct."

"Well, my instincts tell me she's just what she said she is. An innocent victim like all the others."

"And your brother didn't realize what he was doing when he got involved in selling women and children into the sex trades?"

She shuddered. "Of course not."

"Then explain something to me. Who else knows you have his smartphone, and how did they find out?"

"I don't know," she admitted. "But I won't believe my brother really understood what he was doing. And I think whoever came after the smartphone took Soledad as well."

"Why?"

"Why?" she echoed. "I don't know. I don't understand the minds of sociopaths—that's more your style."

His short laugh was humorless. "Afraid I don't qualify as a sociopath, Parker, despite what you think. I can't fault you for your loyalty . . . wait a minute, yes I can. Your loyalty has brought down a shitstorm on us, and if we don't get that smartphone back, then whatever information is on it will be available for the Guiding Light and anyone else to use. Which means the human trafficking will continue, and you'll bear some of the responsibility."

She said nothing, turning her head to stare at the deepening countryside around them. There was nothing she could say. Ryder was right on one count—if she'd turned her brother over, then any information he had would have stopped with him. If she'd simply handed over the damned smartphone, then all this could have been resolved. Her brother was far enough away that Ryder couldn't get to him, but the infrastructure of the human trafficking would be compromised, and it would be a lot harder to rebuild.

"You're right," she muttered.

She could feel his eyes on her. "What did you say?"

She turned to look at him. He looked dangerous in the bright sunlight, unshaven, sunglasses shading his wolf's eyes, and unwillingly she remembered the feel of him on top of her, inside her, his mouth between her legs, and she wanted to curl up and die. From shame, and from wanting more.

"I said you were right. If I'd just handed over the phone all this could have been avoided. My brother would have had to stay out of reach of the police, but that could have been accomplished, and he deserves at least some punishment for what he did, even if he didn't recognize how awful it was. Exile from the US is the least of what he should suffer, no matter how much the family will miss him."

"The family or you?"

"Not me. I hadn't even seen him in almost a year. I don't have anything to do with my family."

"Then what makes you think he's still the lily-white soul you think he is?"

"I told you, you're right. I have no idea who he really is at this point. I'm just trusting my instincts. He's the only member of my family who's still worth anything, and I'm not ready to write him off."

He sighed. "All right, I'll get off your case. But you're in for some nasty surprises."

"I think I've had enough nasty surprises to last me," she said, leaning back and closing her eyes. The wind ruffled her hair, cooled some of the sweat, and this was probably the closest she was going to get to air-conditioning. "Wake me when we get there."

By the time Ryder pulled into the tiny village and brought the jeep to a halt, Jenny was ready to scream. The roads had been so bumpy and rutted there was no way she could sleep, and making idle conversation had been out of the question. All she could do was brood. And remember the feel of him inside her.

She opened her eyes reluctantly, looking around her, and was half tempted to close them again. Their stopping place could barely be called a village. There was a run-down cantina, a tiny store with a gas pump that looked as if it was pre–World War II, and chickens wandering the dusty road. "Where are we?"

"A little town called Talaca. Apparently when the Guiding Light come down from the mountains, they end up here."

Alarm shot through Jenny. "And we just waltz in?"

"We drove in, Parker. And they're not here now. Not yet. Want a beer?"

"What?" Her voice rose an octave. "Are you crazy?"

"Nope. And you're not staying out here alone. If you don't want beer I'm sure they have juice or something, but I think a beer would relax you."

She gritted her teeth. "I'm perfectly relaxed."

"Sure you are. That's why you've been clenching your fists for the last four hours."

"It was a bumpy road," she said self-righteously.

"It's a bumpy life. Out of the jeep, gorgeous. We have things to do."

Gorgeous? Did he just call her *gorgeous?* She was a lot of things—attractive, even pretty by some people's standards, but she could hardly be called gorgeous. She looked at him to see if he was mocking her, but he was fiddling with something in the jeep. She watched in horror as he pulled out a large and nasty-looking handgun, tucked it in the back of his jeans, and then pulled on a rough jacket.

"You know, anyone watching from the cantina will know you're carrying a gun," she pointed out in a cranky voice.

"I'm counting on it." He came around to her side of the jeep. "Are you climbing out or do I have to make you?"

"How do you think that would look?"

"Like a man making sure his woman obeys him," he said lazily.

"I'm not your woman!"

"I didn't say you were. I said that's what it would look like. Now stop arguing and get out of the fucking car. And keep your mouth shut once we're in the cantina. In case you haven't realized it, Calliveria is a man's world, and women should be seen and not heard."

She unfastened her seat belt and climbed out, simply because she knew he'd haul her out if she didn't. "You know I really hate you, don't you?" she said bitterly, trying to stretch her aching muscles.

"Sure you do, Parker. You hate me about as much as I hate you."
There was something in his voice, and she looked up quickly, but his
expression gave away nothing.

"Well, as long as we understand each other," she said stiffly.

He laughed, the bastard. "I wouldn't go so far as to say that." He
took her arm, and she tried to yank free, but he simply tightened
his grip as they climbed up the front steps of the run-down cantina.

The place was empty. An electric fan spun lazily overhead, stirring
up a haze of dust motes in the late afternoon sun. All Jenny could think
of was some of the old westerns she'd watched—she half expected to see
dance-hall girls and gamblers. The bar, however, was a simple length
of wood at the far end of the room, and by the time they reached it a
pretty young girl in a low-cut blouse had appeared, smiling at them.

"What can I do for you, *señor*?" she said in Spanish, not even
bothering to glance at Jenny. And what woman would, she thought,
if there was a man who looked like Ryder nearby—anyone else
would fade into insignificance.

"*Dos cervezas*," he said. "And maybe you could help us."

"Of course, *señor*," she said, and her eyes drifted over Jenny for
a moment, then dismissed her. *Bitch*, Jenny thought amiably. The
two lukewarm beers appeared on the scarred wooden countertop.
"It's not often we see *turistas* in Talaca." She was clearly fishing for
information, but Ryder didn't seem inclined to deny her.

"We're looking for my girlfriend's half sister. She and Soledad
had a fight, and the last we heard she'd come down here. Of course
Jenny wants to find her and apologize, but we have no idea where
she is. Perhaps I might show you a photo?"

"Of course, *señor*. But I have seen no strange women around
here for weeks. Your 'girlfriend' is the first."

Jenny could hear the virtual quotes around the word *girlfriend*
and her temper rose. Obviously a man like Ryder could have anyone

he wanted, and the girl at the bar wanted to make Jenny understand that any hold she had on him was tenuous at best.

But that was minor compared to the shock of hearing him call her Jenny. She'd always been Ms. Parker, or plain Parker, and to hear him call her by her first name was oddly unsettling.

Ryder had passed a photograph of Soledad across the bar, and Jenny wondered where he'd gotten it. Then she mentally kicked herself. There had been cameras all over the house in the Garden District—they would have had a dozen photographs.

The young woman glanced down at the photo, then back up at Ryder. "I have never seen her before." She glanced at Jenny. "They do not look much alike, do they?"

"She was adopted," Ryder said easily. "Are you certain you haven't see her?"

"I am afraid not. Is there any other way I can help you?"

"You can tell me where we might find a place to stay for the night. We've been driving all day and I'm bone tired, and my woman doesn't drive on roads like these."

His woman felt like snarling. She'd driven through rain forests in Costa Rica and mud season in Vermont—these roads were a piece of cake compared to those.

"Then she is lucky to have a big strong man to take care of her," the girl purred.

Oh, gag me with a spoon, Jenny thought.

"I'm afraid there are no rooms here, and this is a very poor village. The nearest town would be thirty miles to the south, but you came that way."

Of course she'd been watching, Jenny thought. She would have seen not only the gun but also the hostile dynamic between the two of them.

She'd had enough of being silent. "We're not fussy," she spoke up, and she felt Ryder's start of surprise and disapproval. "We just need a bed for the night, and we'll leave first thing in the morning. Even a single bed will do—we like to cuddle."

Ryder coughed, but the girl behind the counter didn't notice. "There is no place," she said. And then her forehead wrinkled. "Unless . . ."

"Unless what?" Jenny said.

"Are you afraid of ghosts?"

Jenny just looked at her, and the girl shrugged. "Maybe they won't bother you. There is an old convent on the edge of town. Missionaries used to live there, teach the local children, take care of the sick. The jungle is starting to take over by now, but various travelers have stayed there with no problem."

"Who are the ghosts?" She didn't believe in malevolent ghosts, though she was open enough to otherworldly energy. She could practically hear Ryder snort in disbelief.

"The priest and the women from town who helped out were killed by the Guiding Light a couple of years ago. It is said you can see lights at night, sometimes, and that Father Pascal is looking for the lost children."

"Lost children?" Jenny echoed, horrified.

"Some of the children who attended the school never returned that day, and no one knows what happened to them."

"I think we'll take our chances with the ghosts," Ryder said, taking over the conversation and smiling at the girl. Really smiling, using all his latent charm, and Jenny wanted to scream. He'd never smiled at her like that, never made the slightest attempt to charm her. "We're really bone tired."

"You need food? Come back and I will cook for you. This is my uncle's cantina, and he pours the drinks in the evening while I take care of the tables. I can bring you something to eat during my break if you like."

Jenny really didn't like the girl. "No, thank you," she said sweetly before Ryder had a chance to answer. "I can cook for my man." She used the term deliberately, just to goad him, but he didn't even blink. He probably approved of her territorial stance.

"Yes, thank you . . . ?" Ryder prompted.

"Rosario," she said sweetly, and Ryder smiled at her once more. "If you change your mind I will be here. If your girlfriend is too tired you can always come alone."

Over Rosario's dead body, Jenny thought grimly. She drained her warm, bitter beer, shuddered slightly, and then grabbed Ryder's arm. "Let's go, sweetheart," she said brightly. "I want to get settled for the night."

"Women," he said, not a tactful statement in a room with only women inside. "How do we find this convent?"

So Ms. Jennifer Gauthier Parker didn't like it when he flirted with other women, Ryder thought as he drove down the narrow, rutted road leading from the village. Then again, she didn't like it when he flirted with her, so that didn't mean anything. His companion was tired and cranky and he couldn't really blame her. Six hours in the open jeep over these roads would make anyone cranky, himself included. They needed to get settled for the night, get something to eat, and then get a good night's sleep.

"You didn't care much for Rosario," he said lazily. "Jealous?"

"Oh, please," she protested. "Go spend the night with her—I'm sure that would make both of you very happy, and it would give me peace of mind."

"You want to stay all alone in the haunted convent?" He took the left turn, deeper into the overgrown forest.

"I'm not afraid of ghosts," she said flatly. "Besides, these were good guys who were killed. I'd think the Guiding Light would have more to fear from them."

"Good point. But I don't think you can count on the ghosts to keep the Guiding Light away from you. You'd be a plum asset—the daughter of a rich American gangster . . ."

"My father is not a gangster!"

"Close enough. They could get a nice ransom for you, and that's one of their stocks in trade. I don't think ghostly priests would be able to stop them."

He could feel her reaction without having to look at her. "Rethinking the idea of sleeping alone?" he murmured. "That's wise."

She ignored him. "What if my father refused to pay my ransom? I'm basically persona non grata in the household, and I doubt he'd be willing to fork over much money."

"Even though you put everything on the line to save your baby brother?"

"That was my choice, not his. I don't want his gratitude and I'm not expecting any. He knew I didn't do it for him."

"Who did you do it for? Surely you're not so stupid that you think your brother's an innocent."

"I'm not stupid. My brother may not have been innocent, but he didn't know what he was getting involved in. He deserved a second chance."

"To do the same thing all over again? How many people have to suffer until you decide he's past redemption?"

She flushed. "If you must know, I did it for my mother."

"This is the first I've heard of a mother."

"Everybody has one, at least in the beginning. My mother died when I was thirteen and Billy was seven. I felt responsible for him." She sounded brittle and matter-of-fact, but it was easy to read the pain beneath the cool words.

"Tough age to lose a mother," he said mildly enough.

"There's never a good time."

"So after she died you decided you'd be Billy's little mother, and now you're willing to put lives on the line when you discover you've nurtured a sociopath."

Dead silence. "Why are you such a nasty son of a bitch?" she said finally. "Did I run over your dog? Okay, yes, I did something wrong. Something very wrong, I take full responsibility. But it was done out of love."

"So are a lot of bad things. Love and religion are two of the most dangerous things in human existence."

Another long silence, and he kept his eyes on the road. He was being a nasty son of a bitch, and he wasn't sure why.

"You must lead a very sad life," she said finally. "Faith and love don't do bad things; people do. They get confused, they make mistakes, because, unlike you, they're human. I'm sorry no one ever loved you when you were young—you might not be such a cynical asshat if someone had."

He had to stop baiting her. "I said religion, not faith. And I didn't say love was bad, just dangerous."

"At least you admit the existence of love," she said in a brittle voice.

"I'm open to the possibility."

"Bully for you."

He made one more turn on the increasingly overgrown road, and he saw what must have been the old convent before him. The South American jungle had begun to encroach, and there were vines and foliage crawling over the old stucco walls, greenery everywhere. "Home sweet home," he said.

Parker was looking up at it doubtfully. "Maybe we ought to keep driving."

"We were never going any farther. The Guiding Light has used this place whenever they come down from the mountains, and right now they're not more than ten klicks away."

"We're that close to a rebel army composed of criminals? Just the two of us? Who do you think you are, Rambo?"

"Soledad is with them, remember? If she's a prisoner do you want to abandon her?"

"Of course not! I just don't see how the two of us . . ."

"Don't worry your pretty little head about it," he said, deliberately goading her. "I have a plan." He put the jeep in park, looking at the dispiriting landscape.

"I've got a plan," she said. "To stab you in your sleep."

She surprised a laugh out of him. "Then you'd be up shit's creek without a paddle."

"That's the only thing that's keeping you alive, mister," she said smartly, unfastening her seat belt and climbing out of the jeep. There was a large courtyard to one side of the building, and she started toward it.

He almost reminded her of her bag, then decided he'd given her enough shit for one day and grabbed it himself. "You really going to cook for me?" he said, coming up even with her.

"Hell, no. I just didn't like that skank."

He was amused at the idea. "Why not? She was very pretty," he added, just to see her reaction.

"She's a snake," Parker said succinctly, and then shuddered. "There aren't any snakes or spiders here, are there?"

He'd seen spiders as big as dinner plates in Calliveria when he'd been here in the past, but he suspected this might be one subject that was a little too intense for her. Murder attempts and human trafficking were bad enough—yucky wildlife was beyond the pale.

"You don't like snakes and spiders? Wuss. We're more likely to be visited by jaguars."

"You can fight them off," she said. "I suggest you cook dinner as well, unless you want to risk poisoning."

He almost mentioned the spiders, but thought better of it. "You're just lucky I packed provisions."

"Not lucky. You're a very thorough man." She suddenly turned away, her face growing red, and he knew what she was thinking. She was remembering the sex last night, and if a shaft of arousal hadn't hit him he would have been amused. Hell, he was amused. Except he wasn't going there again, not if he could help it. She had a very bad effect on his attention span—she was far too distracting, and he needed to keep his brain working. "We'll find a couple of rooms that aren't too disastrous, eat dinner, and then settle down. Tomorrow we'll head up into the mountains and see if we can find the Guiding Light."

If he expected her to brighten at the mention of two rooms, he was doomed to disappointment. Didn't she know what she wanted? Either she wanted him in her bed or not, and she couldn't have it both ways.

But he knew what she was thinking, whether she'd admit it or not. She wanted him. She'd had so damned many climaxes the night before there was no way she couldn't want more, though she'd seemed a bit shell-shocked by the whole thing. He might almost have thought she was a virgin—hell, she was tight enough, but he knew he was big. And he hadn't given her much of a chance to participate—he'd wanted to fuck her into a little pool of pleasure and enjoy himself at the same time. She'd been right—it had been his way of trying to make up for what he'd had to do to her earlier that day, but he wasn't about to admit that to her. Particularly when the pleasure for him had been just as shattering.

Shattering? That was a stupid-ass way to look at it. Intense, that was it. "Come on, buttercup. Night's closing in." He started up the side steps, coming into a kitchen that looked like it had been inhabited by frat boys on a spring break. There was garbage everywhere, mostly empty beer bottles and trash, and he looked around thoughtfully.

"I guess the Guiding Light has been here," she said. "God, that name is so ridiculous."

"Call them La Luz, then. But don't underestimate them—they're thugs and killers." He kept himself from saying she ought to know something about that—he'd been too hard on her already, and he was beginning to suspect why.

His circumspection had been a waste of time. "Yes, I know I've been surrounded by thugs and killers all my life. I make no excuses for my family," she said in a tired voice. "Though I've never had proof of the killer part."

"I didn't say anything," he protested.

"But you were thinking it."

"Don't tell me what I think," he growled. "Let's find you a room, and then I'll see if there's a generator here. It's wired for electricity so maybe we'll be in luck—otherwise we'll have to make do with candles."

"And you think there'll be candles left in this place."

"I come prepared, remember."

The halls were strewn with trash and beer bottles as well, and some of the greenery had begun to intrude through a couple of the open windows and louvered vents near the roofline. Lucky she wasn't claustrophobic as well, or he'd have a basket case on his hands. As it was, he wasn't crazy about the closed-in feeling of the place himself. In another year or so the jungle would take over the building completely.

He found a couple of small rooms that were marginally clean, though one had vines coming through the window. He dumped her bag in the adjoining room. "I imagine you're going to want to clean this place up a bit."

"You think?" Her sarcasm amused him.

"I think," he agreed solemnly. "Just put the trash in the next room down—there's no way we can clean the entire place, and La Luz will just come back and trash it again. We need a clean place to sleep—the rest of it will have to take care of itself."

"One place to sleep? Or two?" She didn't look happy about the idea, but she was accepting it, and he gave her a lazy smile.

"Despite your insistence to Rosario that we like to cuddle, I thought you'd be happier with your own bed tonight. In case you didn't notice I left my bag next door. Now you can always talk me into changing my mind—far be it from me to disappoint a lady."

"Go to hell," she said without much heat. "This room will be just fine. I don't suppose there's anything like a broom around here?"

"Improvise. I'll see what I can do about dinner and electricity."

She waited till he was gone, then turned to look at the tiny room in dismay. The only furniture was a very narrow bed, and she realized this must have been one of the nun's rooms back when this was a working convent. A good thing too—the walls must be imbued with virtue and chastity. No place for her to be thinking about last night, the feel of him inside her, the way she could still feel him.

She started with the trash, newspapers and beer cans and old boxes, scooping them up and dumping then in the abandoned room next to them. The bed in that one was splintered and the mattress slashed open, and she simply threw the garbage in there and shut the door.

She was left with a room full of dirt and an old mattress. The first thing she did was push open the louvered window and haul the mattress halfway out. She beat at it, watching clouds of dust emerge and then settle back down on the ticking, but she kept at it, sneezing, until she was satisfied that at least half a pound of dirt was gone.

She pulled it back onto the metal bedsprings, listening to them creak in protest, then surveyed the dirt on the floor. "Improvise," he'd said. Heading out into the hallway, she picked up a discarded newspaper and wadded it into a large, loose ball, then used it as a makeshift broom, herding rather than sweeping the top layer of dust and dirt out into the hallway and away from their doors.

She surveyed the darkening room with satisfaction. She left the windows open to allow at least a breath of fresh air in the room, then headed into the hallway. If Ryder wasn't able to turn on the electricity, it would be dark before he could get to his room, and she didn't want anything encouraging him to share hers.

His was in worse shape, and it took three trips to the newly designated trash room to clear out the trash. His mattress had a slash in it, but it was still in one piece. She lost only a little bit of stuffing as she beat some of the dirt out of it, and by the time she was sweeping the place, it was growing very dark indeed. Was he going to leave her here in the dark while he wasted his time doing whatever he was doing? One thing was for certain—she wasn't going after him in this shadowy place. She didn't quite trust him on the subject of eight-legged creatures, those that she refused to name. She would go back to her own room and sit tight, wait until the lights came on or he brought her a candle.

The shadows had grown deep in her room, and she pulled the louvered windows closed. Enough air seeped through, and she didn't fancy sleeping with a jungle a foot away from her bed. She didn't know how fast the foliage grew, but she had a sudden horrifying vision of lying in bed and waking up bound to the mattress by the invasive vines like in some 1950s horror movie.

She shuddered, sitting down on the mattress. Why hadn't she brought a flashlight with her? The only things in her bag were a couple of changes of clothing and not even the grace of a nightgown. Thank God Ryder had no intention of repeating last night's debacle, despite that box of condoms he'd shown up with. She could still remember the expression of disgust on his face when he woke up, and his succinct "God damn it to hell." As curses went it was mild, but the tone of voice made it equal to the most profane. He was even more horrified by what had happened last night than she was. There was no way he would be coming near her again.

As for that disgust, she knew perfectly well that it had been directed at himself, not her. Knew it in her head, but in the long run it made no difference. It had felt like a stab in the heart when she'd woken up, warm and sleepy and splendidly sated. He'd ripped all that lovely feeling away and ruined it. What had he said . . . "love causes nothing but trouble"? Then again, what did love have to do with what happened between them? It was sex, it was an accident, it was her own stupid fault and she had to stop thinking about it . . .

"Don't move, Parker."

She looked up and saw Ryder standing in the door, his gun pointed directly at her head.

Chapter Seventeen

Jenny stared at Ryder in utter horror. His face was emotionless in the shadows, the gun hand steady as it pointed at her head. He was going to kill her, and she had no idea why, unless that had always been his plan. He'd just wanted to get her away from everyone so that he could shoot her and dump her body, and then no one would ever find her. She opened her mouth, to beg, to scream, but nothing came out. She should fling herself to the floor and cry for mercy, but it wouldn't do her any good. He was an implacable man, and he'd made his decision. At least she knew it would be fast. She opened her mouth again, and his cold, deadly voice stopped her.

"I said, don't fucking move," he said again in that chilling, flat voice. "Stay absolutely still."

Why didn't he just shoot her? Did he get some kind of enjoyment from dragging it out? Did he want to see her cry, did he . . . ?

The gun spat fire a second before the noise deafened her, and she felt something hit her neck, hard, knocking her onto the ground, and she lay there, motionless. She could feel the warmth and wetness of blood and knew she was dying, smothering beneath an unknown weight. "Why?" she managed to croak.

She felt rather than saw him stride into the room, and a moment later the weight was lifted. She felt weak, boneless, waiting for the second shot, but he'd put the gun away, and he was squatting down beside her, and there was a concerned expression on his face. "Are you all right, Parker?"

"You . . . you tried to kill me!" she said accusingly.

"Don't be an idiot. I'm a better shot than that. Look over there."

She looked, and it took her a moment to focus in the shadows. A huge snake lay on the floor beside her, the head nothing but a pulpy mass, and she began to scream.

Ryder pulled her into his arms, slapping a hand across her mouth to try to silence her. "We don't need to advertise our presence to the entire countryside," he muttered in her ear. "You're fine, the snake is dead."

She struggled, terrified. She had to get away from it, get away from him. "Don't!" Her voice was muffled from behind his hand, and he loosened it slightly. "I . . . Let me go."

Instead, he simply scooped her up in his arms, carrying her from the room, back into his. She was crying now, sobbing in reaction and horror. She hated snakes, even more than she hated spiders. She couldn't even look at photographs of them without wanting to throw up, and one had fallen on her; she had its blood on her clothes, and she yanked at her shirt in panic, until he caught her hands. He sank down on the narrow bed and held her still, his voice soft, soothing, until the panic fled and all she could do was collapse in his arms, weeping uncontrollably.

It took her a long time to realize he was holding her with surprising tenderness, one hand on her hair, his fingers stroking her tear-streaked face. She could feel his warmth, his strength enfolding her trembling body, and she slowly began to relax, knowing instinctively that he wouldn't let anything harm her. She was safe. She was home. She closed her eyes, burying her face against his shoulder, breathing in the scent of him, the warmth of him, the unexpected peace of him.

It was pitch black when she finally could speak. "I know what you're going to say," she managed in a rusty voice. "You're going to say 'Jesus, Parker, it was only a boa constrictor.'"

"Anaconda," he corrected. "And there's no such thing as 'only' when it comes to giant anacondas." He didn't loosen his hold on her, and she was glad. She wasn't ready to be on her own.

"I thought you were going to shoot me," she said in a very small voice.

He sighed, and his chest moved beneath her. "I know you did. Why?"

She shook her head against his shoulder, still not looking up. "I don't know. Because I annoy you?"

"If I shot everyone who annoyed me, then the world wouldn't have a population crisis," he said. "And you don't annoy me that much."

For some reason that made her lift her head and manage a shaky smile. "I don't?" she said hopefully.

"It's not you who's annoying, it's my reaction to you," he said finally.

"What does that mean?" she asked, confused.

"When you figure it out, let me know." He released her, and she had no choice but to relax her stranglehold on him. "No generator— it was stolen long ago—but we've got candles and flashlights and a cistern full of rainwater. I think we need to wash the blood off you."

She almost panicked again, but then he'd hold her again, and she wasn't sure that was a very wise idea, simply because she wanted him to so much. "Blood?"

"The snake's."

She couldn't help it—she let out a little moan of distress.

"Don't worry—there's a bathtub, and even if it's not hot, in this

187

climate it'll be warm enough for you to wash. If I were you I'd just dump the clothes. I'll get dinner while you bathe. That sound good to you?"

"Yes," she said in a small voice, torn. On the one hand she wanted every trace of the snake gone from her. On the other, she didn't want to leave Ryder's side.

But she wasn't going to have him scrub her back or keep her company while she bathed. "Where's the tub?"

"Don't worry, it's just off the kitchen. I'll be right there if you need me."

She didn't want to need him. She didn't want to need anybody, but that was before she came to a place filled with monster-sized snakes who'd crush her and swallow her and . . .

"Stop thinking about it. It's dead, and trust me, they don't travel in herds. You're safe as long as you're with me."

She knew it, and it was the most unsettling thing she could think of. He was safety, he was home, he was everything she needed. "Okay," she said in a small voice.

Before she realized what he was doing, he'd scooped her up again and was carrying her through the darkened halls of the place. She closed her eyes, knowing she'd imagine snakes in the shadows everywhere she looked, not opening them until he set her down next to a large old-fashioned bathtub. He turned on the tap and began to fill it, then turned to leave. "I'll see if I can find you something you can use for a towel, and I'll bring you your clean clothes. Just get in the tub, and I promise not to look."

He'd already seen everything, touched everything, but she didn't say a word. She waited till he was gone, leaving the door open a crack, and she surveyed the shadows. Nothing moved, and there was no furniture for a creature to hide behind. She reached for her T-shirt, and saw the blood on her hands, sprayed across the front of her shirt, and she froze. She was still standing there when Ryder returned, an old lantern in his hand as well as her satchel. "I found this in the kitchen—either it belongs to the rebels or they were used to the power going out. Either way there's enough light . . ." He stopped, looking at her. "You need to take off your clothes," he said patiently, moving to turn off the tap.

Once more she tried to reach for her bloody shirt, but her hands dropped helplessly. "I can just get in, clothes and all . . ."

"And end up washing in snake blood?" he said heartlessly. "I don't think so." He came up to her, and before she realized what he was doing he'd pulled the T-shirt over her head. She didn't even pro-test, not when he unfastened her pants and pushed them down her legs along with her underwear, not when he unfastened the white bra that was now stained with red. She shuddered.

But there was nothing sexual in his touch—he was efficient and businesslike, and when she was finally naked he scooped her up and set her down in the lukewarm water. "I know it feels warm but it's colder than your body temperature, and if you stay in there too long you'll start shivering. Do you need me to wash you?"

"N . . . no," she said, cursing her slight stammer. "I'll be fine."

He nodded. "Call me when you're ready and I'll come get you. I'm just on the other side of the door, making us something for din-ner. There are a lot of canned foods—I can manage to whip us up something."

"I'll be fine," she said firmly.

"Of course you will."

Ryder left the door ajar. He could see her from the corner of his eye anytime he wanted to, a mixed blessing. She was looking a little shell-shocked, and while his own reaction to things like snakes was prosaic, he wasn't fool enough to underestimate the effect of true phobias. And even a snake lover might have problems with a dead anaconda falling on their head and covering them with blood.

But he could hear the sound of water splashing, smell the scent of the lavender soap he'd found her, and he knew she was managing, maybe better than he was.

It had taken ten years off his life when he'd walked into her room and seen that anaconda reaching toward her. The thing had to be at least a foot in diameter and God knew how long, and if he'd been a couple of minutes later, it could have twined around her neck, shutting off her screams and her breath and killing her.

He didn't want to think about that. Parker was one of the most alive people he knew, full of piss and vinegar, at least when he wasn't hurting her. To think that her vibrant life could have been snuffed out in seconds . . . unsettled him. He was used to death and its unexpected swiftness. He just hadn't really thought about it for Parker. Letting her come with him had always been a risk, but he'd assumed that risk was from the rebel soldiers and the devious Soledad. He'd forgotten about the indigenous wildlife.

He glanced back into the bathing room. She was moving slowly, rubbing the soap along her shoulders, and he wondered if he should offer to wash her slender back. No, that would be a very bad idea. He'd already played with fire when he'd stripped off her clothes, and it had taken his iron will not to pay attention to her lithe body, her perfect breasts, her long legs, and the soft curls between them. Last night had been a onetime occurrence. He'd brought the condoms because life had a habit of throwing you curves, but the more he thought about it the more determined he was to leave her strictly alone, and the reason was both simple and deeply troubling.

He liked her too much. He liked her smart-ass reaction to him, he liked her bravery. The woman had been shot, had her house blown up, had been hit on the head—and she just kept going with no sign of weakening. Even the trauma of the pain he'd given her hadn't lasted long. He'd been forced to hurt other women before, not as badly as he'd hurt Parker, and they'd looked on him with such horror he'd known his best bet was never to go near them again. Parker had bounced back with surprising speed, her fear leaving her, responding to his touch with anger, and then with something else.

She'd been the one to kiss him. She'd started it last night, a fact he knew shamed her. He could have explained to her that it was only normal—the two of them were trapped together in a dangerous situation, and it heightened adrenaline and hormones.

There was also an intimacy between the giver and receiver of pain, whether it was for a little healthy kink or the need to find out information. It left them both vulnerable, much as he hated to admit it. He now felt more responsible for her, almost protective.

Fortunately she'd come to her senses, and she wasn't about to kiss him again. God knew he wasn't going to put moves on her—he'd already traumatized her enough. No, he'd let her be. He didn't have room in his life for anyone, and Parker was the kind of person a man made room for. If he'd had any sense he would have insisted she stay home, but he'd been stupidly easy to convince. Granted, she could identify the cell phone without its distinctive case, but it wouldn't have taken much for him to figure it out once he caught up with Soledad.

He should have left her behind. But someone had tried to kill her in New Orleans, twice, and he was no closer to figuring out who it was, or why. Leaving her in Remy's care wouldn't have set his mind at ease. Remy was one hell of an operative, but Ryder didn't trust anyone as much as he trusted himself.

So he'd brought her into a different kind of danger, forcing him to realize she was too big a distraction whether she was with him or thousands of miles away.

What was it about her? He couldn't afford to let her get to him—it would be disaster for both of them. He was going to stick to her like glue from now on—this was far too dangerous a place for her. He was going to feed her and sleep beside her like a brother and keep her safe until he could get her back to the States and get her out of his life. The plan was simple.

The question was, could he follow it?

He was right, Jenny thought. The lukewarm water was chilling after a while, but at least she felt clean, rinsing off with fresh water from the tap. There was no towel, but she dried herself on her clean clothes and pulled on a pair of cargo shorts and a baggy T-shirt. The bra had been the only one they'd provided, and it was stained with . . . snake blood. She shuddered in remembered horror. She'd either have the fortitude to wash it tomorrow or she'd just do without. Her modest 34B wasn't going to be that much of a problem beneath the loose shirts they'd provided her, and Ryder was going to be too busy to notice.

She pushed open the bathroom door. He was standing over the stove, and amazing smells were coming from the cast-iron frying pan. "Well, aren't you domestic," she said in a wry voice, attempting to reclaim her sangfroid. It came out a little shaky, but close enough, and he simply raised an eyebrow.

"Red beans and rice, Calliverian style," he said. He took the frying pan and set it down on the scarred wooden table. "No plates, though I found a couple of spoons. We're going to have to eat it from the pan."

"That's a little unsanitary, don't you think?" The moment the words were out of her mouth she regretted them.

He gave her a slow grin. "I think we've shared enough germs already that this isn't going to make a difference." He frowned. "How's your head?"

"My head?"

"You got shot, remember? You had a graze on the side of your head, and then that bitch bashed you . . ."

"Soledad wasn't the one who hit me. I told you, I saw her across the room looking terrified seconds before I blacked out."

"People who've been knocked unconscious quite often don't remember the last few seconds or even minutes before they were hit. Your memories aren't reliable."

"I remember everything," she snapped.

His responding smile was disturbing. "So how's your head feeling? Show me where the bullet grazed you."

She didn't bother fighting him, pushing her hair off her face so he could see the healing graze along the side of her head. "It's fine. Not even a headache."

He nodded. "What about your leg? It's easy to get an infection down here and . . ."

"My leg is fine. Jesus, I'm sorry I ever said anything about germs," she protested. "The leg is just about healed, see." She turned so he could look at the place on her calf where the shard of wood had been. "It only hurts when I poke it."

"Then don't poke it," he said.

"Good advice," she said with heavy sarcasm. "Now that we've finished with my medical exam could we eat?" She dropped down on the bench opposite the frying pan. The concoction inside looked like garbage but it smelled divine. "I'm hungry enough to eat a goat."

"That can be arranged. People raise goats for food around here." He took the seat opposite her, handed her a wooden spoon, and dug in with his own ladle.

"What does goat taste like?"

"Goat," he said succinctly. "Eat."

It was delicious. Spicy and rich, even without any meat in it, and the only problem was that her large wooden spoon kept hitting against the ladle he was using. By the time they'd finished every scrap, she was deliciously full. He took the empty frying pan and dumped it in the sink. "Bedtime," he said.

Jenny had just been feeling at peace with the world when his words sent her into a controlled panic. "I don't . . ."

"Stop worrying. I'm not about to jump your bones."

In fact that hadn't been her worry. "The snake . . ."

"You're sleeping with me. I dragged a second bed in so you can sleep in pristine glory. Those rooms used to belong to the nuns—you can just pretend you are one and you'll be fine."

She greeted this news with mixed emotion. "The question is, who's the bigger snake, you or the anaconda?"

He laughed at that. "You're welcome to stay in your old room. I got rid of the corpse but I didn't bother to clean up the blood. That shouldn't . . ."

"Don't!" she said with a shudder. "I'll sleep with you." His slow grin was demoralizing. "You know what I mean," she snapped.

"Your virtue is safe with me, gorgeous. Just promise me one thing."

She looked at him warily. "What?"

"Don't decide to kiss me in the middle of the night if you don't want that virtue tarnished."

"Not likely," she sniffed, ignoring the fact that she'd done just that the night before. Throwing herself at a man was a onetime occasion, a dire mistake that she wasn't going to repeat, even if it didn't feel like that big a mistake. "But if my virtue is safe then why did you buy the condoms?"

"Have I disappointed you?"

"No," she said flatly, believing it. "I'm just curious."

"Accidents can happen. Any more questions?"

"No." It was far too dangerous a topic of conversation, and she was shocked at herself for starting it.

"Good." He rose, picking up the lantern, pausing long enough to blow out the candles that had illuminated his cooking. He looked . . . to use his mocking word, he looked *gorgeous* in the light of the flames. Tall and lithe and dangerous, with his long shaggy hair and beard-roughened face, his wolf's eyes watching her with steady intensity. She doubted the light was as kind to her, but she told herself she didn't mind. Ryder had a lot more experience than she did, and he was hardly likely to be swept away by the atmosphere.

She followed him down the darkened hallways, struggling to keep up with his long stride. The last thing she wanted was to give him the excuse to carry her again, but with her bare feet on the dirty wooden floors, she couldn't keep from thinking what else might be around to terrorize her. He headed past her room into his, and she noticed with relief that he'd hacked away the intruding greenery and thrown it out the window, closing it so that the louvers let in the cooler night air, and she hoped little else. He'd brought a second cot in, but the room was so tiny there was no place to put it but immediately next to the first one, which didn't silence her fears.

"You take the inside wall," he said.

"Why?"

"Because I need to be the first line of defense if anyone figures out where we are and decides to come for a visit, okay?"

She couldn't really argue with that. "What if they come in the window?"

"Then we're both screwed. Don't worry—it's highly unlikely that anyone will find us in one night. I just like to be thorough."

"Okay," she said in a small voice.

There were sheets on her bed, but not on his, and she wondered where she found them. She didn't bother to ask, climbing over his bed to reach hers. Pulling the top sheet up to her ears, she closed her eyes, but she could still feel him watching her. A moment later he'd turned out the lantern, and she heard the bed creak as he sat down on it, close enough that she could reach out and touch him. The idea was unnerving, though not nearly as bad as spending last night in his arms. That had been catastrophic.

"Stop thinking and go to sleep," he said in a low voice, the sound dancing along the cool night air. "I told you, you're safe."

And that, she thought, was the problem. Some small, stupid part of her didn't want to be safe. Some idiot part of her brain wanted him to pull her into his arms and hold her against his warm, supple skin. She wanted to kiss him again. She wanted to lie beneath him, with him all around her, pressing her down into the mattress . . .

Her eyes flew open. Now wasn't the time for erotic dreams or romantic imaginings. Now was the time for common sense and a good night's sleep, no matter how she felt about the man lying next to her. He was her guardian, her protector, not her lover.

She needed to remember that.

Chapter Eighteen

Her screams ripped Ryder from sleep. He didn't hesitate, moving so fast she wouldn't know what hit her, covering her flailing body with his, putting his hand over her mouth to silence her. She was still half asleep, and her panic was fierce as she fought his restraining body. She bit his hand, hard, but he didn't pull away. There was no telling exactly where La Luz was, but he was willing to bet it wasn't far, and he'd slept so lightly it could barely be called sleep, listening for any untoward noise: something moving through the underbrush, the crackle of leaves underfoot, the silence of the ever-present jungle birds. There'd been nothing, but he wasn't convinced, and Parker screaming her head off could alert an otherwise ignorant group of soldiers.

He was reasonably sure of one thing—the so-called rebels weren't far from the village of Talaca. He was counting on it; the only way they were going to regain possession of that fucking smartphone was through La Luz. Tomás had confirmed that they definitely had it, and Soledad as well, though he couldn't be sure whether Soledad was a hostage or complicit in the crimes of La Luz. It didn't matter— Soledad could do what she wanted, as long as he got that smartphone back before anyone else could put its information to use.

And he didn't need Parker screaming her bloody head off, alerting everyone to their presence. He needed the upper hand in their negotiations, and that didn't include them coming in while Parker was having a nightmare.

"Cut it out, Parker," he whispered in her ear. "You want everyone to know where we are?"

His words must have penetrated her foggy brain. She stopped flailing immediately, lying beneath him still as a stone. "You okay?" he breathed in her ear, not moving his hand from her mouth. "Nod if the answer is yes."

She managed a brief nod beneath his hard hand, and he slowly removed it. She'd bitten hard, but there was no blood, for which he supposed he should be grateful. In fact, the bite had turned him on, but he wasn't about to tell her that. She was already too skittish.

He levered himself away from her, moving next to the wall, his hands still on her, getting her used to the feel of him.

"Not this again," she managed a semi-caustic tone, and he smiled in the dark. She was a tough one, all right.

"Just shut up and go back to sleep. I'll keep the monsters away." *Unless I'm one of the monsters you dream about*, he thought, wondering why it bothered him. He did what he had to do and wasted no time with guilt or second thoughts.

"And who protects me from you?" she said in a quiet voice.

"Yes, who's going to protect the poor, innocent little girl who lied, covered up for an international trafficking cartel, protected a felon responsible for the worst kind of crime against humanity? How capricious and cruel of fate to have put you in my hands, where I've done my best to feed you to snakes."

"Shut up," she said fiercely.

"Oh, gladly. Why don't you tell me what a conscienceless bastard I am? How cruel and heartless and unjustified my actions are? In fact, why don't you take the jeep and drive back to Puerto Claro?

I'm sure you can find a plane to take you back to the States. It would make my life easier and less annoying if I didn't have to babysit you. Just draw me a picture of the phone, and I'll see you on your way."

"I don't remember. I'll know it when I see it."

"I expect you will. The question is, will you tell me about it, or just make a play for it yourself? Because if you do I'd be annoyed. Very annoyed, and you don't want to see me when I'm pissed off."

"I already have," she said flatly. "I wasn't impressed."

He almost laughed out loud at that. He knew he could be frankly terrifying, and a good little pro bono lawyer like Jenny Parker would never be stupid enough to underestimate him, but he had to give her credit for at least trying to appear unmoved.

"That the kind of fairy tale you tell yourself when you're trying to go to sleep, Parker? Trust me, this big bad wolf has teeth, and if you're half as smart as I think you are, you'll watch your step."

"And do what? Not have nightmares? I'm afraid that's out of my control."

"Not out of mine. You start to dream, I'll feel it, and I'll distract you."

Her eyes flew open in sudden alarm. "What do you mean by that?"

"Whatever you want it to mean, gorgeous. I can think of a dozen ways to distract you, most of them pleasant."

"*Pleasant?*" she echoed. "You call sex *pleasant?*"

"Who said I was talking about sex?"

That shut her up as a wave of color swept up her face. Even in the murky darkness he could see it, and it took all his self-control not to smile. She was so damned easy to play when it came to sex. She was a total opposite from the women he liked to fuck. He wanted partners who were comfortable, knew how to get what they wanted, and made no excuses. Parker was like a semi-virgin, and she'd seemed almost shocked by her climaxes last night. If he didn't think it was just wishful thinking, he'd have guessed she'd never had an orgasm with a partner.

Though why should it be wishful thinking? He didn't give a shit about Parker's sexual past or future—it was the present that interested him. The present he had no intention of taking advantage of. "Go to sleep, Parker," he said finally. "Tomorrow's going to come much too soon, and we're going to have a long day."

She grabbed the change of subject like a lifeline. "What are we doing tomorrow?"

"Finding your little lost chickadee and the smartphone she stole."

"She didn't . . ."

"I'm not interested in arguing, I'm interested in sleeping. Unless you have something better in mind? No? Well, then, shut up and close your eyes. I'll keep you safe."

Now why did he say that? He shouldn't give a shit whether she felt safe or not. But bottom line: he did. No matter how annoying, how troublesome, how deceptive she'd been, he felt responsible for her, not just for her bodily safety, but for her peace of mind.

And she believed him. He could feel the tension drain from her body, feel her soften against his, making him even harder. She wasn't wearing a bra, and the soft fabric of the T-shirt was simply temptation personified. Too fucking bad for both of them—sex was off the table for tonight, and if he could hold to his resolution, for the future as well. She was different from the women he fucked, and he'd liked it. He just wasn't going to get used to it.

"Are you always such a bastard, Ryder?" she murmured sleepily.

"Yes. Go to sleep."

She did. He lay beside her, awake, watching over her, until the dawn light filled the room.

Jenny felt when he left the bed, and it took all her self-control not to cling to him. She opened her eyes in the murky light. "Where are you going?"

"Hunting," he said.

"For food, or for the Guiding Light?"

"Just checking out the lay of the land. I want to find the smartphone and your little friend and get the hell out of here before things get dicey. Sleep some more—it's very early."

"And rebel guerillas don't get up early?"

"These ones are fat and lazy. They're not out for government reform, they want money, and once you lose your idealism you start sleeping late."

"Does that mean you're still idealistic?"

His laugh was humorless. "I never was. I just don't need much sleep. You, however, are better off staying in bed. Once I find a trace of La Luz, we're going to have a long day. And don't worry about snakes—they're solitary predators, and I killed the local one."

"Did you have to say the *s* word?" she said with a sleepy shudder.

"Go back to sleep."

She dreamed of his hands on her. She dreamed of snakes and rain forests and blood. She dreamed of her baby brother, and the deeper she slept, the more anxious she felt. Something was wrong, something was profoundly wrong, and she didn't want to wake up. She intended to stay exactly where she was, safe and sound, until Ryder returned, at which time she'd give him holy hell for having taken so long.

Something jabbed her in the back, ripping her from an erotic half sleep, and she froze, unease washing over her. She slowly rolled over to stare into Soledad's uncompromising face.

"Oh, thank God," Jenny said, collapsing back on the bed with relief. "It's just you. We've been so worried . . ."

"Do not waste your time. We know why you've come here,"

Soledad said sharply, none of her usual sweetness visible. "Where's your lover?"

"He's not . . ."

Soledad slapped her across the face, the sharp blow a shock so severe that Jenny froze. "Do not lie to me. We had people watching in Puerto Claro. I should have known you weren't the plaster saint you pretended to be. Tell me where Matthew Ryder has gone, or next time I hit you I will use my gun."

Jenny pulled herself up to stare at the innocent young girl she'd trusted. She looked years older, with her hair pulled back and the gun in her small, capable hand, and Jenny straightened her shoulders. All right, she'd been a trusting fool. Everyone had told her, and she hadn't listened. There was no avoiding the truth now. "Unfortunately for you, Ryder's a lot smarter than I am," she said bitterly. "He never trusted you. He's out looking for you and your soap-opera friends right now. You could have just waited for him to come to you."

"Soap opera friends?" Soledad echoed, confused. "You make no sense." She rose, gesturing with the gun. "And we didn't come here for Ryder. We came for you. Get out of the bed."

There were just the two of them in the room, but Jenny didn't doubt that Soledad had backup. She scooted across the two beds carefully, still in her shorts and T-shirt, and set her feet on the floor. "What do you want with me?"

"Any number of things, *chica*," Soledad said. "Leverage, for one. Plus I imagine your father will pay very well for your safe return, which makes you twice as valuable."

"I think you overestimate my father's affection for me. I doubt he'd pay a plugged nickel for my return."

"A plugged nickel?"

"*Nada*," Jenny said. "Nothing, zero, not a red cent. My father and I parted company a long time ago. I despise people who use guns and violence and lies to get what they want."

"And yet you are in love with Mr. Ryder," Soledad cooed. "How does that make sense?"

It was like a blow in the stomach. "I'm not in love with anyone, particularly a bully like Ryder," Jenny protested. "He can go to hell along with the rest of you."

"Sooner than we will," Soledad said with a catlike smile. "I intend to see to that."

Jenny understood the feeling in her stomach now—it was fear. "What has he ever done to you?"

"You were on the boat when it was raided—you saw the bodies. We have a score to settle with Ryder and his friends." Soledad nudged her with the barrel of the gun. "Where are your shoes?"

"In the kitchen." If Soledad was alone could she fling that iron frying pan at her head? Was there anyway she could outrun her?

"Do not even think about it," the woman said, reading her thoughts. "I wouldn't kill you, but I would hurt you very badly. Too many men put a value on you to waste your life, but that doesn't mean I can't hand you over to my men to teach you a lesson. If they get too rough I can always lie and say you're up in the mountains being held by rebels, though I must admit the loss of revenue would be annoying. Still, it might be worth it."

"Why do you hate me?" Jenny asked, dazed. "I was trying to help you."

Soledad's mouth thinned. "Everything you did got in my way, and you were so determined to help the poor South American girl that I had no chance to escape from you. I couldn't be sure you had the smartphone, or I would have simply cut your throat, but it's a good thing I didn't give in to temptation. I have people who can crack the phone, but they aren't here and I can't wait. In the meantime you'll have to hope some man is willing to pay ransom for you."

"I can't think of a single man who would care much about me one way or another."

"You undervalue yourself. Your father will pay for you—no father ever turns his back on his only daughter. Your brothers are also good for a ransom. And then there's Ryder."

"Who doesn't give a flying fuck about me," Jenny said bitterly.

Soledad sighed noisily. "You are so very tiresome. Ryder will risk everything to get you back. Which will give us Ryder, who has his own value. No, today will be a very fine day's work, I think. Come along." And she stabbed her in the back with the gun, hard.

Jenny swallowed her grunt of pain. "All right," she said. "But you'll find out how wrong you are when no one comes to find me."

"Maybe. But even if he's already tired of you he still wants the smartphone, and I'm counting on you to help me break into it. Your brother has it so protected that I can't find anything."

"Why would you think I'd know anything about it?"

"Because he's your brother. You'd know passwords he could use."

"I don't think I can help you."

"Oh, I think you can. I have friends who can be very persuasive."

Why did everyone want to hurt her? Jenny thought. How the hell had she gotten involved in this mess? It all led back to Billy and her father, two people who'd do nothing to ransom her from a militant army of thugs. Billy didn't have the money, and her father simply didn't care.

"How did you even know I had the smartphone?" She rose to her feet at Soledad's gesture. She towered over the smaller woman, but even if Soledad hadn't held a gun Jenny wouldn't have made the mistake in thinking she could best her. All the watered-down martial arts training she'd gone through in her teens would be nothing against the determination of one small, vicious woman.

Soledad laughed. "How do you think? Your brother told me."

Ryder was in a particularly foul mood, one he attributed to simple lust. After all he'd spent the night pressed up against a nubile female, one who interested him far too much, and he hadn't done a damned thing about it. A case of blue balls would put anyone in a temper.

His life had gotten so fucking complicated since he'd met Ms. Jennifer Parker, Esquire. He wasn't the kind of man who let women mess up his life, and Parker should have been nothing more than an inconvenience, one he could pass off to someone else, but from the very beginning he wasn't letting anyone else near her. He was still furious with her about her lies, furious that she'd covered for her nasty little fuck of a brother, but he could understand. Reluctantly, of course, because he'd always made it a rule never to sympathize with the bad guys.

Parker didn't quite qualify as a bad guy, no matter what she did. She was just a misguided optimist who thought she could save the world. Definitely not the woman for him—he knew the world was long past saving.

Why would he even think of that? There was no such thing as a woman for him—women screwed things up, complicated them, distracted men and got them killed. Women operatives were a different matter—the ones he'd known had been so cold-blooded they could probably mate and then bite their partner's head off once they were done.

When it came right down to it, men were more susceptible. Once they were deluded into thinking they were in love, then all bets were off. He had little doubt that many of the Committee operatives, both in the US and in Europe, would toss a mission in favor of a woman's life. He'd never make that mistake. Collateral damage was an ugly fact of life, and he wasn't about to let some misguided streak of sentimentality get in the way of procuring that smartphone.

She'd insisted on coming along—if she paid the ultimate price it wasn't any skin off his ass.

"Yeah, and pigs fly," he said out loud, disgusted with himself. "You are one sorry son of a bitch, Ryder." So okay, he'd do his best to keep her alive. But if something happened to her, those were the dangers she'd signed on for. Once she'd covered up for her brother, let him escape the justice he deserved, she'd sealed her fate.

But even so, he wasn't going to let anything happen to her. He moved deeper into the jungle, every sense alert for signs of La Luz. His first stop this morning had been the cantina, and Rosario had been extremely helpful. She would have been more than happy to relieve him of his acute state of horniness, but he wasn't tempted. No, Parker had gotten under his skin, and for some reason she was all he wanted right now. It was a temporary affliction—he'd get over it the moment they got back to the States, but all his commonsense lectures to his libido did absolutely nothing. If he'd ever possessed something as useless and vulnerable as a heart, it would have refused to listen, but he could imagine what another man, a better man might be feeling. He wouldn't be off beating the bushes, leaving his woman alone and unprotected in an abandoned convent.

Good thing he wasn't that man, good thing she wasn't his woman. He didn't believe in all that crap anyway—love was a trap at worst, a business arrangement at best. Parker would be lying in bed, sound asleep, dreaming about God knew what. Him again?

Well, tough shit. He had things to do. He needed to find some sign of the Guiding Light, and if that nagging feeling at the base of his skull weren't so irritating, he wouldn't give it a second thought.

But one reason he was still alive was because he knew things. His senses were so highly trained he knew instinctively when there was trouble.

Parker was nothing *but* trouble. He had work to do—he couldn't be babysitting her on the slight chance that something was wrong.

He turned, looking back the way he'd come. The overgrown track made for tricky walking, and he could just imagine her going down in a heap, a victim of the wrong shoes or the wrong terrain.

And why the hell did he keep thinking of her when he had so many other things to do? He needed to forge on ahead, look for signs of La Luz, and ignore the uneasy feeling in the pit of his stomach.

Fifteen minutes later he gave in. She was perfectly fine, there were no more snakes, and La Luz was in a small town somewhere up the road. The most Parker was suffering from was boredom.

Hell, he was bored too. He'd drag her along with him, listening to her gripe—yeah, that was it. Because leaving her alone in the last outpost from hell wasn't really an option.

He turned in his tracks, and a moment later he began to run.

Chapter Nineteen

Soledad hadn't come alone. There were three large men in the hallway and another half dozen wandering around the place, turning things upside down. They'd bound her wrists in front of her with some kind of plastic tie, and it seemed as if Soledad took particular pleasure in hurting her. Jenny was more troubled by the gag and blindfold and her awful feeling of helplessness. A moment later she was shoved forward, stumbling her way toward some kind of vehicle, and then she was picked up and tossed into what she could only guess was the back of a truck. The hands that had thrown her had touched her between her legs, squeezed her breasts, much to the amusement of all the men, until a sharp command from Soledad silenced them. Not that Soledad had any interest in protecting her dignity, Jenny thought. She simply wanted them on the road.

Men climbed into the back of the truck around her, and she knew she was lying at their feet, no shoes, no bra, trussed like a rabbit and completely vulnerable. "Not yet," Soledad had warned them, and Jenny had to put up only with the occasional kick that was far from accidental.

It was a long, bouncing drive, one that gave her plenty of time to berate herself for her epic stupidity. Why had she trusted Soledad? Why had she been so certain the woman had been an innocent victim of the traffickers? Ryder hadn't believed her, and he was experienced in things like this, and yet Jenny had refused to listen, so certain her instincts were right. If she'd been this far off when it came to Soledad, what other mistakes had she made? Was her brother more than the foolish participant in something he didn't understand, or had he lied to her? Why in the world would he tell Soledad that Jenny had the smartphone and put her in that kind of danger?

Billy had always been so sweet, unlike her older brothers, who could be as vicious as their father. Only Billy had still seemed to care about her, and she couldn't give him up without a fight. Surely she couldn't have been that wrong about both Soledad and her baby brother.

It seemed as if they drove for hours, though Jenny could tell by the feel of the hot sun overhead that it couldn't have been that long. She should have been starving but she'd lost her appetite, the softly murmured threats from the soldiers convincing her she'd never want to eat again. Fortunately her Spanish was of the schoolgirl variety, and she didn't understand half their nouns and verbs. She was pretty sure that was a blessing. If she had she might have panicked.

As it was, an almost unnatural calm settled over her. She had no more illusions about Soledad—the young woman would happily feed her to the sharks once she got what she wanted from Jenny. It was up to her to take as long as possible to unlock the phone, something that was going to be difficult. She wasn't used to dissembling, and she'd been able to come up with Billy's passwords when she first got the thing. The contents were incomprehensible—encrypted files, Excel spreadsheets, an address book full of code names. Unfortunately, all that probably made perfect sense to Soledad, and it must be important if they would go so far as to kidnap her.

Where the hell was Ryder when she needed him? How long would it take him to return to the convent and find out she was gone? What would he do then—shrug his shoulders and decide she was no longer his problem?

No, whether he gave a damn about her or not, he still needed the smartphone. Even if he was tempted to leave her to Soledad's tender mercies, he still had to get what he'd come for, and he wouldn't leave her behind.

He also wouldn't jeopardize his . . . his mission for her sake. He'd warned her of that when she insisted on coming with him. If he didn't find them soon Soledad would lose patience, and what Ryder had done to hurt her a few days ago would pale in comparison with what the soldiers were suggesting. Rape was considered a fate worse than death, and gang rape would be unbearable. If it came to that, though, Jenny had every intention of surviving, if for no other reason than to slap her baby brother upside the head. She was a survivor—always had been, always would be, and sooner or later Ryder would show up. She could hold out until then.

The air was thinner when they finally stopped the truck, and Jenny felt bruised everywhere from bouncing around on the floor of the truck bed as well as the occasional kicks from the guards. They hauled her down with rough hands, but this time there were no insulting touches, and she suspected Soledad was watching. Someone took her arm, and she picked her way carefully on the unseen dirt beneath her feet. She was picturing some kind of jungle camp when she heard a door open and felt a sudden, shocking blast of air-conditioning.

"Bring her inside," Soledad ordered. "We have work to do."

Someone ripped off her blindfold, and she cried out behind her gag as the tape pulled her hair, but the sun was so bright all she could do was blink owlishly, her eyes refusing to focus. When they did she almost thought she was imagining it—the clean, elegant lines of the wood-and-glass house perched up high, backing up to a steep ravine. She staggered forward when someone pushed her in the back, tripping over the flagstone pathway, and stepped into the darkened, air-cooled comfort of the place. The sudden flash of cold made her dizzy, and she stumbled slightly as she was shoved forward once again.

One soldier was still with her—the rest of them were left outside—and he dragged her into a large living room, pushing her down on a low ottoman so that her knees buckled beneath her. "Stay," he said in Spanish, and ripped the gag off.

"As if I have any choice in the matter," she said caustically, but she was smart enough to keep it under her breath. The room was spare and sleek, with white leather sofas and thick white carpeting. It looked as if it belonged in a design magazine, not like the headquarters for terrorists disguised as revolutionaries.

Soledad came up to her, and Jenny could recognize the phone in her hand with its distinctive New Orleans Saints case. How could something that supposedly held so much evil information have a football logo emblazoned across it? It was like having Sesame Street handguns.

"You are to help me with this. No one here knows anything about technology, and I cannot even begin to guess what his password is."

"I'm sure there's more than one," Jenny said. "It's going to take a while to get through them all." In fact, her brother had been fairly unimaginative when it came to protecting his smartphone, more proof that he was no criminal mastermind but simply someone who'd gotten in over his head. If there was any way she could avoid putting all that information into Soledad's criminal hands, then she would. Decoding it wasn't going to do Jenny a damned bit of good—her father wasn't going to pay one cent to get her free, and neither would her two older brothers, so it wasn't going to save her life. As for Billy—how could he have told Soledad? They must have known each other, but it was hard to believe her brother was naïve enough to believe Soledad's saintly act.

Then again, she'd believed that saintly act herself. If Billy had been telling her the truth on board the ship that morning, then he'd hardly let them hurt her, would he? But then, he was out of reach, somewhere halfway across the world in a place where he couldn't be extradited, and he needed to stay there, particularly since she'd told Ryder about him. And if he had lied to her . . . She didn't want to think about that.

"We have time," Soledad said smoothly. "We're waiting for your boyfriend to come and rescue you."

"Why bother? No one's going to pay ransom for him. And he's not my boyfriend," she added belatedly. At least she could reasonably assume that the Committee didn't negotiate with terrorists.

"We're not going to ransom him, we're going to kill him. The Committee is well known to us, and they're not likely to simply let things slide. The smart thing for Mr. Ryder to do would be to return to the States, but he won't, not unless he has you with him."

"He doesn't care about me one way or another!" Jenny protested.

"Probably not. But he's not going to leave you to my tender mercies, whether he cares or not, which is a good thing. He knows too much about our workings for his own good. His death leaves the American Committee in disarray and gives us time to set up the trade routes once more."

"Trade routes?" Jenny echoed in deep loathing. "You're talking about human beings!"

"I'm talking about a commodity," Soledad said in a silky voice. "You're such a . . . what do they call it . . . a bleeding heart. These people are nothing to you. The life I give them is better than the toilet they live in now. But no, you must save everyone. I tell you now that this is impossible. You cannot save these people, and most of them come willingly. If something happened to me then someone else would simply take my place. Your Committee friends tried to wipe it out, but they only succeeded in removing the Corsini family from the mix. There are always people to take over, people like your brother."

"My brother didn't know what he was doing!" she protested, ignoring her nascent doubts. "You or someone must have tricked him."

"And you're such an excellent judge of character, aren't you?" Soledad cooed. She held out the phone in front of Jenny's nose. "Get to work."

Jenny gave her a chilly smile. "You're going to have to untie me first."

"You can dictate the names to me."

"That will take twice as long."

"I am very fast on a phone keyboard."

Shit. She was going to have to string her along instead of simply pretending to work on it. She'd make it as tedious as possible. "Do you suppose I might have some iced tea? My throat is parched."

Soledad sneered. "Parched, is it? Such fancy words. You'll get tea and something to eat once you've broken into the phone."

"If you're doing the typing, then I'm going to have to do a lot of talking," she said, her voice hoarse.

"Then you should begin."

It was easier than she had thought. She gave her every name in the family, from their mother to their brothers to their second cousin twice removed, with alternative spellings and substituting numbers for letters. Each one took up a goodly portion of time, and she could see Soledad grow more and more frustrated. "This is no good—your brother isn't as sentimental as you. He cares nothing about family. What else would he have used?"

She went on through his college years at Tulane—the name of his fraternity, each of his friends, first name and last, numbers and letters. The sun was beginning to set, and she hadn't allowed Soledad to get anywhere near the encryption, and while her voice was raw and her stomach empty, she'd lost the ability to worry about it. She just had to keep coming up with plausible choices for as long as possible, long enough for Ryder to rescue her. Assuming Soledad was right and he would risk his life for her.

No, he wouldn't risk his life for her, but he would for the smartphone and the information it contained. She was collateral damage—he'd save her if he could, but not at the expense of getting what he wanted.

"Enough!" Soledad snapped, rising from her chair. The sun was setting over the valley beyond the large picture windows, sending shadows through the room, and Soledad's innocent beauty was looking jaded and sinister. "You are proving useless. If I didn't believe you were lying, I would shoot you in the head this minute." She came up to her, her small body vibrating with rage. "Perhaps I should give you some incentive."

"Perhaps you should give me a glass of water," Jenny shot back.

It was a mistake. Soledad's eyes narrowed. "Manolo, bring me that baseball bat you play with."

The words were enough to send terror through Jenny's insides. The baseball bat appeared, and though it looked incongruous in Soledad's small hands, it didn't look any the less lethal. The woman swung it experimentally, far too close to Jenny's head. Jenny didn't move.

"You realize if you hurt me too badly I won't be able to think because of the pain," she said in a deceptively steady voice. "I'm doing the best I can—what would I have to gain by not giving you the right words? I'm trying everything I can think of—our family, our pets, his favorite foods. Sooner or later I'll hit on the right one— you just need to be patient. If you let me type them in myself you wouldn't be so frustrated."

Soledad's smile was horrifying in its sweet evil. "What would you have to gain? You're a smart woman—you know your own value to me is getting into the phone. It doesn't matter if you're dead when Ryder gets here—he won't make it as far as this house, and he'll never know if we've already killed you or not."

"I wouldn't underestimate Ryder if I were you."

Soledad swung the baseball bat again, and Jenny could feel the wind whip past her face. "I wouldn't underestimate me. You can remain stubborn and try to put off telling me the right words to get into the phone, and you can suffer a great deal of pain. Or you can work harder, come up with the right answer, and you'll have a swift death."

"Meaning you won't hand me over to your men."

"Of course not," Soledad said, righteously, and Jenny knew she was lying. "If you come up with the answer. Otherwise the men are bored and lonely and there are no women up here. I have to give them something to keep them happy, don't I?"

"What about the ransom idea? My father would pay a lot of money for my safe return."

"You already told me he wouldn't pay a penny. The Guiding Light has decided that hostage taking isn't worth the trouble—the payoff is small compared to what we can make with the immigrants."

"Immigrants? Is that what you call them? They're sex slaves."

Soledad shrugged. "They're leaving their country for a new life. And America is the land of opportunity, though they go other places as well. I have sold my body since I was nine years old, and look at me now."

Jenny stared at her in shock. "You're victimizing children the same way you were victimized?"

"So tenderhearted. You know nothing of what life is like. And your mewling protests are annoying me. I'm tired of you. I will give you the night to think about how helpful you can be, and if you don't have the answers in the first hour tomorrow, I will start by breaking your foot and working my way upward." She slapped the baseball bat in her hands.

"Why don't you let me take the phone with me and I can work on it tonight?"

"What kind of idiot do you think I am? You would destroy this rather than let me get the information from it. Why do you think I refuse to let you put your hands on it? It will stay right here, and you will come up with the key to unlock it, or you will be very sorry indeed. Have you ever heard the sound it makes when you break a bone with a baseball bat, Miss Parker? It makes a very satisfying crunch before the person starts screaming. I might start with the knee—you're stronger than I would like, and I want to be sure I get to smashing your pelvis. Unless you've found sudden inspiration."

Jenny's dry throat had closed up at Soledad's dreamy words, and it was hard for her speak. "I'll figure out the password. I promise."

Soledad's lovely mouth curled in a catlike smile. "I know you will, *chica*."

She was half dragged, half pushed through the spacious house, her bare feet stumbling on the cold stone floor, until she was thrust into a vacant room. It had the same floor-to-ceiling windows as the living room, and in the gathering darkness she could see the steep ravine beyond the narrow deck. "Don't make the mistake of thinking you can escape," Soledad warned her. "The sliding door is chained shut from the outside, and if you were fool enough to try to break the window, my men are patrolling the grounds. And they are very, very hungry, Miss Parker. They have orders to help themselves if they find you someplace you should not be. Sleep well."

She shoved her, and Jenny went sprawling, unable to help herself with her arms still bound. A moment later the door was closed and she was left in darkness.

It was a large room, devoid of furniture except for a mattress on the floor, covered with an old blanket. It probably had either fleas or bedbugs, but she couldn't afford to be too picky. After all, chances were good that tomorrow she'd be dead—what difference would a few bug bites make?

She didn't bother to get to her feet as she heard the door being locked behind her, plunging the room into dusk-tinged shadows, she simply crawled over to the mattress, ready to collapse.

It was covered with a filthy sheet, and there were blood smears on it. Who had spent the night here before? She didn't bother to ask where they'd gone—she doubted they'd been rescued by a grateful family. She yanked off the sheet with her bound hands and then collapsed on the mattress, shivering in the air-conditioning. Tomorrow she'd have to come up with something, but one password led to the next layer of encryption, and she had no idea how long she could string Soledad along. She suspected that the woman was looking for an excuse to use that heavy wood baseball bat, and the thought of it cracking her knee filled her with terror. She was going to have to give up something, at least enough to keep Soledad at a distance.

For what? To wait until she heard the gunshots that signaled Ryder's execution? The thought made her sick to her stomach.

She'd rather have a clean shot to the head than be turned over to Soledad's men. Death before dishonor—she laughed at the stupid idea. She could survive anything, would survive anything. There was only one question. If Matthew Ryder was dead, did she want to survive?

She could still feel him inside her body. She could still feel his steady, solid heartbeat beneath her as she slept in his arms, safe in a world full of danger. She wanted to be back in bed with him, hiding her face against his shoulder as she came down from what his clever hands, his mouth, his body could do to her.

She brought her wrists up to her teeth, trying to tear at the cable ties, but they were too strong, and she dropped them back in her lap. The room had been stripped, and the small toilet and sink off to one side would provide nothing to cut through the tough plastic that was digging into her wrists. She could try to kick out the window, enough to get a piece of glass that could cut the bond, but then Soledad's men would hear her, and she didn't want to think what would happen next.

What had she meant—that Billy had told her about the phone? Why would Billy have anything to do with that monstrous woman now that he knew exactly what he'd gotten himself into?

Unless her stupidity and blind faith had been monumental, and Billy had lied to her. Was it possible? Had she been wrong all this time, shielding her brother when he was a worse criminal than her older brothers? She wanted to bang her head against the wall, scream and cry and rail at her misguided trust. How could she have been such an idiot?

Still, she only had Soledad's word for it, and Soledad could have fooled Billy as she fooled her. Anything was possible, but for the first time she was going to look at things with clear eyes and no emotion. Whether she wanted to believe it or not, Billy could have played her. And it was up to her to right the wrong.

If she ever got out of there. In that dark, awful room everything seemed completely hopeless, and all she could do was curl in on herself. She needed to sleep—it was the only way she'd be able to face Soledad the next day, face the threats and the baseball bat. Whether she could face the possibility of Ryder's death was unthinkable.

For now, though, she had every intention of crying herself to sleep.

Chapter Twenty

Matthew Ryder was in a thoroughly savage mood. There were seven men guarding the ridiculously upscale house perched above the ravine that served as temporary headquarters for La Luz, and he'd killed three of them, incapacitated another, and one more might or might not make it. He didn't care. He had a job to do, and he'd learned long ago not to let things get to him, at least not until long afterward, when the nightmares would come. That left two men, and the ones he'd killed weren't equipped with radios. It would be a close call whether the dead men were discovered before he made his way out of here, but he figured he had till daylight at the very least.

It was easy enough to tell which room held Parker—only one had chains looped around the handles on the sliding door. He wasn't crazy about dangling over the ravine, but he'd always been good at picking locks, and he disposed of it in record time, dropping the chain silently onto the deck.

He could see her on the floor, huddled on a mattress, and he took a deep breath to keep rage from blinding him. He couldn't tell whether she was hurt or not, but he slid the door open silently, slipping into the room and closing the door behind him.

Christ, it was freezing in there! This ridiculous palace of glass and steel came equipped with air-conditioning, unheard of in this part of Calliveria, and someone had turned it on high. Parker had a thin blanket around her, but she was shivering in her sleep. He was going to kill Soledad—Madsen had given him his orders, and even without official sanction he wanted to rip her throat out and actually enjoy doing it. She was deliberately freezing Parker, and he could see where the cable ties cut into her wrists, and his rage grew hotter. Pulling out his knife, he knelt down beside her sleeping body, ready to slice through the bonds.

She erupted like a crazy woman, and it took all his control to keep her from cutting herself on his knife. She fought him, all silent fury, but he subdued her quickly, grabbing her bound wrists and holding them above her head as he covered her body with his. "It's me," he hissed in her ear, barely a whisper of sound, but she'd already recognized the feel of him, and she collapsed beneath him, panting slightly, her eyes gleaming in the darkness as she stared up at him.

"Hold still," he said unnecessarily, and reached up to cut her wrists free. He could see the pain wash over her as the blood began to flow back through her arms, and he rubbed them, slowly, carefully, kneading the painful stiffness out of them.

"What are you doing here?" she whispered.

"Saving your ass," he mouthed back.

"It's a trap. They know you're coming. There are men out there looking for . . ."

"They're dead," he said flatly. "The ones who are still alive are patrolling the outer edges of the property—they won't find the bodies till tomorrow."

She tried to sit up. "Then let's go . . ." But he pushed her back down again.

"We're not going anywhere until I finish my mission."

"The smartphone," she said wearily.

He didn't answer. "We'll stay in here until they unlock you tomorrow morning. As soon as you're out of the way, I'll take out the guards. Where's the fucking smartphone?"

"On a table in the living room. I tried to talk Soledad into letting me work on it during the night but she refused." She swallowed. "You were right about Soledad."

He didn't bother replying to the obvious. "What was she having you do?"

"She wanted me to break the password, but none of the logical ones worked."

He didn't believe her. It had taken Jack less than forty-five minutes to hack into the phone once they'd found it beneath Parker's mattress, and the password was the name of Billy's pit bull. There was no way she wouldn't have tried it during the time she had the phone, no way she could have missed the obvious. So she was lying to him as well as to Soledad.

It pissed him off, big-time. He caught her wrists in one hand and hauled them back over her head. "Feel like telling me the truth for once?"

She glared at him, and despite his annoyance he was glad she hadn't lost her attitude. "If you're not getting me out of here then go away," she snapped, a little louder.

He slammed his other hand over her mouth. "For Christ's sake, be quiet. We don't want anyone coming in to check on you."

"Why not? You can kill him, grab the phone, and we can get the hell out of here."

"I'm not fucking Rambo, Parker. I need the phone, I need to deal with Soledad, and I need to get you out. I can't just go in with guns blazing."

"I thought that's what you did to get up here in the first place."

"I used my bare hands," he said, the words flat and unemotional, but something in his tone must have tipped her off. She was silent for a moment, and she'd stopped trying to free her arms.

"I'm sorry."

The words shocked him. "For what? For being a pain in the ass? You can't help it."

"No," she said evenly. "I'm sorry you had to kill."

He shrugged, angry with himself that he'd given so much away. "It's all in a day's work."

"No, it isn't," she said. "And you killed for me."

He didn't bother setting her straight. His job was to take out Soledad and any of her men he could, and to bring back the smartphone. Saving Parker was simply an added benefit, if you could call it that. He wasn't even sure his boss, Peter Madsen, would approve.

She looked up at him in the air-cooled darkness. Her body had softened beneath his, accommodating his bigger one, welcoming it, and he knew he was getting hard. She'd know it too, soon enough. "Do you want to get off me?" she said after a moment. "I don't think now is the time for a quickie."

"We're locked in here for the next four hours at least. I can't think of anything better to do."

"You're out of your mind! If you think I'd let you . . ."

He covered her mouth with his, silencing her whispered protests, holding her by her wrists while he kissed her with slow, deliberate thoroughness, kissed her until she was breathless and panting and trembling beneath him, kissed her until she was pliant, and her wrists twisted in his hand until she held him and she arched up beneath him.

He lifted his head. He had to stop this, he had to get away from her. But he stayed where he was, cradled between her legs. "This is a very bad idea."

"Yes," she said, pulling her hands free from his grip and sliding them around his neck. "But we're probably going to die tomorrow. Do it anyway."

He was a man of considerable resolve and willpower, but not, apparently, where she was concerned. He groaned, setting his forehead against hers for a moment. And then he sat back, reaching for the hem of her T-shirt and pulling it over her head with one swift motion.

She had perfect breasts, full and high, and he stared down at them for a long moment as the moonlight filtered through the clouds, providing just enough illumination. He half expected her to try to cover herself, but instead she reached up for his shirt, tugging it free from his jeans, pulling at it, so he yanked it over his head and tossed it somewhere in the darkness.

"We shouldn't be doing this," he said in a low voice.

"I know," she said.

Of course she did, and she wanted this anyway. By now his hormones had gone into overdrive, sharpened by the danger and death all around them, and he could think of no earthly, practical reason not to take what she was offering, what he wanted so badly.

He leaned down and caught one turgid nipple in his mouth, rolling it on his tongue, letting his teeth graze her, and he felt the start of desire shimmer across her body. He caught her other breast with his long fingers, pinching lightly, and she let out a silent gasp as her nipples grew even harder beneath his dual attentions.

Last time had been fast and hard in the darkness, and he hadn't had time to fully appreciate her. Now they were lost in a place with no present, no past or future, and he could take his time giving her the attention she so richly deserved. She was lithe and luscious and utterly delectable, and he wanted to drown in her scent, her taste, her sweetness.

He licked his way down her stomach, tasting the sweat and fear and arousal, and he wanted nothing more than to give her what she'd suggested—a rough quickie, just to get the edge off so he could enjoy her in a more leisurely fashion. He wanted a fast release, for him if not for her, and leisure might be more than they could afford. He yanked her shorts down her long legs, bringing her underwear with them, and she was naked and vulnerable beneath him. He reached for his own belt buckle.

But her hands were already there, unfastening him, and his hard cock thrust through the straining zipper once her deft fingers had managed to unfasten it.

He knew he was big, intimidatingly so, and he half expected her to shy away, but her cool, long fingers encircled him, tugging slightly, and he uttered a soft groan in response.

"Keep that up and this will be the quickie you were so keen on," he warned her, and she immediately stopped her light, squeezing touch, much to his regret.

He slid his hand down between her legs, wanting to ready her, but she was gloriously wet, and he felt his cock jerk in reaction. She reached up her hands, sliding them up his arms and then tugging at him.

"Please," she whispered. "I'm tired of feeling sick and frightened. Make me forget that we could die tomorrow. Make me forget everything."

He couldn't have been gentle if he wanted to be, and he didn't. Sliding his hands under her butt, he lifted her enough to bring her to the perfect angle for his sudden, deep thrust.

She didn't make a sound. She didn't need to—he could feel the resistance and then welcome inside her hot, wet cunt, pulling at him, and he wanted to slam into her, to rut his way to the mind-blowing climax that was starting in his balls and spiraling outward.

She'd already had a small orgasm—the contractions of her sex had stopped his forward progress, and he still had a good three inches to go. He didn't want to hurt her, but he needed to get inside her, all the way in, to drown himself in pleasure and pain and forgetfulness, to wipe out the staring eyes of the dead men, to fill this woman with his seed, his life, to take back what he'd lost.

He braced himself over her, kissing the side of her mouth, letting his tongue trace her lips, slip past her teeth to coax her tongue forward, kissing her as he'd never kissed anyone before. He moved his mouth to her ear, biting into the lobe, and she made a muffled sound of pleasure. "I need more," he whispered. "I need you to take more of me."

He felt her hesitation, and he kissed her mouth again. "I'll help you," he murmured, licking the side of her neck, and he slid his hand down between their sweat-slick bodies to find the bud of her clitoris. She trembled in his arms as he slid his finger over that sensitive spot, and he pulled his cock out, then sank in again, a little bit deeper, but still so far from reaching home. He did it again, feeling the flutters along the walls of her sex, drawing him in deeper, and he couldn't know whether that whimper was of pain or desire. He was almost home, and he knew he should hold back rather than risk making her uncomfortable, but need was raging through his body, and he needed his entire cock deep, deep inside her.

He pulled out, pushing in gently, then pulled out again, and she reached up and caught his arms in her tight grip. "No," she said. "I want all of you. Give it to me."

He couldn't have stopped himself to save his life. He rubbed her clit, her vaginal walls grabbed at him, pulling him in deeper, and unable to help himself he shoved all the way in, slamming her hard into the mattress, drowning in her body.

She hadn't made a sound, and he was sure he'd hurt her, and a good man would have pulled away, but he was a bad man, a man burning with need for the surcease only she could provide, and with each hard thrust she answered him, her knees cradling him. He reached back and pulled her legs around his hips, and he sank in deeper still. He drank in her gasp of pleasure and pain, reveled in the feel of her fingers digging into his butt, pushing him, and then he was there, shooting into her, an endless orgasm milked by the trembling, grasping walls of her sex as she threw back her head in a silent scream.

He didn't have the wherewithal to cover her mouth, and he didn't care. If they'd accidentally alerted Soledad's two elite guards, then it would be as good a way to go as any. Sex couldn't get any better than this, than the ridiculously innocent sweetness of her. He would die happy, but there were too many things they hadn't done yet. He hadn't taken her from the back, standing up, sitting down. She had barely touched his cock, and he needed her to put her mouth on him before he could die a happy man.

He pulled out of her, and she made an unhappy noise. He was unhappy as well—despite the power of his orgasm he was still mostly erect, and he knew he could keep on.

She, however, looked as if she'd been hit by a truck, and he wasn't about to push her any further. Instead, he rolled over and pulled her into his arms, and she lay sprawled on top of him, naked, limp, totally satiated. He brought her closer, as she snuggled up against him, and he could feel her warm breath against his skin, the pounding of her heart as it began its slow return to normal, the dampness of her face against his skin. She was crying, and he didn't want to know why. Maybe for what could never be.

It would be two thirty in the morning—he had an instinctive knowledge of the time of day burned into him. No one would come until at least six and with luck a lot later—he'd had enough time to watch the guards' routine, and they wouldn't bother to check in until later. He could afford to lie here with his woman in his arms, if only for a short while.

Even if she wasn't really his woman. Right then it felt like she was, when he'd never felt that way about anyone before. Dangerous thoughts, and he wasn't going to pay any attention to them. Except for the next couple of hours, when he could be at peace.

Until he had to rise and kill again.

Chapter Twenty-One

When Jenny awoke she was alone on the thin mattress. The room was empty, and for a moment she wondered if she'd dreamed it all. Until she realized she was stark naked beneath the scratchy wool blanket and wet between her legs.

She staggered to her feet, heading for the small toilet off the sparse bedroom, and managed to clean herself up. She lifted her head to look at her reflection in the mirror. Her brown hair was a tangle around her face, her lips were swollen, and she could see a love bite at the base of her neck. She was a woman in danger for her life, and instead she looked like a well-stroked cat, slumberous and contented. She had to be out of her mind.

Where the hell had he gone, she thought as she swiftly yanked on her clothing, trying not to think about how they had come off the night before, trying not to think about him. She was infatuated with him, nothing more, and given the highly dangerous situation she was in, it was little wonder she'd clung to him like the savior she wanted him to be.

Except she had the gloomy feeling she would have clung to him no matter what the circumstances. Her attraction to him went deep—it had been haunting her a long time—and whether they were safe in a hotel room or in imminent danger, she reacted to his touch as she'd reacted to no one else.

Where the hell had he gone? Had he decided she was collateral damage after all? Why hadn't he woken her, told her what his plans were? Now all she could do was hope Soledad wouldn't notice the whole atmosphere of saturated sex in the room.

She sat on the mattress, drawing her legs up and wrapping her arms around her knees. She could still feel him inside her, still taste his skin on her tongue. *Fuck it.* If she was going to die she'd die with some of him still inside her, and she would revel in it.

Could she trust him to save her? Could she trust anyone but herself? Clearly her instincts about people were dead wrong—she'd been so sure Soledad was an innocent victim, so certain Ryder was nothing but a danger. Was she wrong about her baby brother as well? Someone had tried to kill her back in New Orleans, and it couldn't have been Soledad, who'd been put in almost as much danger.

Someone had hired a killer to shoot at her. Someone had blown up her beloved cottage and almost taken her with it. While she could believe it of her unnatural father, it wasn't really his style. Besides, a man like Fabrizio Gauthier, no matter how estranged he was from his children, would never endanger that child's life. Blood meant too much to him.

The workings of the Committee were complicated and devious enough to have done it, but again, they would have been more efficient. If they wanted her dead she'd be dead.

Or it could be an enemy of her father's, looking to hit him in a vulnerable place. But everyone knew they were estranged, and killing one of his sons and heirs would make far more sense.

Which left one more possibility, one so unacceptable that she wasn't even going to consider it. That kind of betrayal would be too awful to bear.

She heard the sound of the door being unlocked, and she braced herself. Soledad had sent two guards, and despite her efforts at being cooperative, they dragged her back into the living room, shoving her down on the sofa.

Soledad was sitting at a table, dressed in a pale designer suit, her hair in an elegant chignon while she sipped at a cup of coffee. She barely looked up when Jenny was hauled into the room, continuing to read the paper in front of her.

The phone still lay on the coffee table. So did the baseball bat, a warning. At least it meant that Ryder hadn't managed to get the phone and abandon her. She still had a chance.

"I see you somehow managed to get your hands unbound," Soledad observed in a cool voice.

Shit, she'd forgotten about that. "I used my teeth."

"Very sharp teeth," Soledad said. "I'll remember that. Though if I'm any judge of character, and unlike you, I am, I'd say you spent the night with a lover, not worried about your very limited future."

Jenny managed a creditable laugh. "And just how did that happen? I'm afraid none of your thugs are my type."

"No, my men know better than to go against my wishes. I'm just wondering if we have another visitor at the compound that my men have managed to overlook. Ramón!"

One of the guards who dragged her in immediately stood at attention. "Yes, Madam."

"Madam?" Jenny repeated with an unwise laugh. "Who do you think you are, Evita Perón?"

Soledad's smile was pure evil. "You really think you are wise to bait me?" She turned to the guards. "Go out and search this place. Check in with those useless outside guards to see if they've seen anything. Go now! This one will be no problem for me to deal with."

Jenny waited until the two men left. "I'm a lot bigger than you are, Soledad, and my hands are no longer tied. And I'm really pissed."

Soledad finished her coffee, then folded her hands on the table, giving Jenny her full attention. "Yes," she said. "But I have a gun and no morals. I would kill you for the fun of it. You would hurt me only if it were a matter of life and death. Which, I promise you, it is."

"You want me to attack you?" Jenny said incredulously, trying to ignore the baseball bat that was just out of reach.

"After you break into your brother's fucking smartphone," Soledad said sweetly. "And it depends on my mood and how long you make me wait. If you're quick, then I'll do the same, a single gunshot to the head. If you drag it out like you did last night, then I will smash every bone in your body. And if you think you'll be in too much pain to talk, you're wrong. No matter how much pain you're in, there's always more coming, and you'll be able to tell me what I want even if I've broken every bone in your body."

"Might I suggest you leave my jaw intact? Otherwise you might not understand me when I spill state secrets."

Soledad shook her head. "Did no one ever tell you to watch your tongue when you're in a dangerous situation? And trust me, your position is extremely precarious. If I get too angry I'll simply shoot you and wait until I get back to Puerto Claro to have a professional hacker break into the phone. I have things to do up here, but I can change my schedule if you annoy me enough."

"Here's an idea—why don't you simply ask my brother. He's working for you, isn't he?" It was a wild guess, but closer to the mark than she would have wanted.

Soledad looked startled for a moment, and Jenny felt her stomach tighten further, particularly when Soledad laughed. "You think your brother works for us? How delightfully naïve you are."

Sudden hope rushed through her. "You mean he doesn't?" she said, not caring if she was letting Soledad see her vulnerability. "He's innocent?"

"You idiot. Your brother doesn't work for us—we work for him.

Though I can hope to change that in the near future, he's a necessary evil. He took over from the Corsini family, and he knows the routes, the connections, the players. With the information contained on the smartphone we can put him out of business, which obviously is not in his best interests. He wants this phone back as much as you and your Committee friends do. Maybe more."

It felt as if she'd been slapped in the face. "I don't believe you," she said, knowing in her heart that it was the unacceptable truth.

"Don't you? Well, you've always been good at believing what you want to believe. I'll give you one hour to break the phone—otherwise I will begin to break you."

Jenny picked up the smartphone with real hatred. She had been so certain it would prove her brother's marginal involvement with the human trafficking. Maybe Soledad was lying to her, trying to rattle her. But Jenny's faith had been shaken.

Jenny rose from the sofa, holding the phone in her hand. "Sit down!" Soledad snapped, and Jenny could see the small gun she held in a freshly manicured hand.

"I need to pace," Jenny said, edging closer to the row of windows. The air-conditioning had been turned off that morning, and one of the sliding doors was open, leading out onto a narrow deck that hung out over the deep ravine cut into the rainforest around them.

"And I need you to sit down," Soledad snarled.

"Some fresh air," Jenny pleaded. "That's reasonable, isn't it? After all, there's nowhere I can go except down, and I'm not ready to give up yet. I'm going to stay alive as long as possible."

Soledad regarded her for a long moment. "You're right," she said. "There's nowhere to go out there. Go and enjoy your last taste of fresh air."

Well, Jenny thought, she may be stupid when it came to trusting people, but Soledad had the foresight of a gnat. The cell phone was going to go sailing into the ravine, hopefully to smash against some rocks but at the very least to be lost forever in the tangled jungle. The moment she threw it Soledad would shoot her, and she wasn't ready to die yet, but when push came to shove the phone was going over the edge, and maybe, just maybe, she'd go too, rather than give Soledad the satisfaction of killing her. And satisfaction it would be—she could practically feel Soledad's murderous intent. The sweet young woman had disappeared, leaving a poised, beautiful monster in her wake, and Jenny wasn't about to underestimate her.

If only she could reach the baseball bat things would be easier. She could smash the phone with it, smash Soledad with it before she could get off more than one shot.

But that one shot would kill her, and she hadn't given up on Ryder yet. He had to be somewhere around, hiding from the guards, waiting for his chance. Unless he'd already been captured and killed.

If he had, Soledad knew nothing about it, or she'd be crowing in triumph. There was still a chance she might survive this cluster-fuck her father and brother had thrust her into, though the chances were looking slim. She just had to stall for time.

The deck was narrow—just wide enough for a table and chair, and the drop over the side was terrifying even to a woman with no fear of heights. Then again, the height wasn't the problem; it was the landing. She sat in the chair and began keying in random numbers, her back to Soledad, her attention on the shiny screen.

She heard the door open behind in the living room, and she glanced up to see one of the guards return before she turned back to the phone, her feet drawn up and resting against the low railing. Whoever had designed this house had no sense of safety.

"The password is *beastmaster*."

She froze at the sound of Ryder's voice, then at the words. She turned to find him standing in the middle of the room, pointing a gun on Soledad. The guard lay at his feet, and Soledad had a gun trained on Ryder.

Jenny jumped up, shoving open the sliding glass door, about to run to him, when common sense stopped her. "Stay there, Parker!" he snapped.

"How sweet," Soledad said. "I thought she looked particularly well fucked this morning, though I don't understand how you happened to get in and out, if you'll excuse the pun, so easily. However, I'm afraid your girlfriend miscalculated. You can shoot me, but not before I put a bullet in her head."

Ryder didn't even glance at her. "That's not my concern. My job here is simple—retrieve the cell phone and terminate the South American head of the trafficking cartel."

"Which would be me," Soledad said smoothly, seemingly not disturbed by his words.

"Which would be you," he agreed.

"And you are not concerned about your girlfriend? Americans are so squeamish about collateral damage. Do you really want to see her head blown apart in front of you?"

"You're holding a twenty-two. It won't blow apart her brain," he said in a laconic voice.

"She'll still be just as dead."

He wasn't even looking at her—it was as if they were in the midst of an academic argument, not talking of life and death. "You underestimate my resolve. And you'd be wise not to think of me as American. I'm Committee."

Soledad's smug smile faded slightly. "Isn't this what they call a standoff, then?" she said in her pure voice. "Put the gun down, Mr. Ryder, or your girlfriend is dead."

"Now why would I do that?"

"Because if I kill your girlfriend you'll be forced to kill me, and I won't be able to answer any of the thousand questions you must have," she cooed.

"I don't mind," said Ryder, and his gun spat fire at the same moment Soledad's did.

It was a blur of noise and light and action, as Jenny felt Ryder crash into her, slamming her against the decking as his body jerked, but everything seemed to move in slow motion—the repetitive gunfire, Ryder diving in front of her, the phone falling onto the deck and skittering toward the end, and Soledad sprawling onto the white carpet, an expression of disbelief on her innocent face as bullets pierced the designer suit and blood began to spread outward, soaking into the rug.

And then time flipped back to normal, as Ryder rolled off her and went straight to Soledad's limp body, feeling for a pulse.

Jenny grabbed the phone and shoved it in her pocket before she pulled herself upright, using the railing to do so. She looked over the edge with a shudder before pushing away. "Is she dead?" she asked in a raw voice.

Soledad's eyes were wide and staring. "Close enough," he said, not turning to look back at her. "You in one piece?"

"Your concern for my well-being warms my heart," she snapped.

"Don't be a baby. Are you hurt?"

"No."

"Then stay put. I'm going to find us a vehicle and we're getting the hell out of here."

"And what if she'd managed to shoot me? Would you be taking me with you?"

"Depends on how badly you were injured," he said callously. "Stay put. There's at least one more guard roaming around. If you need to throw up then throw up here. I don't want you wandering around this place—there may be booby traps."

Jenny immediately swallowed her incipient bile. How did he know her that well? "I'm fine," she said icily.

"Of course you are. You gonna give me the phone?"

"What do you think?" she replied.

"I can take it from you. If you think you're going to be smart and throw it over the balcony, then think again. Remember, I know the password. My people found it when you were wandering around the house on Magazine Street, and everything's been downloaded and decrypted. We can make a case against your brother without it, but it would be a lot more trouble."

"Sure," she muttered.

He caught her chin in one hard hand. "Promise me you won't throw it over the balcony."

"I promise."

To her shock he place a swift, hard kiss on her mouth, and a moment later he was gone, leaving her alone with a dead woman and the one thing that could destroy her brother.

Chapter Twenty-Two

Jenny stared at the smartphone in her hand. He was right, he could have taken it from her, but he probably thought she was too shell-shocked and grateful that he'd saved her life to disobey him.

He had saved her life, she realized. If he hadn't knocked her aside Soledad would have shot her, and at such close range it would have been fatal. Instead, he'd knocked her aside as he'd shot back, and now Soledad lay dying on the once-pristine white carpet, and Jenny couldn't bear to look at her.

Instead, she stared at the phone. It symbolized everything—her trust in her brother, her blind hope that he really was innocent. It was still a possibility, but a weaker and weaker one.

Had Soledad lied? Was it possible her brother could really have been behind it all? She'd been wrong about Soledad. She stared at the phone like it was a snake, an evil, murderous thing that was going to crush the life out of her family. She'd promised Ryder she wouldn't throw it over the balcony, but that didn't mean she couldn't destroy it some other way. And what would happen if she did? Would she be saving her innocent brother from a punishment that far outstripped the lesser crime he'd thought he was committing? Or would she be protecting a monster who deserved everything he got? Ryder said they'd already downloaded and decrypted the information—they would still have a strong case even without the actual phone itself. She turned to pick up the baseball bat and then froze.

Soledad was standing, holding on to the table for support, weaving slightly, her eyes crazed. In her hand she held the gun.

Jenny felt like a rabbit caught in the stare of a rabid coyote. Ryder had gone off somewhere and left her to die. Had he done it on purpose, knowing that Soledad was merely wounded? Had he left her gun behind just so there wouldn't be any loose ends? Did he want her dead?

Whether he did or not, that was going to be the outcome, as Soledad swayed, trying to get her gaze properly focused. "Give me the phone," she said in a guttural voice, and there was blood trickling out the side of her mouth.

A number of responses came to mind, such as "come and get it" or "in your dreams," all of which would have signed her death warrant. In fact, she was so terrified she couldn't speak, couldn't move, could simply stand there waiting to be shot.

And then the sheer stupidity of that hit her, breaking the thrall. She dove for Soledad's feet, sliding on the bloody carpet, moving so fast the dazed woman didn't have time to react, and she went down with a crash, firing the gun wildly. Jenny didn't count the bullets, she simply rolled away, snatching up the baseball bat as Soledad rose to her feet again, like fucking Rasputin, and on sheer instinct and adrenaline Jenny slammed the bat against her head.

It only seemed to daze the woman. She staggered toward her, but Jenny was already at the very edge of the room, by the sliding doors, and she had nowhere to go but out on the ledge, where there'd be no escape from Soledad's gun.

She was backing onto the decking as Soledad advanced on her, cornering her, when she heard the *click click* of an empty gun, and relief swamped her. Jenny's eyes met Soledad's crazed ones a moment before the woman heaved the gun at her head, stunning her, and then Soledad jumped her, overwhelmingly powerful in her insane rage.

It was over in an instant, so quickly Jenny wasn't even sure how it happened. Soledad clamped her strong, bloody hands around Jenny's neck, squeezing fiercely, and Jenny could feel the air cut off, the blackness begin to close in. The baseball bat was trapped between them, and she turned, shoving at Soledad as hard as she could in blind panic. Soledad's hands fell away from Jenny's throat, and in the next moment she went backward over the low edge of the railing, twisting and turning in the wind as she fell in a silent, graceful dance.

Jenny sank back in the chair, still clinging to the baseball bat, panting, shocked, wanting to scream herself. And then she saw the smartphone lying in the middle of the carpet, in the pool of Soledad's blood.

She'd promised not to throw it. She hated that small piece of technology—it stood for her brother's betrayal and every horrible thing that had happened, up to and including the fact that she'd just killed a woman.

She stood up dazedly, walked over to it, and slammed the baseball bat in the center of it, over and over and over again, until she felt arms come around her, strong arms, forcing her to stop, to drop the bat. "I think you killed it," Ryder said in her ear, sounding incredibly calm. "Where's Soledad?"

She was surprised she was even able to speak. Her voice came out in a curiously raw monotone. "She's gone."

"What do you mean?"

"I knocked her over the side of the balcony. She wasn't dead, and you'd left the gun behind. Did you do that on purpose?"

He said nothing, and since he still had his arms around her, holding her back against him, she couldn't see his expression. "Are you hurt?" he said instead. "You have blood on you."

Jenny shook her head, not caring whether he could see it or not. "It's Soledad's blood. I hit her with the baseball bat."

Something rippled through the body behind her, and she had the horrified suspicion it was laughter. "And you dumped her over the balcony?" he said in an even voice.

"No. She still came after me, but she ran out of bullets, and then she was trying to choke me, so I shoved her, and that's when she fell."

He turned her in his arms, with surprising gentleness, tilting her chin up so he could look at her throat. His face was expressionless but his fingers were gentle. "You'll have some bruising," he said. "But you're in one piece, and that's what matters. Let's get the fuck out of here."

She looked up at him dazedly. "You didn't answer my question. Did you leave the gun behind on purpose?"

There was no change in the emotionless face, but his eyes darkened, and her brain woke up enough to regret her words.

"I promise you one thing, Jenny," he said, and she'd never heard him call her by her name before. "If I decide you're going to die I'll kill you myself. I don't leave things to fate." His words were cold, clipped. "Either come with me now or take your chances with the rest of the Guiding Light when they show up." He stepped away from her, removing his protective warmth.

She couldn't summon any words, so she simply nodded, following him out into the bright, cheerful sunlight, leaving the house of death behind.

Chapter Twenty-Three

The ride down the mountain was made in complete silence. Ryder had commandeered an ancient jeep, in worse shape than the one they had first used, but it bumped its way over the barely perceptible roads without complaint, splashing through deep channels of water that sent sprays of mud up the sides and over Jenny, bouncing over gravel and stones and small tree trunks without hesitation. She'd managed to unearth a seat belt, but Ryder was driving like a bat out of hell, and if she didn't know better she would have suspected he was driving fast more out of rage than necessity.

It wasn't until they were down on level ground that she noticed the fresh blood on his hand as he shifted gears, the blood that had accumulated all around the stick shift. "You're hurt!" she said involuntarily, startled.

"Yeah, so what?" he snarled, stomping on the accelerator. "It's nothing."

"Nothing? You're bleeding."

"What the fuck do you care?"

She was emerging from her horror-filled thoughts to stare at him. "If you bleed to death, then chances are I'll die out here as well," she shot back furiously. "Pull over and let me see how bad it is."

"It'll be a cold day in hell, gorgeous," he muttered. "It's just a through and through in the fleshy part of my arm. A couple of Band-Aids will fix it."

"In that case stop and we'll find the Band-Aids," she snapped.

"This jeep doesn't come with a first-aid kit."

"Then I'll find something to bind you up. Stop the fucking jeep!" A distant part of her brain wondered at her language. Her father had always hated it when she swore, and she'd never dared use anything stronger than *damn* and *hell* in his presence. But right now it was a holy fuck of a day.

Ryder slammed on the brakes so fast that Jenny would have gone through the windshield if she hadn't been wearing her seat belt. He was wearing a loose jacket, and if she hadn't been so caught up in her own horrors, she would have noticed the dark patch of blood on the upper arm. She unfastened her seat belt with shaking hands, then started rummaging through the front of the jeep. "Take off your jacket," she ordered, coming up with a beer-can opener, a bandanna, three oily rags, and a roll of duct tape.

"You think you're putting any of those filthy rags on me and you can guess again. Unless you're trying to kill me. Which I suppose would serve me right since I deliberately left the gun with Soledad, hoping she was strong enough to shoot you before she died."

It sounded absurd when he said it. "Shut up," she muttered.

"But why? I thought you wanted the truth. Of course I left the gun with Soledad. I should have known three bullets center mass wouldn't kill the bitch, but then I thought I'd spare your tender sensibilities by leaving her as she lay rather than turn her over and finish her off with a head shot. Of course I was hoping she'd be able to reach the gun she fell on and take care of you, but things don't always work out as we plan, now do they?"

"All right, I'm sorry I asked!" Jenny said. "It's just that you never make mistakes, and leaving that gun behind . . ."

He sighed. "Leaving that gun underneath Soledad's body was the very least of my mistakes in the last week."

"What was the worst?"

"You."

Okay, she was a glutton for punishment. She knew that answer was coming long before he said it, and she didn't even flinch. "Are you going to take off that jacket?" she said in a dangerous voice.

In answer he shrugged out of it. He was right—the bullet had gone through the fleshy part of his upper arm, tearing across the skin. "That's not harmless," she said. "You've got muscles there." She could feel a sudden warmth in the pit of her stomach. Of course he had muscles in his arms—he'd held her, carried her, rocked her when he'd killed the snake.

"I'll live," he said dryly.

"There's a stream up ahead. Do you think it's safe to wash it off?"

He shrugged, and the gesture didn't seem to cause him any pain. "I'll take antibiotics when we get back to town." He slid out of the driver's seat and stalked toward the stream, and Jenny followed after him, bringing the bandanna and the duct tape. He was kneeling by the stream, splashing water up his blood-streaked arm, and she could see the tear was still oozing blood. Coming down beside him, she began to wash the bandanna in the stream, hoping to get some of the dirt off it.

"If you think you're wrapping that around my arm, you can guess again," he drawled. "It'll still be filthy."

"It's the cleanest cloth I have."

"I think we should use your panties."

She looked at him in shock, certain he was kidding. He wasn't. "They're relatively clean, and considering their proximity to holy virgin territory they're probably supernaturally blessed. You can count the instant healing as your first step toward a miracle."

"I wasn't a virgin."

"Well, you fuck like one."

The words were so cruel they took her breath away. She turned her face so he wouldn't see how he affected her, and muttered, "I'm not taking off my underpants to bandage your arm."

"Softhearted, aren't you?" He pulled a handkerchief out of his back pocket and presented it to her. "Then use this. I won't enjoy it half as much, but then, I'm not in a very good mood."

"I know you don't give a damn, but if your bad mood has anything to do with me then I'm sorry," she said, feeling stupid.

"You mean when you accused me of trying to murder you? I'm hardly going to get all butt-hurt over something like that—I don't give a flying fuck what you think of me." He leaned back, most of the blood gone from his arm except for the fresh rivulet beginning to slide down.

She took the handkerchief from his hand and examined it briefly. If it had been dirty she actually would have considering taking off her underwear, but it looked clean enough, and she wrapped it around his bicep as far as it could go. "Your muscles are too big," she grumbled.

His laugh wasn't entirely devoid of humor. "First time I've been told that."

She pressed the handkerchief hard against the wound, expecting him to curse in pain, but he didn't even take a deep breath. He was watching her out of those blue eyes, wolf eyes, she reminded herself. The eyes of a predator who feels nothing, not mercy, not sorrow, not love.

She peeled off a strip of duct tape and wrapped it around his arm, holding the handkerchief in place, then followed it by rows and rows of the stuff. "There," she said, sitting back to admire her handiwork. "You look steampunk."

He gave her a look of disgust. "Just in case I get shot again, if you're not going to donate your panties, then you can always close a wound temporarily with just the duct tape."

"You'd end up looking like the Tin Woodman in *The Wizard of Oz*."

"If I only had a heart," he said briefly, and the knife in her stomach twisted again. "Let's get the hell out of here."

"How far is it to Puerto Claro?"

"Depends on what route we take, how many stops we make, whether we have to hide out for a while. We can't drive main roads, people will be looking for us. Sooner or later I'm going to have to find us something to eat or we'll never make it, and this thing is going to run out of gas. So we'll get there when we get there, sweetheart." The endearment was a cynical slap in the face, and she wanted to kick him. "So shut the hell up and let me drive."

It must have been later than she thought. Even though it was the middle of the summer, shadows began closing in around them in another hour, and the temperature began to drop. She was starving, she had to pee, and she was freezing to death in her thin cotton cargo shorts and braless T-shirt, but the last thing she was going to do was complain. Sooner or later he was going to have to answer nature's call—despite all evidence to the contrary, he was only human—but he seemed content not only to keep driving but also to hit every bump imaginable. It was almost dark when he turned off the barely recognizable road and drove the jeep into the underbrush.

"We're stopping here for now," he announced.

She looked around her. "No Motel 6?" she inquired sweetly.

"Sorry, gorgeous, but we're roughing it. Go find yourself a tree—you've been squirming in your seat for the last hour."

She was past the ability to be embarrassed. "If you knew I had to go, then why didn't you stop sooner?"

"You didn't ask," he said simply.

Jenny made a growling noise in the back of her throat. At least the post-twilight shadows afforded her more privacy, and she didn't have to go too far from the jeep. By the time she came back he'd grabbed a duffel from the back and dumped it on the ground in a clearing a ways off from the jeep. She tried hard to control her shivers, but as usual Ryder was ahead of her, tossing her his blood-soaked jacket.

"Put that on," he ordered. "You're freezing to death."

"It's not b . . . b . . . bad now that we've stopped driving," she said, trying to disguise her chattering teeth.

"We're not having a fire, so you're going to have to figure out some other way to warm up. You can have my jacket or me."

She grabbed the jacket. "You think the rebels would see the fire?"

"I think anything's possible. We just need to get through the night. There's a small village a mile or two to the left, and I'm going to see if I can get us some food and gasoline."

She stared at him. "Have you been here before? How do you know there's a village nearby?"

"I can smell smoke and farm animals on the wind."

Jenny took a tentative sniff. "I can't smell anything."

"You don't have my training. Just sit tight and I'll be back."

"You're leaving me?" she shrieked.

"For God's sake, lower your voice! You never know who's around," he said irritably.

"And again I say, you're leaving me? To those mysterious marauders?"

"I'll leave you my gun."

"No!" she said in horror. "I've already killed one person today—that's about my limit."

He came over to her, and she'd forgotten how very large he was, how intimidating he could be. "You're going to sit your sweet little ass down over there, wrap yourself in the jacket, and keep my gun in your hand. If anyone shows up and it's not me, you're to shoot first and ask questions later."

"What if you don't come back?"

"Don't make me think you care one way or another, gorgeous. And you may as well accept the fact—I always come back. You can't get rid of me until I'm ready to let go. You're going to have an hour or two of sitting alone, and then I'll be back and you can entertain yourself hating me."

"I don't hate you," she said in a very small voice.

"Oh, yeah? You could have fooled me." He shoved her down on the ground, wrapped a jacket around her shoulders, and put a gun in her hand. It was the same gun she'd had before, but back then it had simply been a tool. Now she could see Soledad's face as she'd gone over the balcony, and she wanted to throw it at him.

He must have sensed her rebellion. "You want the Guiding Light to have a crack at you?" he said in a cool voice. "I'll be back in time to kill them before they could finish with you, but if they happen to find you, you'd be in for a very unpleasant time."

She tightened her grip on the gun. "Don't be long," she said.

For the first time in the entire horrid day, he smiled at her, and even though it was tinged with cynicism, she felt some vague stirrings of hope. "One might almost think you cared, Parker." And then he'd melted into the underbrush as if he'd never been there in the first place.

One or two miles, he'd said. One or two miles through this dense foliage, following the scent of something she couldn't smell. And then one or two miles back, following nothing but whatever kind of path he made on his way out.

He was never coming back for her. He hated her for doubting him, hated her for all the trouble she was. Traveling on his own would be a lot easier without her tagging along—he could hike or hitch a ride to the port city and fly out from there, complete with the sad tale of how she'd been murdered by rebels. Her father would probably breathe a sigh of relief as he made a substantial contribution to the church in her memory. If there was one thing you could say about her villainous father, he was a devout Catholic.

Who else would mourn her? Daisy, her paralegal, might be more worried about where her next paycheck was coming from. Her two older brothers wouldn't give a damn.

As for Billy . . . she still didn't know what to believe, and at this point she didn't care. She'd gotten herself into this unholy mess because of a misguided need to save him, save someone who'd done something unforgivable, and her act of covering up for him was unforgivable in itself. Maybe she deserved all this.

It had all been for nothing. Ryder hadn't seemed the slightest bit discomfited by the loss of the phone, but then, he'd already known about it, had already hacked it. Which meant there had never been the need for her to come with him, never been the need for him to hurt her. He'd already known most of the answers to what she'd been hiding, and he'd hurt her anyway, the sadistic bastard.

Except he hadn't hurt her since. When they'd had sex he'd been almost tender with her, if such a strong man could be tender. She would have thought he'd feel wracked with guilt, but Ryder wasn't the kind of man who let guilt faze him. Then again, what did she know about what kind of man he was? She was an idiot when it came to people—Ryder might be a secret saint or a sociopath, and whichever she guessed would probably be wrong.

She drew her knees up to her chest, huddling under the blanket, as his cruel words came back to her. "You fuck like a virgin," he'd said. She could think of a thousand comebacks now that it was too late, but in truth she just wanted to put her head down and cry. She hadn't really liked sex, had never liked it, until Ryder had crawled into her bed, and his touch had been such a revelation she'd been foolish enough to think it was mutual.

He wasn't going to come back for her. Why should he? She'd destroyed his piece of evidence, she'd lied to cover up for her brother, she fucked like a virgin. What possible use would he have for her? He'd know well enough her father wouldn't be grateful for her return, particularly since Ryder was going after Billy. So what possible use would he have for her? He'd be much better off on his own.

He was probably lying when he said he could smell civilization a few miles away, just using it as an excuse to get away from her. There were wild animals in the jungle, jaguars and pumas and . . . and snakes.

She hugged her knees tightly. Maybe she was going to die from one of those snakes, maybe that explained her lifelong, irrational fear. Deep inside she'd always known they'd bring about her death, and she'd been terrified, knowing those coils would wrap around her, slowly, squeezing the life from her, crushing every bone in her body so that he could swallow her whole . . .

"Stop it!" The sound of her voice in the jungle was a shock. Her throat hurt from Soledad's clawlike fingers—if she hadn't shoved her away Soledad might have killed her. But she hadn't meant for Soledad to go over the ledge—it had just happened. If only she didn't keep seeing Soledad's pale, surprised face as she went spinning, gliding downward to smash against the sharp rocks of the ravine. She would see that face in her nightmares when she was in her eighties, she knew it. She'd killed a woman. A woman who'd already been shot, an evil, murderous woman. None of that made a difference. In the end she'd taken a life, and she felt forever changed.

"Come back, Ryder," she whispered out loud. "Please don't leave me here."

Only the sound of the night birds answered her, but that was its own comfort. If someone else was moving around in the jungle the birds would grow still and silent. She didn't have to worry about the Guiding Light sneaking up on her, she didn't have to worry about anyone surprising her . . .

"Wake up, gorgeous," Ryder said. He was squatting down beside her, and she could just manage to see him in the darkness.

"I'm awake," she said, certain she couldn't have been sleeping.

"Sorry it took so long, but we're getting out of here. There's a bigger road just ten miles away, and then it's straight on to Puerto Claro. Get up. I've got food in the jeep."

"Okay," she said sleepily, shrugging off the jacket and struggling to stand up. Her legs didn't feel like holding her, and Ryder caught her as she stumbled, holding her against him for a long, breathless moment.

He was so big. So hard, so warm—no one could possibly hurt her if he was looking out for her. He let her go, and she made her way back to the jeep, walking carefully, knowing he was following her with his eyes.

It wasn't until she was safely buckled in that she spoke. "Thank you."

He barely glanced at her. "For what?"

"For coming back."

If she thought that would ease the tension between them she was mistaken. "Rather than abandoning you in the middle of the South American jungle? It was tempting, but I figured if I did that it might piss off your old man."

"Then you shouldn't have come back. He cares a lot more for Billy than he ever did for me, and I don't think you're going to keep your hands off my baby brother."

"No, I'm not." He put the jeep in gear. "So I guess I should have left you behind."

His tone was flippant, but she was in no shape to know whether he was serious or not. "I guess you should have," she said wearily. "Why weren't you angry that I destroyed the phone?"

He hesitated for a moment. "We have enough information downloaded from it to put your brother away for the rest of his life. The important thing was not to let it fall into the wrong hands."

"I see."

He turned to look at her. "Come on, gorgeous. Don't sound so defeated. You'll have plenty of time to fight with me once we get to the plane."

"Stop calling me that. And I am defeated. If you're looking for a fight you won't find one from me," she said, leaning her head back against the seat and closing her eyes.

"That'll be a refreshing change," he said, concentrating on the road as he maneuvered his way through the dense greenery. "Just keep your head down if we come to a town. One *norteamericano* driving alone wouldn't garner that much attention. A pretty woman would get everyone talking."

She looked over at him, trying to read his expression. He looked older somehow, bleaker than when she had first met him. No, that wasn't true—he'd looked just as grim when he'd scoured the container ship for bad guys. His long dark hair was pulled back from his face, his dark-blue eyes were hooded and unreadable, his mouth flat. He hadn't shaved in several days, and she could still remember the feel of his stubble against her sensitive skin.

"What are you blushing for?" he demanded irritably.

"It's almost pitch dark—how can you tell I was blushing?" she shot back.

"I notice you're not denying it," he pointed out.

"I'm not denying anything. How long till we get to the main road?"

"How the hell should I know? I didn't even know it existed. With luck it'll be a couple of hours to Puerto Claro."

She didn't allow herself to groan aloud at the thought. "In fact, we'd probably be better off heading straight for the plane," she said finally. *No time alone with a bed in between us, no watching eyes.* "That would probably be the smartest idea."

"Maybe," he said. "But every time I get around you, I start acting stupid, and I don't see that that's about to change anytime soon."

She stared at him. "What do you mean by that?"

"I mean every time we're alone we end up in bed together, and that's not a good thing. I get sloppy, you get emotional, everything gets fucked, including us."

"Am I supposed to laugh at that?" she said icily.

"Better than crying. Close your eyes and try to sleep. I promise to wake you up if I decide to stop sooner."

"Don't worry about me," she said stiffly. "I'm fully able to take care of myself. I killed Soledad, didn't I?"

He was silent for a moment. "She would have died anyway. Don't beat yourself up over it."

"I'm not," Jenny said fiercely. "She was an evil, horrible woman who deserved to die, and I'm not sorry. I'm not."

He glanced at her, and before she realized what he was doing, he'd reached over and unfastened her seat belt, hauling her up against him as he drove one-handed, his arm around her.

She didn't fight him. She started crying, silent tears streaming down her face. She had no idea who she was crying for—whether it was for the sweet young woman she'd thought she'd known, for her own blind innocence, for the man who held her so comfortably and let her weep into his T-shirt. It was for all of them, and she lay against his shoulder and cried.

━━━⌣━━━

She was in rough shape, Ryder thought, holding her trembling body against his as he maneuvered the jeep along the dirt track. It was a rare trick, steering with one hand and keeping the drive smooth enough that she didn't bounce out of his arms, but he could do it, simply tightening his hold when he reached a rough section. She was holding on to him, her fingers clinging to his T-shirt, and he could feel the dampness of her tears soaking through the thin cloth. Funny, he'd never seen her cry before, not even when he was deliberately hurting her. She hadn't even cried during sex, though he'd known she'd wanted to. Women had a habit of crying after a really good climax, and he'd made sure she'd had several the two times he'd gotten her in bed.

And then he'd taken it all away by telling her she fucked like a virgin. What had gotten into him? He wasn't always such a bastard, but for some reason she brought it out in him, and he kept saying such cruel things to her.

But he knew what had gotten into him. She had. She was the greatest danger to his peace of mind that he'd ever run into. She made him want things he couldn't have, care about things that didn't matter. She was . . . lovely, and there was no room in his life for lovely. Everything in his life was hard and gritty and lonely, and he'd made peace with that long ago. Every day he was with her he was offered a view of another kind of life, one he'd turned his back on, and no matter what he did he couldn't put her out of his mind.

She fell asleep before she even stopped crying, and she let out a few remaining shudders as she slept against his shoulder. The ride was rough, but she'd adapted. Sooner or later she'd get back to her elegant suits and her pro bono work and her safe life, and he wouldn't have to think about her again.

But he would. He had the gloomy suspicion he'd think about her every day for the rest of his life. The only consolation being that it was unlikely to be a long life—his profession didn't lead to old-age pensions and retirement villages.

He moved his head down and placed a soft kiss on her tangle of hair. She didn't have to know she had somehow become his kryptonite. He'd get her back to New Orleans, hand her over to Remy, and deal with Billy Gauthier. And then she'd never want anything to do with him again.

It was for the best. She needed to keep her distance—when she was around he made stupid mistakes like not taking Soledad's gun away. She could have been killed because he'd been too worried about her reaction if he searched Soledad's body. She'd resolved that, and lost part of her soul in doing so. You couldn't kill someone and remain unchanged, and he'd done that to her. She would have to live with that for the rest of her life, and his memory would be inextricably tied up with the knowledge that she'd taken a life.

He needed to get the hell out of New Orleans. The Committee branch was up and running, Bishop would be back from his goddamn honeymoon, and Peter Madsen could damned well reassign him. Right now Eastern Europe sounded just about right, someplace dark and depressing and cold. Just like his nonexistent heart.

The wound in his arm was throbbing beneath her head and he welcomed it, proof that he was alive, proof that he could still hold her for a few hours longer. Once they left Calliveria everything would be back the way it was. For now he could hold her, let her tangled curls blow against his mouth, and drive on into the night.

Chapter Twenty-Four

By the time they reached the small private landing field, Parker had woken up, pulling away from Ryder and huddling in on herself. He was half tempted to haul her back, but his instincts had told him she'd reached her limit. All he had to do was tell her she was in shock, and there was a good chance she'd erupt from the unnatural quiet that surrounded her like armor, but there were times when shock and denial were old friends. He'd let her be for now—there would be time enough to knock her out of it once they reached New Orleans.

He didn't think he could sleep once they got on the plane, but he did, halfway into his scotch on the rocks. He woke when they were about to land, the lights of the Crescent City like a welcoming beacon, and he glanced over at Parker, still huddled in her single seat at the back of the spacious cabin, the one reserved for the non-existent flight attendant. She still had that glazed expression on her face, and he suspected she hadn't slept during the six-hour flight. The moment they touched down she began to unfasten her seat belt, but he glared at her and she leaned back, dropping her hands. The last thing he wanted was for her to end up flat on her face if the plane had to come to a sudden stop.

The car was waiting for them, gassed up and with the keys over the visor. He tried to take Parker's arm when they started down the short stairs but she pulled away, walking ahead of him, and he ground his teeth.

A moment later he caught up with her, yanking her against him. "Sulk all you want," he said, deliberately trying to goad her into a reaction, "but I'm not risking you running off into the night."

To his annoyance she didn't try to break free. "Why would I do that?" she said in a listless voice. "I can't very well walk to town, can I?"

"You're in shock," he said, going for the big guns. "Who knows what you'd do." He waited for her hot denials.

"Maybe I am," she said dully. "Can you drop me at a hotel?"

"No."

She didn't argue about that either, simply letting him settle her into the front seat of the car and fasten the seat belt around her. The sky was growing light in the east, and he usually loved that time of day. Right then he wanted the night to be eternal.

What the hell was he going to do with her? She couldn't go to a hotel—she had no luggage, no ID, nothing. Taking her to her father's house was out of the question, given that Ryder's next visit wasn't going to be of the social kind, and while her intel jacket had the names of close friends and favorite relatives, he knew that showing up with her in this state would be something she'd never forgive. There was no choice but to take her back to the house on Magazine Street and hope she'd come out of her fugue state on her own.

Part of him sympathized. He'd killed more people than he could remember—no, that was a lie. He remembered every one of them, up to and including the three men at Soledad's compound. They haunted his dreams and even his waking hours, and he was trained for this kind of work. For an innocent like Parker the memory of Soledad going over that balcony would be a permanent scar.

It didn't matter that she would have died anyway. Should have been dead, except that the truly wicked never died easily—it was as if their very evil gave them the ability to withstand things that would kill an ordinary mortal. He should have realized that Soledad wouldn't go that easily.

Parker said nothing when he pulled into the underground garage on Magazine Street, though she made no effort to climb out of the car. He came around the side and opened the door for her, taking her arm, and she followed him docilely enough, still with that shuttered expression on her face, and he wanted to shake her. Instead, he led her into the house, nodding at the security camera as he led her up the three flights of stairs. The house was empty—Remy had his own apartment in the French Quarter and Jack had a house in the suburbs, of all things. Only Ryder lived in the house full time, Ryder and enough security and booby traps to outfit Fort Knox.

When they reached the third floor she started toward the bedroom she'd used, his old bedroom, and then stopped, and he saw her absently rub her arm, the arm he'd hurt when she'd last been in the room.

"Not there," he said, moving her to the other side of the hall. The room he'd taken over was small, unfinished, and the only piece of furniture was the king-sized bed that fit his tall frame the best. She stood just inside the door, not even looking around her.

"You can spend the night here," he said gruffly. "I'll take my old room."

She said nothing. Her face was unnaturally pale, and he could see the streaks of her earlier tears, though now her warm brown eyes were flat and expressionless. She'd get over most of it, he told himself. A good night's sleep in a decent bed and she'd be ready to move on.

He was almost out the door when she spoke. "Are you going to kill my brother?"

He stopped, not turning to look at her. "If I have to. I don't think it will be up to me. We already dumped the evidence from the phone, and the FBI will have a warrant out for him if he's fool enough to return to this country. Otherwise someone will find him overseas."

"And kill him," she said dully.

"And kill him."

She lifted her head. "Could you stop them?"

"Not even if I wanted to."

She nodded, as if she expected nothing less, and he took a step toward her, his frustration boiling over. "Look, you can hate me all you want. The fact of the matter is your brother is a vicious criminal who's victimized women and children, and he deserves anything he gets, just as Soledad did. Don't waste your sorrow on monsters like them—save a little for their victims and the ones who died because of them."

"I'm not mourning Soledad and Billy," she said in a voice so soft he almost couldn't hear it.

"Then what are you mourning?"

"Loss," she said, turning her back on him and walking to the window. "The loss of my brother, loss of innocence, loss in the belief that I knew what I was doing. You."

"What about me?"

She kept her face averted, her back straight. "I'm mourning the loss of you."

He moved so fast Jenny wasn't prepared, spinning her around and pushing her up against the wall with none of his usual tenderness. He caught her face in his hands and kissed her, open-mouthed and carnal, rough when he'd been sweet, and she felt her whole body come alive again, the blood surging through her veins, her heart pumping. She put her arms around his waist, pulling him against her, and she could feel he was hard, aching for her. She closed her eyes as feeling washed over her, need and sorrow and pure longing so hard and powerful she thought she might explode from it.

He slid his hands down, caught the T-shirt and ripped it in half, the stretchy cotton shredding beneath his grip, and she caught her breath, shocked. He put his arms around her hips and lifted her up so that her breasts were at the level of his face, and he put his mouth on one and sucked, hard, using his teeth, as a shaft of white-hot longing went straight between her legs to the very center of her being. She wanted him there, needed him there, and she panted as he pulled her legs around his hips, her sex pressed against the hard rod of his erection, too many layers of clothes between them as he moved to her other breast, taking it in his mouth with a roughness that made her whimper in longing and need. A moment later he pulled away, and she went flying through the air, ending on her back on the huge bed, staring up at him in shock as he ripped off his clothes, then crouched over her like a predatory beast. "I don't care if you're afraid of me," he growled. "I don't care if you've been hurt. All I care about is fucking you as hard as you can take it. I'm going to make you come so hard you'll feel like you've died and gone to hell. I'm going to fuck you so hard that no one will ever come close. You'll never get me out of your mind, out of your body."

She stared at him out of wide eyes. "You said I fuck like a virgin," she said.

"I said a lot of things, and most of them were lies. There's only one truth between you and me, and that's sex. Take off your pants, or I swear to God I'll rip them off you."

She reached down for the zipper, shucking out of them quickly, staring up into his wild wolf's eyes. He put his hand between her legs, and she knew she was wet with longing, and she arched up as he slid a finger into her, then two, and she shattered so quickly, so unexpectedly that she cried out.

And then he was lying on top of her, stretched over her, kissing her, his cock pressed between them, and she reached down to touch him, marveling at the feel of him. The skin was silky smooth around the iron-hard erection, and she let her fingertips trace the veins, the size of him.

He kissed her mouth, slowly, deliberately, his tongue making lazy swirls inside her mouth, his teeth biting down on her lower lip, his hand sliding down her stomach to touch her once more, and she could feel the excitement building almost instantly, and she wanted him, so, so badly.

"I need you," she whispered, her voice raw. "I need you inside me."

"Then take me in your mouth."

She should have been shocked at his words. Instead, they sent a thrill of forbidden desire through her at the very thought, and she pushed at him until he rolled onto his back.

He was beautiful, that part of him that was so unfamiliar to her. She reached out her tongue and ran it over the top, tasting the sticky, sweet fluid, and then she put her mouth over him, taking him inside her, sucking on him with a fierce delight. She wanted this, she wanted him, she wanted him to come in her mouth, she wanted him around her and over her and inside her. The feel of him inside her mouth was strange and hypnotic, and she moved up and down on him, trying to take more and more of him inside her, but he was too big, and she was going to choke and she didn't care, she needed all of him.

And then he plucked her off him, pulling her free, and she cried out in protest. "No!" she said. "I want more . . ."

"I'll give you more," he said, and flipped her onto her stomach, pulling her hips up to meet his as she felt the broad head of his cock at her slick entrance. He began to push inside, and the sensation was so powerful she began to contract around him, but he just kept pushing, so deep, so deep she could almost taste him, and she slammed her head down on the mattress, holding on as he pounded into her, each thrust pushing her further, until he reached between her legs and caught her clitoris between his fingers, pinching lightly, and she screamed as her body was flooded with sensation, and she was lost in it, drowning in it, dying in it.

A moment later he followed her, shoving his cock in so deep that the tiny pinch of pain only added to her pleasure as she felt him flood her, and his arms came around her stomach, holding her against him, as his own climax joined hers.

When he pulled out she almost cried, expecting him to move away from her, but instead he simply sank down on the bed and brought her with him, tucking her against his sweating, shaking body. She knew she should do something, say something, but she was beyond rational thought. All she wanted to do was bury herself against him, let go of all the sorrow and pain that had tied her in knots. She loved him. He was an ornery son of a bitch with a nasty tongue and she loved him, and it would do her no good at all. He'd saved her life, over and over again, he'd held her when she wept, he'd taunted her into fighting back, he'd treated her like an equal, and whether it made sense or not she felt tied to him, flesh of his flesh, blood of his blood. He was going to destroy her brother, and she had no choice but to watch him do it. Even destroying the cell phone couldn't stop him.

She couldn't imagine a future with him. First off, he wouldn't want one. And how could she live with a man who destroyed her baby brother, even if he richly deserved it. It didn't matter. All that mattered was right now, and she pressed her face against his sweat-damp skin and gave up. For now it was the best she could do.

Chapter Twenty-Five

When she woke up the sun was high overhead and she was alone in the big bed. Of course she was. She managed to crawl out of bed—every muscle ached. The ride in the jeep wouldn't have been enough, but he hadn't let her alone that morning. They'd made love two more times, once in the shower, once over the side of the high bed, and when she'd gone to sleep after the final time he stayed with her, their bodies wrapped so closely together she couldn't tell where he ended and she began.

She didn't know how long she'd been alone. The bed felt cold and empty, her body felt drained. She took another shower, hoping it would give her some energy, and she found some of the new clothes still in the other room. She ignored the bed where he'd held her down and hurt her. What the fuck was her problem—Stockholm syndrome? She'd fallen in love with a man who'd tortured her, a man with a mean streak and a nasty tongue, and all her common sense didn't make a bit of difference.

She didn't have time to think about that, about him, about her. She had to get word to her brother that he mustn't—absolutely mustn't—come home, or the man she loved would kill him. At least she had the dubious relief that Ryder didn't give a shit about her. Yes, he'd spent a lot of time in bed with her, but she wasn't fool enough to think it meant anything. If she disappeared he'd forget all about her, and that was exactly what she was intending to do, once she warned Billy.

Ryder had said something to her, but in her sleep and sex-dazed mind she couldn't remember. He'd probably ordered her to stay put, but that was the last thing she intended to do. He didn't want her hanging around, mooning after him—he just didn't want her to warn Billy.

As for her, she didn't know what to believe. If Billy could safely go to prison, she wouldn't do anything to stop it, but that likelihood was almost nil. Ryder would kill him if he could, the other inmates would take their rage out on him, and Billy would never stand up to the rigors of prison.

He was the only member of her family who still mattered, who still had a soul, and she couldn't give him up so easily, not without concrete proof that he'd lied to her. She'd promised her mother she'd watch out for him, and letting Ryder get to him would be tanta-mount to breaking her mother's trust. As long as there was a chance, no matter how unlikely, that Billy had been tricked and manipu-lated, then she had to save him. If she wanted him to stay alive, then she needed to get him to lay low, and there was only one person she could turn to for help.

Her father.

It was easier than she expected getting out of the Magazine Street house. She knew there were security cameras all over the place, but she knew the back stairs led to the garage. She wouldn't steal a car, but the moment she got out on the street she could call a taxi and be gone before anyone even realized she'd left. It was the last and only thing she could do for her brother—dump the problem in her father's lap, and then she could safely disappear.

It went like clockwork. No one seemed to notice as she slipped down the stairs, there was no sign of Ryder or any of his fellow Committee members, and by the time they were likely to notice, she was gone, she'd be halfway to her father's house outside the city. She could only hope he was there—if he was off somewhere she'd leave him a message and have done with it. She'd already risked her life and betrayed her principles for her baby brother's sake. There wasn't any more she was willing to do.

When the taxi pulled up in front of her father's ornate, slightly garish house, a cross between Tara and the Parthenon, she could see the Bentley and the Cadillac in the wide, circular driveway, and she knew Fabrizio was home.

She climbed out, overtipping the driver, and smoothed down her hair. She'd found another of the sundresses someone had bought her, and she'd dressed accordingly. Her father disapproved of women in pants, and she wasn't interested in wasting time fighting with him. She simply needed to pass on the warning and leave. After that it was up to him.

The door opened before she could knock, and Tonino, her eldest brother, stood there, massive and unwelcoming. "So the prodigal child has come home," he said. "What new trouble are you bringing us?"

"I think you bring home enough trouble as it is," she said, pushing past him into the cool interior of the house. "Where's Fabrizio?"

"I don't think he wants to see you."

"Well, I don't want to see him. But I need to warn him about Billy."

"What about Billy?" Tonino demanded.

"He screwed up, Tino," she said, automatically using her ancient nickname for him, when she was six years old and he was her lordly teenage brother. "He's part of the human-trafficking ring the police busted a couple of months ago, and they've got evidence against him."

"Tell me something I don't know."

Jenny took in a shocked breath. "Were you part of it too?"

Tonino looked annoyed. "Of course not. That's filthy money— we don't do things like that. Besides, our organization is already in place. But you know Billy—he's still a kid, young and arrogant, and thinks he knows everything. Our father is very unhappy with him."

"I need to see Fabrizio. To warn him."

Tonino shook his massive head. He was built like a bull—well over six feet tall and two hundred fifty pounds, he looked like the same man who'd played football for Tulane. "He's with someone."

"I can't wait," she said, striding deeper into the house's interior.

"Guess you're going to have to, Sissy." Billy's voice came from the shadows, and Jenny froze, turning slowly to face him.

He looked the same—boyish, handsome, enthusiastic, and she almost went into his arms, until she noticed the petulant expression around his mouth.

"Billy," she said breathlessly, panicked. "You were supposed to be overseas, out of reach of the US authorities."

"No one's ever out of reach of the Committee, and I have you to thank for that, don't I?" he said in a sour voice. "If you'd given me back the smartphone when I asked for it then all this would have been avoided."

Her heart sank. "I couldn't," she said miserably. "Don't you realize what you did? You sold women and children into slavery. Most of those people won't live that long, and yet you're sitting on a profit made off them."

"And a very nice profit it is," he said with a shrug. "It's their choice. They could have stayed in the pigsty villages and died young, or they can enjoy civilization for a few years. I know which one I'd pick," he said with supreme indifference.

"You're a monster," she breathed, shocked.

"Don't be ridiculous. I'm a businessman, like my father and brothers before me."

"Not like me," Tonino spoke up. "It's dirty money."

"You're a pussy," Billy said maliciously. "You can't make an omelet without breaking eggs, you can't make a profit without stepping on some toes. My partner and I know what we're doing."

"Your partner?"

"Soledad. You had no idea she was working for me, now did you? It took her too damned long to find the telephone after you refused to hand it over, but in the end she got it."

"I smashed it," Jenny said.

The momentary darkening of Billy's eyes was terrifying. And then he smiled affably. "That's all right. Most of the information is outdated by now. In fact, you've probably saved my life. No one will be able to prove anything even if they had the records I'd stored on that phone."

"The Committee does."

"Does what?" Billy demanded irritably.

"Has all the records on the smartphone. They dumped the information while I was staying in the house, and they'll use it to hang you. You need to get out of here before you're arrested."

Billy laughed. "No one's arresting me. You forget—Father's paid for half the New Orleans police force. I'm not going anywhere until I feel like it. In fact, I'm safer from the Committee right here."

Jenny looked at him as she saw the last vestige of her family crumble in front of her eyes. "How could you do this, Billy?" she demanded brokenly.

"Give me a break, Sissy! You always were such a bleeding heart. I told you, I'm ambitious. Father's always discounted me, and I decided it was time he was taught a little lesson. No one should ever underestimate me."

"You've betrayed all of us with this shit," Tonino exploded, taking a step toward him.

"Never." He turned a winning smile on Jenny. "I love my family, and you, sister mine, most of all. I could never hurt you."

Relief swamped her. Thank God. Someone else had to have been behind the murder attempts . . .

"That's why I hired someone else to kill you," Billy continued blithely, as if it made perfect sense. "After all, you were the only one who knew I'd been part of the trafficking, and you wouldn't give me back my cell phone. I don't know why you were so selfish about it, Sissy. I wouldn't have had to hire someone if you'd just been reasonable."

Jenny swallowed, as something inside of her died. "I'm . . . I'm sorry."

"Jesus, Billy," Tonino said.

"No need to be sorry, Sissy. Everything's taken care of. Even the Committee can't touch me here, and I have the money to go any-where I want. The only problem that remains is you."

"Why me?" This all had a strange, Alice-Through-the-Looking-Glass kind of feel about it, her brother acting as if he were making perfect sense when every word out of his mouth was insane.

"Because you know the truth. Sooner or later you're going to tell the wrong person and I'll get caught, and I really can't let that happen."

"You're my brother. Why would I want you to get caught?"

"Oh, you wouldn't want me to," he said sweetly. "You just can't keep your fucking mouth closed."

They were alone now in the giant foyer of her father's garish house. Tonino had disappeared; it was just the two of them, and she felt sick inside.

"What are you going to do about it?" she asked, very calm and reasonable.

"I'm going to have to take care of you, of course. Father will understand. Family is family but business is business, and business comes first. If I get caught it reflects badly on Father, and he wouldn't want you shooting off your fat mouth either." The hateful words, in such a sweet tone, were eerie. The front door had three locks on it, but there was always the chance she could open it in time, and she could run very, very fast. That, or she could try to get to her father, but she'd be an easier target in the house, and there was no telling whether her father would protect her or not.

"Are you going to shoot me, Billy?" she asked. "Or is someone else coming to take care of me?"

"Unfortunately I don't have time to call someone in. Tonino's probably tattling to Father right now, and he might not think it was a good idea." He reached behind his back and pulled out a Glock 25, just like the one her father carried. "If you kneel down on the floor I promise I won't make it hurt."

She stared at him in horror and disbelief. This couldn't be happening. "You don't mean it," she said, hating the pleading sound in her voice.

"Of course I do." Billy shook his head. "Don't look so surprised, Sissy. I'm just a businessman, like father, cutting my losses. You should understand—you're a member of this family."

"Not anymore," she said brokenly. He raised the gun, and Jenny closed her eyes.

"Keep away from her!" Ryder's voice thundered through the cavernous hallway, and Jenny's eyes flew open as shock and relief flooded her. She made an instinctive move toward him, but Billy intervened, grabbing her and pressing the gun against her temple. It was cold and hard, and all he had to do was pull the trigger and her life would disappear. She held herself very still.

"Who the hell are you?" Billy said disdainfully, glaring at Ryder. "I don't think this is any of your business."

"It wouldn't make any difference to you," Ryder said, moving into the hallway. "Leave her the fuck alone."

She could see Tonino move behind him, and she realized that Ryder had been there all the time.

Billy laughed. "God, what a hero! You must be Ryder—my father told me about you and your pathetic attempts to find me. If you're in love with my sister, then I'm sorry for you. She's a waste of oxygen with no family loyalty. But I'm afraid you don't have any say in the matter."

Ryder didn't even glance at her, his face cold and implacable. "I'm not in love with your sister, Billy. This is a job. You understand that, don't you?"

Billy brightened. "Of course I do. I'm not sure Sissy does—she's looking like you slapped her in the face. Did you think he was in love with you, Sissy? Men like us can't afford to love anyone."

"Ryder isn't anything like you," she said, ignoring the sharp pain in her chest. She wanted to weep. She'd been wrong about everything, about her brother's innocence, about Ryder caring about her.

"Oh, I think he's exactly like me. I'm guessing you slept with him—Father won't like that. You know he thinks women are whores or Madonnas, and you're supposed to be in the saintly category like our mother. I tried to explain to him that all women are whores at heart but he never believed me." He swung the gun toward Ryder, and Jenny froze. He could kill them both with that small handgun, and he wouldn't care. He was a Gauthier after all, amoral and heartless in his casual cruelty. "Don't move any closer to her. I really don't want to have to shoot you both."

Ryder kept moving, slowly. "You're not going to have any choice in the matter. You kill her then you might as well kill me, because I'll rip your heart out if you do."

Billy laughed, and there was a tinge of hysteria in his voice. "And you say you don't love her. You're just as weak as the rest of them!"

"My son, this is enough."

Fabrizio Gauthier appeared behind Tonino, a small, dapper man with the face of a bulldog. "You will only make things worse. Your sister doesn't understand. She has betrayed you and your entire family, but it is already too late. Put the gun down, Billy."

Billy froze. Slowly, like a naughty child, he lowered the gun and set it on the shiny marble floor. He turned to look beseechingly at their father, and for a brief, shocked moment Jenny could see the little boy who'd opened Christmas presents with her, the child with the innocent eyes and sweet mouth.

"The FBI is coming for you," Fabrizio said. "Mr. Ryder has explained that there is nothing I can do to stop them. There is no one left to pay off. I am sorry, my son."

Billy looked shocked. "You aren't going to let him do this to me, are you, Papa?"

"No, my son," said Fabrizio, and shot him three times in the chest.

The flashes of light came a nanosecond ahead of the thunder that echoed around the foyer, and the smell of gunpowder filled the air as Billy stared down at his shirt, now dotted with bright red stains. He looked up again, his mouth moving soundlessly, and then his head exploded with a final bullet.

Jenny began to scream, sinking to her knees on the marble floor, screaming and screaming until someone yanked her hands away from her face and slapped her, and she looked up into her father's furious expression.

"You see what you made me do?" he said in a voice of deadly quiet. "I killed my own son because of your stupidity. You stop this, do you hear, or I swear I will shoot you too." He pulled back his hand to slap her again when Ryder caught his arm, yanking him away.

"Leave her the fuck alone," he snarled, then knelt down beside her. He put his hands on her, pushing her hair back from her shocked, tear-streaked face. "Let me get you out of here."

"And don't let her come back, or I swear I'll kill her myself. My family has shamed me, first my son with his stupid choices and now my daughter who doesn't know the meaning of the word *loyalty*. This is all her fault—blood is first."

"Blood is first and you murder your son," Jenny said in a shaky voice. "You bastard! You're even more of a monster than I thought you were."

"Get her out of here, or I swear I'll come after her," Fabrizio said.

"You won't touch her," Ryder said in a quiet voice, scooping her up in his arms. "Because I can get to you, no matter how big an army you have, no matter how many people you pay off. You'll leave her alone."

"Fine. From this day forward I have no daughter."

From somewhere deep inside Jenny found her voice. "You never did," she said.

And Ryder carried her from the house, leaving the carnage behind.

Chapter Twenty-Six

Jenny was scarcely aware of Ryder as he carried her out into the overcast day. He tucked her into the front seat of the car, fastening the seat belt for her, and within moments they were speeding down the driveway, out onto the road. She leaned back against the seat, closing her dry, scratchy eyes.

She couldn't cry. She'd lost her baby brother, the last person she'd considered to be her family, lost him more thoroughly than she'd lost her other brothers. No one else in her family had considered her worth bothering about, but at least they hadn't tried to kill her. She could see her father's cold, angry face, the gun still in his hand. She really had been raised by wolves, and that madness, that bad blood, ran in her veins as well.

She was in shock. She knew it, welcomed it. She didn't want to feel the dark cloud of pain that hovered, threatening to smother her. She didn't want to think, to feel, to care.

The car pulled out onto the interstate, and she opened her eyes. Ryder was driving fast, way too fast, weaving in and out of traffic, and normally she'd be grabbing the door handle and screaming at him to slow down. It didn't matter. If they ended up in a pile of twisted metal it would make no difference.

She turned to look at him. His face was set, his eyes cold and wintry. He glanced at her, taking his eyes from the road for a moment, and she considered shrieking in protest. She couldn't say a word.

"I should tell you I'm sorry." His voice was low, unexpected. "But I'm not. If your father hadn't killed that son of a bitch then I would have. You know that, don't you?"

She pictured her brother's body lying on the marble floor, the blood pooling beneath him, and she felt nothing. "Yes," she said dully, surprised that her voice worked.

"Whoever your baby brother was, he died a long time ago. That piece of shit would have killed you." There was banked fury in his voice, enough to catch her attention.

"It doesn't matter," she said, knowing she sounded as defeated as she felt. "He was the last member of my family I cared about, trusted. Now there's no one."

"There's me."

She barely heard the words. She jerked her head back to him, some of the fog beginning to lift. "What did you say?"

He didn't answer her question. "Look at it this way—you had a rough start in life. You're a changeling, born into the wrong family. That family is gone now, and you can shut the door on them."

"You think it's that easy? That I don't need to mourn my brother?" she said, her raw voice stronger.

"Of course you do. You need to cry and scream and hit things. You can even hit me if it helps. But you can't change the fact that he's dead and the world is a better place for it."

She wanted to hit him, hit him for the awful truth she couldn't refute. Billy had been a monster in sheep's clothing, and she'd been too blinded by her need for family to look past his smooth exterior.

"You're driving too fast for me to hit you," she said in a low voice.

"I'll keep that in mind." He sped up, and it was beginning to scare her, just a little bit.

"Slow down!"

"Make me," he shot back. He was going over ninety now, and the roads were crowded with commuters and tourists heading back into the city. He dodged into the right lane, passed someone and then crossed three lanes of speeding traffic into the fast lane, and Jenny wanted to scream.

"Slow down!" she yelled at him, no longer apathetic.

"Why?" he shouted back, the noise of the traffic all around them.

"Because I don't want to die."

He immediately slowed down, and she could sense some of the tension leaving him. Which was fine—she was already tense enough for the both of them. "Good," he said. He moved the car over to one of the middle lanes, driving at a comparatively sedate pace. "So where do you want to go?"

She looked at him with disbelief. He was getting rid of her, now that everything was over, and that safe cocoon that had embraced her began to dissolve. "How the hell should I know?" she said, her voice harsh. "I have no house, no clothes, nothing. Drop me at a hotel somewhere."

"I don't think so."

"Then where the hell are you planning on taking me? I won't go back to that goddamn house on Magazine Street."

"Not there."

Oddly enough the traffic was thinning a bit, the highway going from four lanes to three, and she suddenly realized they were driving away from the city, not toward it. "What are you doing?" she said in a calmer voice.

"Taking care of you. You're hurting, and you need someone to look after you. That's what I'm doing." His voice was matter-of-fact, and for a moment she was cold and silent. She was hurting, and he was looking after her. His words broke the dam inside her, and suddenly she began to weep, loud, noisy sobs.

She had no idea how long she cried—at some point he pulled off the road and parked, hauled her to him and held her as she wept, stroking her back in a soothing gesture. Eventually her sobs slowed, turned into shuddering hiccups, and then into shaky breaths, and he moved his hand up to push her hair away from her wet face.

He'd pulled her over onto his lap, and she'd never felt so safe, so protected in her life. She looked at his impassive face, and she was so tired. All she wanted to do was stay in his arms forever, but she knew that was impossible. "Why are you doing this?" she said in a small voice.

"Doing what?"

"Holding me. Acting like you care about me when I know you think I'm nothing but a pain in the ass." She felt completely vulnerable, with nothing to hold on to, and she wanted to hold on to him.

To her shock he actually smiled. "You are a pain in the ass. You're also being deliberately obtuse but I'll give you that. You've had a hard day."

"You think? So fucking indulge me. What am I being obtuse about?"

He didn't even hesitate. "I'm in love with you. I'm not even sure I believe love exists, but if it does I'm in it with you, and I've given up fighting. You may as well give up too. Love doesn't seem to respond to common sense and conventional wisdom."

She looked at him for a long moment. "I gave up long ago," she said simply, half afraid to admit it.

"Gave up what?" he said warily, as if he wasn't sure he could believe her words.

"Gave up fighting it." She gave him a tremulous smile. "Let's face it—you're hot. And you save my life, over and over again, you utterly destroy me when we make love, and . . . and I trust you. You're a good man, whether you believe it or not, and I love you."

His smile widened as he shook his head. "This isn't *Romeo and Juliet.*"

"I don't want it to be. They died. We're going to live."

He kissed her then, sliding his hand behind her neck to bring her mouth to his, and she let herself sink into it, into him, so there was nothing but his mouth, his body hard beneath hers, his rock-solid arms holding her, and when he used his tongue she felt the wet hot lick of desire wash through her, as life filled her veins once more.

She pushed back from him, breaking the kiss. "You don't have to love me, you know," she said, suddenly guilty. "I'm not always this pathetic."

"You're not pathetic at all. And yes, I have to love you. I've given up fighting it. Now why don't you curl up and get some sleep while I get back on the highway. The Louisiana State Police are broad-minded, but it's still daylight and I don't think they'd overlook road-side sex. Don't worry—I'll wake you when we find a bed."

Another knot of hope and desire turned inside her. "But what about your work?"

"Remy can take care of the Committee—I'm long overdue for a vacation, and my partner Bishop can get his ass back from his honeymoon. We're going to drive until we feel like stopping, and then drive some more."

"And when we stop?"

"We'll fuck like rabbits. Does that suit you?"

"Yes," she said, slipping back into the passenger seat with a shaky sigh. "And I promise not to cry anymore."

"You can cry all you want. It's hard to lose a family."

"Not when you've found your real one," she said.

He kissed her again, short and hard. "Remember that."

He pulled out onto the highway again, catching her hand in his strong one as they headed west into the setting sun.

About the Author

Anne Stuart is a grand master of the genre, winner of Romance Writers of America's prestigious Lifetime Achievement Award, survivor of more than forty years in the romance business, and she still just keeps getting better.

Her first novel was *Barrett's Hill*, a gothic romance published by Ballantine in 1974, when Anne had just turned 25. Since then she's written more gothics, regencies, romantic suspense, romantic adventure, series romance, suspense, historical romance, paranormal, and mainstream contemporary romance.

She's won numerous awards, appeared on many bestseller lists, and speaks all over the country. Her general outrageousness has gotten her on *Entertainment Tonight*, as well as into the pages of *Vogue*, *People*, *USA Today*, *Woman's Day*, and countless other national newspapers and magazines.

She's just celebrating her fortieth wedding anniversary with her luscious husband, and she lives by a lake in northern Vermont, where she enjoys an empty nest, fabulous grandchildren, and overacting in local theater. She has so many books she still wants to write that she plans to live forever.